COME BACK TO ME

The Bishop Smoky Mountain Thrillers
Book 11

LAUREN STREET

STERLING & STONE

COME BACK TO ME

Chapter One

THIS WAS A MAN WHO NEEDED TO DIE!

So Farrah Hollis would kill him.

Simple as that.

She was, in fact, looking forward to becoming the angel of his particular doom — was *eager* to off the old bastard. She had marked him as a dead man when he got her ass evicted from the coveted window seat on the bus.

The stinky piece of shit.

And oh, did he stink! The old man reeked. Farrah'd always been able to detect the foul aroma particular to old people, and it filled the air around this old guy so thick, she was surprised you couldn't see it hanging in the air like a green fog. She neither knew nor wanted to know what it was specifically about old people that smelled so bad. The rest of humanity pretended not to notice that everybody over age seventy stank, but of course they *did* notice. How could they not? All old people reeked, and it was always the same foul smell. Was it that they had some kind of — she wrinkled her nose — mold or fungus, like toe jam, that grew in the folds of their ancient spotted skin, a goo they never washed off? Maybe. Most of them were too skinny to suspect that the goo was folded up in the layers of their fat. That's what caused a fat person's stink, which was equally as bad, but not the same at all.

After the old man finally made it down the bus steps, Farrah watched him move slowly, leaning forward, shoulders bent, like he was walking into a strong wind. He had a bathtub ring of white hair around a bald head that was splotched with liver spots and other suspicious-looking growths she didn't know the name of.

His eyes were rheumy and unfocused, his hands so gnarled by arthritis that the lumpy fingers didn't even stick out straight from his palm anymore — they angled away from it like brown-spotted turtle flippers. His loose pants were held up with bright red suspenders over a wrinkled shirt crusted with the remains of the last half-dozen meals he'd eaten — so filthy you could have put it in a pot of hot water and made soup.

She shuddered in disgust. Yep, this was a man who needed to die, and she was going to provide that service to him free of charge, all taxes, license, and delivery fees included.

His was the standard whiny old-person voice that always got attention. The I'm-old-so-feel-sorry-for me voice that grated on her nerves and made the roots of her wisdom teeth throb. But it worked like a charm every time. The man had moaned and groaned about his stupid walker being folded up in the back of the bus and how he wanted it near him because it had a little zippered pouch attached to it, a man-purse filled with important things that he *needed*.

At least that's what he said to the bus driver. She knew damned good and well what was in it — Chapstick, corn plasters, maybe some Preparation H for his hemorrhoids — not exactly the essential elements of human survival.

But the bus driver rolled over like people always rolled over when old folks started whining and made Farrah give up her window seat so they could put the old man's stupid walker in it. She had been fascinated looking out the window at the scenery, but the driver made her move to an aisle seat.

The old man would be sorry he'd crossed her. He would pay dearly for that decision.

It took the old geezer a thousand years to get down the steps of the bus and then pilot his stupid little walker thing into the bus station, inching down the sidewalk so slowly, she was surprised he didn't leave a slime trail on the concrete like a snail.

She watched the old guy cross the lobby to the far wall, where a sign above a large doorway proclaimed *Restrooms*. Of course, this little bus station — Sandstone Creek, according to the sign — out in the middle of nowhere Tennessee wasn't progressive enough to have unisex bathrooms. She'd just have to follow the old guy into the men's room. It took him so long to even get through the big doorway that she was afraid anyone watching would mark that she had gone in there right after him. But she looked around and no one was looking at her … because there was no one to look. The place was empty. The other passengers on the bus were still asleep. There was the bus driver, of course. But she could shut the driver up if she had to, would threaten to report his constant nips from the flask he kept in his jacket pocket.

The old man had gotten his walker up to the sink and turned the water on when she came up behind him.

"The bus driver made me move out of the window seat

to make room for your stupid walker," Farrah growled at him.

Apparently, his neck was stiff and he couldn't turn just his head, so he had to rotate his whole body around to look at her. He squinted.

"This is the men's room. The ladies' room is next door."

"That window seat was *mine*, old man, and you stole it."

He looked confused, like maybe he was surprised to hear her say a thing like that. The confusion lasted only a moment, though. Then his ugly face contorted in a toothless sneer that revealed a mouth with a random assortment of blackened, crooked teeth that didn't appear to match up enough to take a bite out of anything.

"You got the deed to that seat, Missy?" he snarled. "Signed over to you so you own it?"

When she said nothing, he turned from her with a satisfied smile, twisting his ugly purple lips. "Didn't think so. I need my walker and I can put it anywhere I want — it's a free country. Ain't no sassy teenager gonna make me move it just so you can look out at the scenery."

"So that's your final word, is it?" Farrah asked, almost chirpy.

"Course it's my final word. And what the hell are you doing in the men's room, anyway?"

"Like you said, it's a free country. I can use any bathroom I want."

He mumbled some garbled expletives under his breath.

"This here's a *men's* room." He gestured with a hand so gnarled and covered with brown spots, it was almost unrecognizable as a human appendage. "That there's a urinal. 'Less you got the 'quipment to stand up and use it, you're in the wrong damn bathroom."

"I'm in the bathroom where I need to be to accomplish what I came here to do. "

"Well, I hope your plan is to take a shit in one of them stalls," he grumbled. He finished washing his hands and *then* started toward the urinal. Weren't those activities supposed to be in reverse order? He didn't seem to know or care. Moving slowly toward the upright porcelain fixture on the wall, he fixed her with an ugly smile, clamped his eyes on hers, and began slowly unzipping his pants with his trembling palsied hand. "You'd best get in there and close the door behind you, 'cause I'm 'bout to use the facilities."

No way was Farrah going to let him drag that shrunken worm out of his pants and dangle it in front of her.

She actually showed him the knife before she'd plunge it into him, lifted the handle up in front of his face so he'd be able to see it with his cloudy eyes. She flicked the little switch and the blade snapped out, vicious looking, six inches long and sharp as a razor. He didn't flinch.

"Them things is illegal," he spat. "I'm going to report you. I'm going to call the law on you. Get you kicked off that bus here in the middle of nowhere."

"No, you're not. You're not going to report anybody or anything to anybody … about this knife or about anything else."

"You think I'm bluffing, do ya?"

She shook her head and stepped up close to him. "Oh, I'm sure you mean every word. But see, here's the thing — you won't be alive thirty seconds from now to report me to anybody."

Then Farrah Hollis shoved the blade deep into his belly and watched shock register on his wrinkled features.

"What the—?" he began.

She pulled the knife out, wiped the blood from it on the sleeve of his shirt, then stuck it in again and again and again as he crumpled in slow motion to the floor. When he face-planted on the filthy tiles, blood puddling all around him, she stabbed him a couple more times just because she loved the feel of the knife slicing through his flesh into his muscles and his guts and whatever the hell else was under his disgusting spotted skin.

She heard a sound then, wondered who … and then realized *she* was making it. It was a tiny giggle that swelled up out of her throat as she got to her feet and stepped over the body to the sink to wash the blood off the knife. Then she slid the blade back into the handle before she put it back in her pocket.

She started to turn then and leave, but stopped. In the mirror over the sink was a reflection.

A witness. How perfect. How utterly perfect.

She turned slowly around and faced the person gaping at the dead body of the old man on the floor.

"You know, we have to stop meeting like this," she said. "People will talk."

Her attempt at humor didn't strike the witness as funny.

She suddenly felt a wave of exhaustion wash over her. Parasites, that's what they were, people who attached themselves to you and would suck your whole life force dry if you let them. She was so *done* with that.

"You can't just keep *showing up*, blundering into my affairs. It's my life, after all, and nobody else's. *Mine*. I took it and it belongs to me."

She smiled.

"I wonder what it would feel like to slide this blade into *you* just like I did into *him*. What do you say we find out?"

Farrah Hollis flipped the catch on the knife and the blade popped back into place.

Chapter Two

MICKY HOLLIS — NOT MICHAELA MARIE, JUST MICKY — stood rooted to the floor in the doorway of the bathroom. Her mind refused to recognize the reality of what her eyes had just seen. She was dreaming. She *had* to be dreaming. Yes, that's what it was, just a dream.

It was a continuation of the nightmare that Micky'd had every time she closed her eyes on the long bus ride from California to Tennessee. A bus ride that was almost over. Her stop was the next one on the line. She'd just gotten off for a few minutes for a potty break and was determined that even though it was late and she'd had almost no sleep the whole time she'd been on the bus, she was *not* going to nod off again. No more nightmares! No *more!* The images from the dreams were too terrible.

She shook her head to clear out the gauzy remnants of sleep so that the scene in front of her would vanish with the other images like smoke from a dying campfire.

Except it didn't vanish.

"You know, we have to stop meeting like this," Farrah said. "People will talk." Then she burst out laughing

Micky shook her head again, willing her senses to reject the unreality of the crazy eyes open far too wide and the pupils dilated so wide, the pale blue was only visible in a little circle around the black.

Farrah's laughter chilled Micky, the callousness of it. And she discovered, to her horror, that not only was what she was seeing real, she wasn't even surprised. She'd known it was coming. It had been only a matter of time.

Micky looked down at the old man on the floor. His body was riddled with knife wounds, half a dozen of them, maybe more, certainly far more than it would have taken to kill him. She'd killed him, and then kept stabbing and stabbing him after he was already dead.

He'd been a grumpy old man, but he'd also seemed frail, barely able to move around. His voice had that little quaver in it that old people's voices sometimes got, that made you think they were either developing some kind of palsy, or whatever was happening was affecting them emotionally in some way that you were too young and stupid to understand.

He'd had trouble getting up out of his seat when the bus stopped, and Micky had offered to help him.

"Need me to give you a hand?"

"Nah, you don't have to *give* it to me. But if you could let me borrow it for a few minutes, Missy, I'd be much obliged."

Micky'd smiled, then reached across him and took the collapsible walker out of the window seat, set it in the aisle, and opened it up so he could make his way to the door. Then she helped him pull himself to his feet. If she hadn't helped him, he wouldn't likely have been able to get off the bus and into the bathroom and back in the few minutes the bus driver had allotted for them at this stop.

If she hadn't helped him, he'd have been stuck on the bus.

If she hadn't helped him, he wouldn't have been able to come into this bathroom — where the merciless killer had ... *butchered* him.

In other words, Micky was responsible for his death. If she'd left him alone, he'd have stayed on the bus, and if he'd stayed on the bus, he'd still be breathing.

No! She wasn't going *there*.

The old man was dead, at the hands of a merciless murderer who was smiling at her, wagging something that looked like a knife handle back and forth in the air, babbling something about her own life.

Micky tuned back in to Farrah's words. "I wonder what it would feel like to slide this blade into *your* body just like I did into his. What do you say we find out!"

The blade on the switchblade snapped back into place, and Micky turned and bolted out of the doorway, raced across the empty lobby, her eyes frantically searching for someone, anyone. But the other passengers had either gotten back on the bus or never got off at all. She'd stood talking to the bus driver after she helped the old man out, and she could have sworn some of the other passengers were getting up to leave too, but she couldn't see a single soul now. Not one person in the empty bus station lobby, not a single sound but the staccato clap of her footsteps as she raced across the floor toward the exit, bursting out into the warm Tennessee night that smelled of magnolia blossoms and honeysuckle.

Her eyes raked the parking lot where a few vehicles sat empty, but still there was not a soul in sight.

Maybe the Rapture had happened, the end of the world that her apocalyptic Sunday school teacher had talked about all the time, where the good people would be taken to Heaven and the bad people left behind on Earth to suffer Satan's retribution. Maybe she was the only person left, just she and the killer whose footsteps she could hear right behind her, gaining on her.

She headed across the empty lot toward the stand of trees beside it, the murderous killer following behind her.

Suddenly, headlights flashed on only a few feet ahead of her and to the left, the headlights of a battered old red pickup truck that she recognized. Oh dear God, yes, she recognized it.

Without breaking stride, she cut at right angles through the parked cars in front of the pickup truck, watched in horrified wonder as the door of the pickup truck opened and the familiar figure stepped out. He'd seen her. Of course he had.

She'd been right all along! She hadn't been imagining it again and again for days. The truck *was* following the bus. A red pickup truck had first appeared outside Kansas City, too far back in the line of cars for her to be certain, but there, always there. She hadn't gotten away after all.

Plunging headlong through the darkness in the woods, she wondered if the man in the pickup truck was chasing her now, too. Uncle Dan. Her sweet and caring Uncle Dan, the one who took her with him to the county fair, held her hand tight even when it was sticky from cotton candy. So tight it hurt. But nobody could see that he was holding on too tight. It just looked like he was determined to keep that little girl safe! Safe.

Riiiight.

She wondered if he had spotted the killer chasing her. The killer who'd butchered the old man in the bathroom, and who had also butchered—

No, this couldn't be real. It had to be a dream. Reality couldn't be this perfectly horrible, couldn't match her worst imaginings this precisely — her uncle finding her after all these months, tracking her down, coming for her. The killer standing there, bloody and smiling — just like before.

No, this had to be something her terrified mind had conjured up out of random, misfiring synapses creating a bad dream. It *couldn't* be real.

There was no old man dead on the bathroom floor in the bus station, and she had not run from his killer. Her uncle had not found her to make her pay for what she'd done.

Those revelations struck her like thunderbolts. She was running from nothing. There was no real danger.

Staggering to a stop, she leaned over and put her hands on her knees, gasping for air. The sweet release of relief began to flow over her in a warm flood, and she wanted to cry and laugh at the same time. It was okay. Nobody was trying to kill her. It was just—

Suddenly, a bloody hand reached out of the darkness. She didn't even feel the knife slide into her, not the first time anyway. But she felt it the second time. And the third. And all the other times after that.

Chapter Three

RILEIGH STOLE GLANCES AT MITCH WHEN HE WASN'T looking. He was driving, so he wasn't looking at her. She, on the other hand, was under no obligation to watch the road ahead to keep the vehicle from careening off any one of half a dozen hairpin turns. Mitch negotiated them like a pro, like a local. She smiled at that.

"What's so funny?" he asked.

"I was just thinking that you've finally learned how to drive in the mountains."

"Finally learned how to drive? I beg your pardon. I've known how to drive for—"

"No, no, no. You missed the key phrase in that sentence. In the mountains."

"Mountains, prairie, desert. Same, same."

"You know damn good and well it's not the same. Just ask all those people from Lubbock or Kansas City who creep along at ten miles an hour, afraid they're going to go hurling off the edge into the abyss at every corner."

"All right, I'll concede that driving in the mountains is

a particular skill set, but it's not one that's taken me almost a year to acquire."

"Oh, you could drive in the mountains soon after you got here, but you have finally developed the," she paused to try to come up with the right word, "the mountain swagger. You have developed a drive swagger. It's an attitude, really. Mostly occasioned by the lack of fear that you're going to go flying off into the air, hang there for a horrifying, Wile E. Coyote-style moment, and then plummet onto the jagged rocks thousands of feet below."

"So I drive with a swagger," he said, as if mulling the words around in his mind like a peppermint on his tongue. "Am I supposed to like that? Was that a compliment?"

She reached over and touched his leg lightly. Just grazed it and then put her hands back in her lap. "Oh, it was a compliment, all right. Definitely, definitely a compliment."

He put his smile on high beam and she promptly melted into a puddle in the front seat.

She wondered if that feeling in her belly, those butterflies would ... no, not butterflies. Something more agitated than butterflies. Grasshoppers. Yeah, that feeling of grasshoppers leaping up and down in her belly just at the sight of him — would that calm down over time? She didn't have an answer to that question, but it hadn't abated so far, not in the slightest, and then there were the goosebumps that sometimes accompanied the grasshoppers. Wait. Would crickets be a better description than grasshoppers? Crickets made music, and when she saw Mitch, the feelings inside her were positively musical.

"So was your steak really cooked properly tonight, or were you just too polite to send it back?"

"A little of both," she said and smiled. Truth was, she had trouble eating when Mitch was around. The sense of excitement stole her appetite, which for Rileigh Bishop was absolutely one hundred percent *not* a good thing. She didn't need anything that kept her from eating. She had yet to put on what she considered the requisite amount of weight to fill out her clothes the way she once did, the way she wanted to fill them out for Mitch.

"The steak was tender," she said, "and juicy."

"And cooked right?"

"Mostly."

"Mostly is not an answer."

"All right. I have trouble with steak and other foods that require more than a little bit of chewing when we're together, because I…" She couldn't finish it. She thought she'd be able to finish it. She'd said a lot of other things to him in the past couple of months, since he dragged her out of that fan in the basement of Shagbark Manor, the one that had been about to slice her in half. Things that had been accumulating behind her lips for months, but somehow telling him that she couldn't eat because of the butterflies/grasshoppers/crickets in her belly just felt like a bridge too far.

She tried finishing anyway. "I'm always so, you know, interested in what you have to say that I don't want to be too busy chewing in case I have some cryptic remark to offer the conversation that will amaze and dazzle you."

"You still didn't answer my question."

Before she could protest, he held up one finger. "But I like that answer so much that I'm going to let it pass. And the amazing and dazzling part, you've got that down."

He turned toward her briefly, flashed his high beam smile, and she melted again.

They had been out to Saturday night dinner at Bonefish Grill in Gatlinburg. Rileigh liked the place because it had a romantic atmosphere, low lighting, candles on the tables, white tablecloths, and waiters with dish towels over their arms. Conversation at Bonefish Grill was subdued, and she didn't feel awkward reaching out across the table and taking Mitch's hand and holding it while they waited to order.

Tonight was the first time in months she'd left the Ace bandage off her severely sprained ankle. Mitch had put his foot down, so to speak. "No more green shoes," he'd said, "not for one calendar year."

So let it be written, so let it be done.

And in truth, her green shoes didn't actually go with her outfit of blue jeans and a button-down shirt anyway, and it was certainly more comfortable to be in running shoes. She wiggled her toes appreciatively, moved her ankle around. Mitch noticed.

"How's it feeling?" he asked.

"Like brand new, like I was issued a recently minted ankle, stamped with the date 'Summer of 2024.'"

"That's some nice flowery language. Now tell me the truth."

"Truth is it doesn't hurt anymore, it really doesn't." She reached down and pulled up the leg of her jeans to reveal a bare ankle. "No bandage. Wrapping the ankle up in that thing and unwrapping it takes a lot of time every morning and night."

His smile widened.

She realized he was thinking the same thing she was. That being able to get into and out of a bandage or any other constraining garment had become a critical decision maker in what she wore when she went out with Mitch.

He reached over and took her hand and squeezed it, then brought her fingers up to his lips and kissed them one at a time. And she found she was delighted by his mountain driver swagger because it meant he could drive faster on these roads than once he could, and she wanted him to get to his house as fast as it was humanly possible.

They pulled up in the driveway of his house, and he killed the engine, leaned over, and kissed her, soft and gentle and tantalizing. He drew back, then took her head in his hands and brought her face toward his, kissing her hard and deep and longingly.

She drew back, breathless.

"Good thing I don't have an Ace bandage to take off," she said.

"Good thing indeed," he said.

Rileigh was careful not to let on that the broken rib she'd gotten the night Shagbark Manor burned to the ground still bothered her a little. It wasn't the first broken rib she'd ever had, and she managed to dismiss the pain that way for a while. But the bottom line was a broken rib was really painful, and she hated watching her family become somber and serious in an effort not to say something unexpectedly humorous and make her laugh. That was the hardest thing. Laughing hurt like hell with a broken rib, and she tried every day to perfect the "it doesn't hurt at all, I'm fine" front she presented to the world. It worked with most people, but not so much with Mitch. That was because Mitch never seemed to take his eyes off her. Not like he was watching her, but like he was, well, *admiring* her all the time. So the slightest wince on her part, and the slightest lifting of an eyebrow or stifled groan didn't go unnoticed by the Yarmouth County Sheriff.

Mama and Jillian might sail right past it, but Mitch almost always caught her. And then there was the fact that he was often the cause of her discomfort, squeezing her too tight. She loved it. She loved feeling his big strong arms around her, smelling the nearness of him. But one little squeeze too hard in the wrong place, and that healing rib screamed. The pain had subsided in the last couple of weeks, and that, coupled with the perfection of her ability to hide a wince or a grimace when it did hurt, had finally seemed to relax Mitch enough that he wasn't constantly holding himself back, making sure he didn't do anything that hurt her. And she liked the relaxed Mitch way better than the one who constantly kept a lid on his emotions and behavior to make sure he didn't squeeze her too tight.

In fact, just in the last day or two, she had seen evidence of the Mitch who let himself go entirely. The Mitch who was caught up in his own emotions and at the mercy of his own passion. The rib was healed enough that nothing he did would actually harm her, and she would gladly exchange a pain-free world for a world in which Mitch caught her up in his arms and made passionate love to her.

Mitch got out of the car, and because they were in dating mode, came around to her side and opened the door. She stood up, and he took her into his arms, held her, and kissed her neck. She let her head roll back on her shoulders in delight. He started to whisper in her ear, but she couldn't hear what he said because the radio in the cruiser parked beside his car in the driveway of his house crackled to life.

"All units respond Code 27 to a 10-66 at the Sandstone Creek Bus station."

Code 27 meant use lights and siren. A 10-66 was a shooting or knifing.

Rileigh and Mitch both froze. The dispatcher was shorthanded tonight. And Rileigh knew it. Deputy Jeb Rawlings was out with COVID, and Deputy Tony Hadley had gone hiking with his brother over the weekend and somehow managed to get poison ivy on his face, arms, and hands, and all over other unnamed parts of his body so extensively that he couldn't even get dressed. The department needed all hands on deck when there was a problem. And apparently, there was a problem.

Their eyes met. The disappointment sank down into Rileigh's belly like cold water sinks to the bottom of a lake. Mitch sighed and let her go, then pulled out his phone and called the dispatcher.

"What's up, Sheila?"

"You're off duty."

"Thanks for reminding me. I'd forgotten. What's going on?"

"Caller to 911 said an old man had been murdered in the bathroom of the bus station. I've dispatched an ambulance. Unit 3 is nearby. Want me to have him call you when he's on scene?"

Unit 3 was Deputy Beau Mullins.

"No, I'm responding."

"*We* are responding," Rileigh said from beside him. She draped a smile on her face like a surgeon's mask and chirped, "This is what we signed up for."

Chapter Four

BOTH MITCH AND RILEIGH WERE SILENT ON THE RIDE from his house to the bus station in Sandstone Creek, a few miles from Black Bear Forge, where an old man had been stabbed to death in the bathroom and a young woman had been attacked in the nearby woods but had survived.

"What possible motive could there be to attack an old man in the middle of the night in a bus station bathroom?" Rileigh asked, expecting no answer. Mitch obliged her with silence.

He was preoccupied, figuring out who on the part-time deputy roster he could he call in to fill the holes left by Deputy Jeb Rawlings and Deputy Tony Hadley so he could actually have an entire day and night off, free from being summoned at the first hint of mayhem. The dispatcher understood, and he knew she found out the severity of a crime before she sent out the call to pull the sheriff in from off duty.

This, a murder and assault, definitely ranked up there in the classification of bad-enough-to-call-the-sheriff, in the eyes of the dispatcher anyway. In Mitch's eyes, the random massacre of half the population of Black Bear Forge wouldn't be sufficient reason to interrupt his time alone with Rileigh.

He squeezed his fingers tight around the steering wheel and managed not to grind his teeth because Rileigh would notice that, and he didn't want her to know how upset he was that — yet again — they had been called in to work some terrible crime when what they wanted was *private* time together. He didn't want her to know how much that meant to him because...

Yeah, why didn't he? What did it matter? He had admitted his feelings for her, told her he loved her. And he did! He'd never felt this way about any woman, not even the woman to whom he was engaged — briefly — while he was still in the police academy. Her image flashed in front of his face: a ditzy blonde with dimples deep enough to eat pudding out of and a thousand-watt smile on the front of a head that had not much of anything inside. He didn't like stereotypes, and dumb blonde was definitely a stereotype, but he was certain that woman couldn't pour sand out of a boot if the instructions were on the heel. It wasn't just that she wasn't the sharpest knife in the drawer. It was that she enjoyed her "blissful ignorance." She had no desire to learn anything new, to use her mind in any way; she was all about the physical, and oh my goodness had she been about the physical.

He'd realized somewhere along the line — no, not *some*where, he knew exactly where. He remembered the day distinctly. She had admired a stranger's gaudy necklace, and he'd commented there'd been enough gold in it "to fill half the gold depository in Ft. Knox."

"A *gold* depository?" she'd asked. "It'd be kinda expensive, wouldn't it — to stick a thing like that up your butt every time you needed to take a dump?"

When he remembered the conversation now, he could laugh about it. But at the time, the realization that she'd been absolutely serious ... well, he had become the Apostle Paul on the road to Damascus, struck down by a vision of what it would be like to be married to a woman who didn't know the difference between a depository and a suppository. He realized quick he wasn't in love with her, he was in *lust* with her, and it had been hot and steamy — and blessedly brief.

He hadn't gotten deeply involved with anyone since then, and that had been years ago. He smiled and looked over at Rileigh. She was looking out the window and didn't see his smile. Just as well. She'd have asked him what he was smiling about, and then he would have had to admit he was smiling about how very, very much he had disliked her when they first met. She had seemed to him to be an arrogant ex-police officer who had reluctantly given up the badge on her chest but clung tenaciously to the authority it granted her. She still behaved like a cop with absolutely no reason to, and he found that offensive on all kinds of levels. But as he had been forced to work with her in the murder investigation into the death of Tina Montgomery, he had been forced to admit she was good at her job, even when it wasn't her job. Damned good at it. She saw things he didn't see, things that went right past him, and the locals would open up to her like a Venus flytrap to a fly. She could get them to tell her anything, and Mitch was lucky, at least at that time, to even get an acknowledgment of "How you doin' today."

In the months since that first encounter, they'd been forced to continue working together until some point, and he didn't remember when that was, that it wasn't forced at all. And it didn't matter because they still worked together. They were a good team, a really good team. She was the best partner he'd ever had.

Partner. The word stuck out in his mind, and he managed not to grimace at it. He had a singular dislike for that particular word because its definition had been hijacked, and now it meant way more than the word had ever been designed to mean. Partner now described couples who once would have been described as husband and wife, or wife and wife, or husband and husband. He didn't care; he just disliked that the word "partner" had been smeared indiscriminately over all of them like a bunion plaster. All of those different relationships, and each of them was unique and special enough to deserve their own word. Partner, that's what she was, his partner, by the original *ordinary* definition of the word, which was the person with whom you worked on particular assignments. But it could be more than that. He let that thought peek into his mind and look around; it made sure the coast was clear before it leapt out into the spotlight, center stage. She could be *more than that*. Did he want her to be? That was a question he wasn't quite yet ready to answer.

So he pulled his cruiser into the parking lot of the little out-of-the-way bus station that only a small local fleet of buses, Short-line Buses, serviced — so you could get on a bus in Dry Ridge and ride the twenty minutes to Fox Chapel for a couple of bucks. He had never met the man who ran the bus line but had heard that just last year the man had convinced Comfort Buses, the big bus line that serviced that whole part of the Smoky Mountains, to include at least one stop at one of the smaller stations. Then he was able to arrange a routing system to take passengers to that spot who wanted to go farther than some place within a sixty mile radius.

Somebody had probably called the boss when the body was found, because a frazzled-looking man spotted Mitch's cruiser pulling into the parking lot and came running toward it.

"This is terrible. It's awful. I've never seen anything like it in my life, my whole life," he said as Mitch was getting out of the car.

"Calm down, sir," Mitch said, "and tell me what's going on."

"What's going on is that an old guy was stabbed to death in the bathroom, holes all over him, blood, oh so much blood. I didn't know the human body had that much blood. It's awful. What if this makes Comfort Buses decide it's not a good idea to stop at the smaller bus stations? Sheriff, you got to figure out who did this, fast."

"I'm on it," he said, then corrected himself with, "We're on it," and he nodded at Rileigh, who smiled at the distraught man.

"How's Clarice?" Rileigh asked him.

"Oh, she's fine," the man said. "So damn busy with them twins, she meets herself on the way out of a room when she's coming in."

"I heard she had twins. Girls or boys?"

"One of each," he said. "My first grandchildren, but I ain't going over there anymore until they're older. As soon as I hit the door, she's begging me to babysit so she can just go sit out in the yard by herself and not do nothing."

"She needs to call Georgia for some moral support," Rileigh said. "Georgia can definitely relate."

Then Rileigh turned to Mitch.

"I'm sorry … Mitch, this is Ralph Parker, he owns Short-line Buses."

The man started in again on how Mitch had to find the murderer quick or he could lose his whole business, which Mitch considered an overreaction, but he kept that sentiment to himself.

As they walked away, Mitch shook his head. There didn't seem to be anybody in this county that one of the Bishop women, either Rileigh or her mother, didn't know, and he knew that Rileigh considered that both the good news and the bad news. The good news: well, you knew everybody. The bad news: well, they knew you, too.

He stepped into the front door of the small lobby that was now crowded with people and saw that Deputy Mullins had set up a perimeter, black and yellow police tape closing off the men's restroom on the back wall. The restrooms on the back wall were accessed by a single door under a restroom sign and then arrows pointing in both directions: a W pointing right, an M pointing left.

Mitch approached the deputy, who already had his notepad out of his pocket to give the sheriff the information he knew the sheriff was about to ask for.

"So, the victim's name is Horace Belcher. I found his wallet in his pocket." Mitch lifted an eyebrow. "Didn't have much money in it, maybe a hundred dollars, but it was still there."

"So, scratch robbery as the motive," Rileigh said.

"For now, at least," Mitch said.

"He's 87 years old, and he lives on Martindale Pike. He was on his way home from his daughter's house on the other side of Stockton."

"Who found the body?" Rileigh asked. The deputy gestured with his chin toward a man sitting by himself with his head in his hands in one of the two rows of seats available for passengers waiting to get on the bus.

"His name is—"

"I know what his name is," Rileigh said and shot Mitch a warning glance. "Let me talk to him."

Mitch nodded and watched Rileigh approach him. The man looked up at her, and his face changed as if he'd seen salvation come floating down out of the clouds from heaven.

"Oh, Rileigh, I'm so glad you're here. This is … this is … blood, so much blood!"

"Take it easy, Paul," she said, patting him on the arm.

"It's just like … can't you hear the screaming?"

"It's all right, Paul, listen to me. It's all right. Take a deep breath."

But she was too late, and the man suddenly got a stricken look on his face and fell to the floor, twitching, in the throes of a seizure.

Rileigh kneeled over him quickly, leaning his head back.

"Who's got a pen?" she asked.

Deputy Mullins gave her the pen he'd used to take notes with, and she put it crossways in the man's mouth to keep him from biting down on his tongue, and then she sat back on her heels and watched the seizure.

"This is Paul Abramson. He started having them after he got back from two tours in Afghanistan," she told the men, "had a closed-head injury. I think the epileptic seizures are just the tip of the iceberg."

Deputy Mullins went outside and plucked one of the EMTs off the second ambulance that had arrived at the crime scene; the first one had already taken the surviving victim into the hospital in town. Mitch and Rileigh gave the epileptic man over to the care of the EMT.

Mitch took a pen out of his shirt pocket and gave it to Deputy Mullins to replace the one Rileigh had taken from him, and he used it to check off the points in the notes he had taken.

"That's the bus driver," Mullins said and pointed to a man in a uniform seated behind a small desk in the corner.

"He didn't see anything. As far as I can determine, nobody saw anything. The bus driver watched the man get off the bus with the help of a woman who was also a passenger, and then the driver was busy with logbooks and didn't see anything else. He didn't see the man walk across the parking lot, didn't see him go into the bus terminal, and I can't find a single soul who was inside the bus terminal when the old man went in."

"So we have a body and no witnesses," Mitch said, sighing.

"That's about par for the course," Rileigh said, offering him a weak smile.

Continuing to consult his notes, Deputy Mullins said that an injured girl — with multiple stab wounds — had staggered out of the woods after the police arrived and collapsed. He called the ambulance, and they took her to Yarmouth County Hospital.

"So she was attacked in the woods?"

"Must have been."

It was too dark to find the crime scene in the woods right now, but the scene was secure. Nobody would go wandering out into it before morning, when Mitch would investigate and see if he could find any evidence.

"Don't mean to be Captain Obvious here, but you think the same person who killed the old man attacked the girl in the woods, don't you," Rileigh said.

Mitch raised an eyebrow. "Seems likely."

Yarmouth County Coroner Gus Hazelton had gone fly fishing in Colorado for a few days, so an autopsy would have to be performed by the forensic pathologist in Gatlinburg to determine the nature of the weapon used.

The deputy flipped his notebook shut, stuffed it back into his pocket, and handed the pen back to Mitch. "That's all I got."

"Good job," Mitch said, shooting Rileigh a glance. He didn't even have to say anything. She knew what their next stop was. The Yarmouth County Hospital to talk to the stabbing victim who had survived.

Chapter Five

The Yarmouth County Hospital was a strange-looking building, but then so were most old rural hospitals. Rileigh had never seen one that hadn't been added on to and remodeled repeatedly over the years until it became a warren of hallways and interconnected passageways, where you had to leave a trail of breadcrumbs to find your way back to your car. Though on a smaller scale than the big metro hospitals, Yarmouth County was indeed a maze. Maybe not a rabbit warren, but certainly a gerbil warren.

Mitch pulled his cruiser to the curb outside the emergency room doors and found the ambulance crew still there. He approached them, and Jefferson Whitley held up his hand in what Rileigh called a *hidey-doo*. Mitch had not responded particularly well to that colloquialism, and she knew he'd never use it himself, but at least he understood now what it meant when other people did.

"What can you tell us about the stabbing victim you just brought in?" Mitch asked.

"She didn't have any ID on her," Jeff said.

She must have left her belongings on the bus. Deputy Mullins didn't mention it, so he hadn't thought to ask about that. Rileigh was about to point that out to Mitch when she saw him typing out a text she was sure was to Beau Mullins. Great minds and all that.

"All I can tell you is: Caucasian female, early twenties, no identifying marks or tattoos that I saw, and multiple stab wounds. She came staggering out of the woods and collapsed in the parking lot. If she hadn't, she'd have bled out. As far as I can tell, nobody even knew she went into the woods."

"Do you know where was she headed on the bus?" Rileigh asked.

"She had a ticket stub in her pocket — final destination was Black Bear Forge."

"Did you recognize her? Look like any family you know?"

Jeff shook his head. "She's pretty. Blonde hair as light as Jillian's." Rileigh remembered then that her sister had dated Jeff briefly in high school.

"Why did she go running off into the woods?" Rileigh wondered aloud. "I take a bus to Black Bear Forge, I get off at the stop just before my final destination, probably to go to the bathroom, and then what? Why run off into the woods?"

"The bus driver told Deputy Mullins that a young woman helped the old man off the bus. Maybe this was her," Mitch said. "And maybe she witnessed the murder and was chased into the woods by the person who killed the old man."

"You didn't hear this from me," Jeff said, "but if you want to talk to her, you better do it fast." He shrugged. "Her blood pressure was in the basement — she lost a lot of blood."

Rileigh and Mitch left the EMT and went into the emergency room. They could see that only one of the curtained-off exam rooms was being used, and it was as busy as a colony of ants — nurses hurrying around, pieces of equipment being rolled in and out. Mitch stopped in front of the enclosure and spoke through the closed curtain.

"This is Yarmouth County Sheriff Mitchell Webster. I was wondering if I can talk to—"

The curtain was instantly yanked back, and there stood Alexander Dowling. *Doctor* Alexander Dowling, for whom the diminutive was not Alex but the far cooler-sounding Zander.

Rileigh rolled her eyes. Dowling was the doctor who had demanded she spend the night in the hospital after the brakes lines in her car were cut and she ran off the road and hit a tree. She'd refused. He'd shrugged, in his infinitely arrogant way, and said that was fine by him — she was welcome to leave, but if she did, her insurance wouldn't cover her emergency room visit. He'd coerced her into staying and had enjoyed every minute of it. Rileigh had babysat Zander Dowling when he was ten years old. He'd been a little shit then, and he was a bigger shit now.

Dowling's smile widened when he spotted Rileigh.

"Hello there," he said. "I figured you and your"—he gestured to the sheriff—"sidekick would be here pretty soon."

"Can we talk to her?" Mitch asked.

"No way in hell," he said. "She's on her way to have some scans." He pulled the curtains wide apart, and two nurses began shoving the rolling gurney down the hallway, with IV bags of both blood and plasma on poles pushed along with it, leaving Mitch and Rileigh standing with Zander. Rileigh tried to get a look at her face, but her head was turned the other way. All she could see was the dirt and leaves still in her hair — light blonde, like Jillian's.

"What can you tell us about her condition?" Mitch asked.

The doctor smiled smugly. "Nothing. That's private medical information."

"We're trying to figure out who stabbed the girl. Did she say anything to you?"

"She was unconscious when she got here. She only came around once."

"Did she say anything when she did?" Rileigh paused, then added, "Anything a person who happened to be walking by could have heard?" to emphasize that he couldn't claim every word out of a patient's mouth was private medical information.

"Nothing that made any sense," he offered grudgingly. "Just slurred something — '*iship*.'"

"*Iship*?" Rileigh repeated the word questioningly. "What does that mean?"

"You got me."

"That's it, just *iship*?"

"No, the word was bigger, longer. It was something like…" He thought. "Like '*Illie iship.*'"

"Billie Eilish?" Mitch offered, and the doctor shook his head

"No, not that, not anything that clear. Just smeared together — '*Illie iship.*"

Rileigh's eyes opened wide when a thought occurred to her. *Illie iship*…

"Could it have been… 'Lily Bishop?'"

The doctor looked at her and considered, "Yeah, I suppose it could have. It could have been a whole lot of other words, too."

Rileigh looked at Mitch, who shrugged. The victim, whoever the girl was, had a ticket to Black Bear Forge. Could she possibly have been on her way to see Lily Bishop?

Chapter Six

"LILY BISHOP."

Big John Clancy's head snapped up when he heard customers at the table near the end of the counter in Red-Eye Gravy mention Lily's name.

He sauntered over to get closer to the table, cleaning off the bar in that steady, swiping motion that he had been using to clean off bars for decades.

Big John was a classic movie buff and he had loved *The Karate Kid*, particularly the part where the old man was teaching the boy how to avoid blows by making the kid wax all the cars in the old man's collection. He'd demonstrated for the boy the proper way to put the wax on, the exact movement of the wax cloth. Then he demonstrated the proper movement to take the wax off — the opposite movement from the one required to put the wax on the car. The boy had shined a dozen or so huge cars using the exact motions he'd been taught by the old man. By the time he was finished, muscle memory had made those movements instinctual. Big John's bar-cleaning technique was the same. "Wax on," moving toward one end of the bar, then "wax off," moving toward the other, cleaning a surface that needed no cleaning, one that had been cleaned already ten times this morning.

As he rhythmically performed "wax on," he heard Turnip Smothers running his mouth.

Turnip Smothers was just about the sorriest excuse for a human being Big John had ever come across. He wasn't just too lazy to work, he was even too lazy to go to the post office to collect the government checks that paid him not to work and paid him to be lazy. He got his mama to do it for him while he lounged around every place that catered to tourists in Black Bear Forge. And when they ran him out, and they always did, he wound up plopped down on a stool at the counter in Red-Eye Gravy until Big John got tired of listening to his blather and ran him out of there, too.

"Nah, it ain't likely you're tracking Lily Bishop," Turnip said. "Daisy Bishop's the crazy one. Why, that old lady's dipstick ain't touched oil since candy bars cost a nickel."

He laughed at his own humor, cackled like an old crone stirring a black vat of witch's brew. The two men seated at a table nearby were listening intently, but apparently they didn't think the remark was any funnier than Big John did, because neither of them even cracked a smile.

Big John studied the men, all in suits and ties, olive skin, dark eyes and hair.

"So, how are Daisy Bishop and Lily Bishop connected, if they are?" asked one of the men. The accent was unmistakable. This guy's native language was Arabic. Big John would recognize that anywhere after two tours in Iraq and another in Afghanistan. Why were two Middle Eastern men asking Turnip about the Bishop family?

"Daisy's last name ain't Bishop, but she and Lily are

sisters. Daisy ain't just normal crazy, though. She's homi-cidal crazy. Why, she took after her niece with a chainsaw!"

The men's eyebrows went up and Turnip sat back on the stool and raised his hand.

"If I'm lying, I'm dying. She sure as hell did. Was gonna cut her head off with it. And she'd already smashed Rileigh's hand with a sledgehammer."

"Smashed her hand with a sledgehammer," repeated one of the Middle Eastern-looking men.

"Swear it on a stack of Bibles ten feet tall. The sheriff got there and shot her, and they locked her ass up in the funny farm."

"You're saying that's *Daisy* — and she has a sister named Lily, is that right? "

"Why sure."

Big John stepped up then and slapped the rag down on the countertop with a *pop* that sounded like a gunshot.

"Turnip!" he snapped, and the man fell instantly silent. Holding his index finger half an inch from his thumb, Big John said, "I am *this close* to making you drop your pants and take off your drawers ... so I can *stuff 'em in your pie hole to shut you up.*"

Turnip looked suitably impressed. Anybody would have been. Big John looked like he'd walked right out of a Popeye cartoon. Six feet, eight inches tall, with arms were bigger than most men's thighs and way more muscled. He had not a single hair on his shiny bald head, a thick black beard, an earring in his left ear — even had a tattoo of an anchor on his upper forearm.

Then Big John turned his attention on the two men.

"Why are you asking so many questions?"

One of them shrugged his shoulders and lifted his hands in a no-reason gesture. The other didn't move.

"Regardless of what Turnip here may have led you to

believe, folks around here don't hold with nosey strangers asking questions about one of our own." He turned on Turnip. "Get your goat-smellin' ass out of here, Turnip. You ain't bought nothing in five years."

One of the men stood. He was tall and lean and looked as mean as a snake. "We're buying for Mr. Smothers," he said and reached into his pocket. Removing a wallet full of cash and credit cards, he took out a twenty-dollar bill and tossed it toward the counter Big John stood behind.

The bill fluttered in the air before it dropped to the floor and Turnip leapt off his stool and grabbed it. Holding it out to Big John, he said, "I ain't had nothing but a cup of coffee, so I got change coming."

Big John gave him a look that surely caused internal damage.

Putting the bill down carefully on the counter, Turnip turned and hurried out the door.

The other seated man got easily to his feet. The one who'd tossed the money at Big John smiled a crooked smile and gestured at the two cups of coffee that Susie had served to them.

"That cover what we owe you?" he said.

"Depends," Big John said.

"On what?"

"On what you're paying me for. If you're just buying coffee, that'll cover it." He paused. "But if you're buying information, it'll cost you a sight more than twenty bucks."

Big John watched their faces change.

"You have information you think we might want to … purchase?"

"This part's for free. The lady you're looking for don't go by Lily Bishop. Name's 'Miss Lillian.' Or 'Madame Lillian' if you're inclined to be formal about it."

The men exchanged glances. The man still holding his

wallet pulled out a fifty-dollar bill and placed it on the bar beside the twenty.

"Where might we find Miss Lillian?" he asked.

Big John burped out a bleat of laughter.

"It sure as shit ain't here in Black Bear Forge," he said. "She ditched her hometown for the big city a long time ago. She's in Nashville now, a place better suited to … her line of work."

He picked up the bills and tucked them into his shirt pocket and said nothing else.

"Nashville's a big place," the Arab man said, pulling out another fifty-dollar bill and placing it on the bar.

"She and her girls work the bars in the Strip District," Big John said. "Ask around. Miss Lillian tends to change addresses more often than folks in other lines of work, but grease enough palms and somebody'll tell you how to find her. "

Big John picked up the second bill and put it in his pocket, then lifted his rag and began his rhythmic cleaning — wax off — down toward the other end of the bar.

The two suit-and-tie men left the place without another word.

The waitress, Susie, had clearly been eavesdropping on the conversation. "Who the hell's Miss Lillian?" she asked.

"When I was a teenager, Miss Lillian *Bichon* ran a house of ill repute in Nashville."

"That was twenty-five years ago — you think she's *still* there?"

"Wouldn't be surprised. Ever see the movie *The Princess Bride?*"

Susie rolled her eyes. "Only about a thousand times. It was my Mama's favorite movie."

"Remember the Dread Pirate Roberts?" Understanding washed across Susie's face, and Big John nodded. "I figure it's probably like that."

In the movie, when the pirate "retired," he passed on his name and reputation to someone else, so there was always a Dread Pirate Roberts sailing the sea.

"Those yahoos will chase their tails around for a few days before they figure out what's going on. Teach 'em to mind their own damned business." He patted his shirt pocket. "Though we do appreciate their generous donation to the Yarmouth County Animal Shelter."

Big John kept the grin in place on his face until Susie went to go wait on other customers. It drained away then. He'd seen men like that before, and he wondered what in the hell they wanted with Rileigh Bishop's mother. Well, he'd sidetracked them long enough for him to give Lily a head's up. He hadn't seen her for more than a week, so she was long overdue for a vanilla milkshake. She'd be in today or tomorrow, and when she came in, Big John would warn her then that two dangerous-looking men had been inquiring about "Lily Bishop."

Chapter Seven

"LILY BISHOP." RILEIGH ROLLED THE WORDS OFF HER tongue, then asked Mitch, "You think that's what she was saying?"

Mitch shrugged. "Maybe."

Opening the squawking screen door for Rileigh, he stepped aside to usher her into Mama's living room ahead of him. He had come over for Sunday dinner with the family, which flipped the relational switch to "dating behavior" from "professional behavior," where it had been set last night when they'd had to cancel their plans yet again to go dashing off to a crime scene.

Mama was clucking around everyone, getting them seated properly in the dining room, as if any of them needed to be shown where to sit. Rileigh noticed the way David Hicks was looking at Jillian and wondered if that was the way Mitch looked at her when she wasn't looking. Surely not. Surely not *that* kind of adoring gaze. But who knew?

It was possible, she supposed. She certainly was guilty of looking at him adoringly sometimes. And she was grateful that she no longer had to pretend it wasn't happening.

They'd given up that charade after the night Shagbark Manor burned to the ground, when Mitch was almost too late to haul her out of the HVAC fan and away from its blades and the flames.

She smiled at the thought — he'd *come out of the closet* big time that night, held her in his arms, trembling, both of them shocked and horrified and still frightened by how close a call it had been. Rileigh had escaped from the burning basement to the only opening available. There was a big fan in it that turned on automatically to the siren song of some automatic thermostat or other that even the Shagbark Manor's owner didn't understand. Mitch had been on the other side, removing the grate so she could get through when, for some reason, the fan had cranked up and sprung to life, which meant within seconds it would have sliced Rileigh into pieces. Mitch had yanked the grate heel off the front of the fan with one enormous pull, grabbed her by the arm, and yanked again as the blade was beginning to turn. They lay together just beyond the whirring blade, listening as the fan spun faster and faster until it was a blur of movement behind the grate. They had laid there together, panting, terrified, Mitch holding her tight, and it was a little while before she even registered what he was saying, his words. "I love you. I love you, Rileigh. Rileigh, I was so scared for you. I love you. I love you." And that broke the dam for both of them. She told him she loved him. And when she thought back on it, she wondered if maybe she didn't even realize it fully until that moment.

No, that wasn't right. She'd known it for months, just wouldn't let herself know it, because loving him made all kinds of things complicated. Well, they were complicated now, and she was surviving nicely, thank you very much.

"Lumps in the potatoes!" Mama decreed, a look of horror on her face.

"No, Mama, there aren't," Jillian said. "You whipped them."

"I'm telling you, there are lumps in these potatoes. It's my fault. I'm getting sloppy in my old age,

"Mama, they're fine."

"More than fine," David Hicks put in. "They're wonderful. Glorious." He shoved a big spoonful of them into his mouth to demonstrate.

"Mashed potatoes ain't supposed to have no lumps in them," Mama said, clearly very upset by her discovery. If they didn't do something fast, that "lumps in the mashed potato" reality might just hang on a nail in her head, where most every other reality nearly flowed slowly through, in one side and out the other. But if a thing got hung up in there, her dementia would blow it all out of proportion, and make her life and everyone else's life miserable while she beat herself up about it.

Rileigh saw the look from Jillian that meant she'd realized the same thing. They had only seconds to respond.

"Mama, is there any more ice in the freezer?" Jillian blurted out at the same moment that Rileigh said, "I need some more lemonade."

Their mother responded to each in turn, looking from Jillian to Rileigh and back to Jillian. The moment elongated, and then they saw the lumps-in-the-mashed-potatoes issue come loose from the hook in their mother's mind and flow gently away downstream.

"Well, I can get you some ice and you some fresh lemonade my own self," Mama said. "I was just about to get up anyway. That butter dish is nigh on to empty, and cornbread ain't no good 'thout butter slathered all over it."

The sisters smiled at each other as Mama got up and left the room.

"Whew!" Mitch said.

"Dodged a bullet," David said.

"Jillian sank the three-point shot," Rileigh said and smiled at her sister.

"Nothin' but net," Jillian acknowledged daintily.

Mama returned without any more butter for the dish, but with ice for Rileigh and a glass of lemonade for Jillian. Rileigh looked around the table, watching the ebb and flow of conversation — four-wheeling in the woods, the pros and cons thereof, dirt bike riding in the woods, the pros and cons thereof, and squirrel hunting, which was mostly cons because Mitch had been so traumatized by the whole process of cleaning the little critters after they killed them the last time they went. Rileigh had been reluctant to bring the subject up again.

She watched the easy way that Jillian and David now related to each other. It made her heart swell in her chest with joy.

When Jillian had first returned, David had appeared on the scene too soon and put on a full-court press, a gentle, kind full-court press, but even so, he had asked more of Jillian than she was able to give in her fragile state. After an ailing FBI agent had spent a week in their home and Jillian'd had to relate in a normal manner to a normal man with whom she had no past and no obligations, she had realized that she needed space. She needed for David to back off. Maybe there was something there. Maybe there wasn't. But it was all moving too fast. And she'd told David as much.

David had taken the news like a champ. He had bowed

out, told her that he was around if she ever wanted to give him a call, and maybe they could have dinner now and then. Or lunch. Or not.

And for five or six weeks, they had barely seen each other at all. Jillian had done a lot of soul-searching, a significant amount of healing, and had many hours of deeply troubling therapy sessions with Dr. Al-Masri that had opened up devastating wounds that'd been festering for thirty years. Sometimes she'd come home from those sessions so shattered, Rileigh feared she had finally been pushed too far, that her sister had been asked to cope with more than she could stand. And then she had started coming back. It had been slow going. Rileigh had watched it with fear and trembling, saw her sister very slowly and gradually return to a semblance of who she had been before her Aunt Daisy had destroyed her life, as surely as if she put a gun to her head.

It had been Jillian who called David and asked him if he wanted to go to lunch with her at Red-Eye Gravy. And David, bless his heart and thank you, Lord, had replied he'd love to, but today wasn't a good day. How about next Thursday?

That one act may have completely erased his bumbling possessiveness when she first came home. Jillian had waited a week, and David had called, said this was a good day. Did she want to go? And she did. Since then, the two of them had gradually rediscovered the beginnings of the feelings they'd had for each other as teenagers. Had it not been for Aunt Daisy, the two of them would have been celebrating their silver anniversary. And as Rileigh watched them now teasing each other, easy and laughing and enjoying life together, she no longer cringed when Mama brought up the subject of that aborted wedding and how she'd sure be glad to crank up that engine again if anybody was interested.

Rileigh noticed that Mitch, David, and Jillian didn't flinch at her mother's attempts to orchestrate their lives back into the proper lanes, that Jillian and David didn't flinch at her stumbling attempts at matchmaking. They just looked at each other and smiled, and she suspected, didn't know but suspected, that perhaps the two of them had been talking about that very subject themselves.

"Earth to Rileigh. Come in, this is Houston control," Mitch said.

Rileigh shook her head. "Was I zoning?"

"I'm not sure where you were," Mitch said, "but it was somewhere other than right here."

"Sorry about that. What did you say?"

"It wasn't what I said, it's what Mama said." Mitch turned to Mama. "Launch it again and see if maybe it hits the target this time."

"I just asked you if you and Mitch had a good time last night at dinner at Bonefish Grill. Did they finally make a steak cooked the way you like it?"

Rileigh looked at Mitch and grinned. "It was good, but it still wasn't cooked like I like it." She held up her hand before Mitch had a chance to speak. "And no, I did not tell them to take it back and cook it again."

Before either Mama or Mitch could scold her, Jillian leapt to the rescue. "When you got home, you said the two of you were called out on a case. What was that about?"

"We were called to a murder and the stabbing at the bus station in Sandstone Creek," Mitch said. "Murder victim was an old man named Horace Belcher. He was stabbed to death in the men's room."

Mama's hands flew to her mouth. "Oh my, the poor man."

"But there was another victim who survived," Mitch said hurriedly, trying to channel Mama's angst before it cranked into high gear. "A young woman whose bus ticket was to Black Bear Forge stumbled out of the woods and collapsed from half a dozen knife wounds."

"Oh my goodness," Mama said.

"But she survived," Mitch said quickly. "She's in the hospital now."

"Who was she?"

Mitch shrugged.

"Don't know yet. Deputy Mullins collected her purse from the bus last night, but I haven't seen it. She was too out of it last night to give her name, but I'm going to try to talk to her tomorrow morning."

Rileigh wrinkled her nose. "Emphasis on 'try to.' The attending physician was Dr. Alexander-I-made-it-through-med-school-and-you-didn't Dowling."

Jillian looked puzzled. "Who's that?"

"I used to babysit the little shit when he was a redheaded terror," Rileigh said. "He's larger and more educated now, but still not a day over six years old."

"He said he spoke to the girl briefly before she passed out, but she didn't make any sense."

"What did she say?" Jillian asked.

"Just slurred words," Rileigh said.

"Sounded like Billie Eilish," Mitch said.

"No, Zander said it sounded more like Lily Bishop."

"No, *you* said it sounded more like Lily Bishop. The doctor said it could have been anything."

"Lily Bishop?" Jillian asked, confused.

"Syllables that sounded like that," Mitch said.

"Jefferson Whitley was the EMT who treated her."

"I dated Jeff for a bit in high school," Jillian said to David.

"Oh, I remember," David said, grinning.

"All he could give," Mitch continued, "was basic information — Caucasian female, early 20s. But he said she had blonde hair that reminded him of Jillian's."

"There's nobody in the world who's got hair that's as pretty and pale blonde as Jillian's," Mama said. But Rileigh noticed that Jillian's face had frozen at the mention of hair that reminded Whitley Jefferson of Jillian's.

And for the rest of the evening, Rileigh noticed that Jillian seemed to be out of sorts, like her mind was somewhere else entirely.

Chapter Eight

MITCH WENT INTO HIS OFFICE EARLY ON MONDAY MORNING to go through the contents of the purse and "luggage" that belonged to the stabbing victim. Deputy Mullins had retrieved it from the bus. There was only a small suitcase, carry-on size, containing clothing — tees and jeans, socks and underwear, basic toiletries. There was also a small purse with almost nothing in it — a little makeup and a wallet with an ID card. Not a driver's license, but an ID card with a name and photograph. The photo was of a young woman with pale blonde hair, whose name was Michaela Marie Hollis, date of birth: September 18, 2004. No address was listed.

The most interesting thing about the contents of Michaela Hollis's purse was what *wasn't* there. No cell phone. That made no sense at all to Mitch. Surely there weren't more than a dozen people under the age of 25 anywhere in America who didn't have a cell phone. But this girl didn't. She had an ID card and less than a hundred dollars in cash. No credit cards. None of the other cards you might expect, either. Student ID. Social

Security card. Grocery Store "rewards" card, Costco or Sam's Club card. Gym admittance card or bus transfer. She had none of those things.

Reminded Mitch of Tecumseh, the native American chief who boasted that he had not been born but had burst fully grown from an oak tree.

Mitch took the purse and suitcase with him to the hospital to return it to the stabbing victim, and quickly discovered that Dr. Alexander Dowling, M.D., was an equal opportunity asshole. He was just as rude and obnoxious to Mitch as he had been to Rileigh when the two of them had tried to talk to the girl the night she was admitted.

Rileigh had told Mitch "Zander's" story. It seemed that the boy's parents didn't want his poor, fragile little ego stifled in any way, stunted by "negativity," and that they believed the best way to ensure that he would grow into the great man he was destined to become was by not disciplining him in any way. Translate that: they let him get away with behaving like a monster, and it was culture shock when Rileigh had shown up on the scene and expected him to behave like a reasonable human being. The family never hired Rileigh to babysit again after they came home from going out to dinner and found their still-furious son duct-taped to a kitchen chair. Rileigh informed them that when the cable television went out in the middle of his favorite movie, he had gone to the garage for a bowling ball and tried to throw it through the television screen. When Rileigh stopped him, he bit her, so she'd duct-taped him to a chair. She said she'd once done the same thing to Georgia — duct-taped her to a chair — but Mitch hadn't yet been able to wheedle *that* story out of her.

Dr. Dowling would likely claim the trauma of that incident had scarred him for life. Maybe that's what turned him into a self-absorbed, arrogant asshole, but it was more likely that the remainder of his upbringing had destined him for that outcome, and Rileigh's intervention had just been too little too late to prevent it.

One way or the other, the doctor was a jerk, totally uncooperative, not the least bit interested in helping Mitch figure out who had almost killed the girl who had been entrusted to his medical care. Mitch had to threaten him to get even a few minutes alone with the girl.

Mitch found her with her eyes closed, pale as the sheet she was lying on. She was a fair-skinned young woman who did indeed have hair as pale blonde as Jillian's. Her skin was so fair that Mitch could see the tracing of blue veins in her temples. He stood beside her bed without speaking for a few moments, trying to figure out exactly what he could say to her, when she opened her eyes, saw him, looking surprised and then frightened.

"What do you want with me?" she asked, her voice as small and fragile as a small child.

"Whoa, wait a minute, I'm not here because you're in any trouble. I'm here to talk to you to find out who did this to you."

"Did what to me?"

"Stabbed you."

"*Stabbed* me?"

"Yes, someone stabbed you. Don't you remember?"

Her eyes took on a faraway look, and he watched an odd, disassociated array of emotions cross her face before she shook her head and said, "I don't remember being stabbed."

"Alright, what do you remember?"

She looked at him quizzically.

He decided to start with a more basic question. Maybe she had lost so much blood, her thinking was fuzzy.

"I brought your purse to you, thought you would want it with you," he said and put the small purse on the bedside table. She didn't look at it. "Can you tell me your name?"

"I'm Micky Hollis."

That was progress.

"And how old are you?"

"Nineteen. I'll be twenty in a few days."

More progress.

"And where were you going on the bus?"

"My sister Farrah and I were on our way from" — she paused then as if she was deciding whether or not she was going to tell him where. Then she merely said vaguely, "California to Black Bear Forge."

Sister? Mitch was surprised. "You were traveling with your sister?"

No "sister" had come forward when they were investigating the murder scene at the bus station or when they were loading Micky into the ambulance. Where had this sister Farrah gone?

"Are you aware that a man was murdered last night in the bus station," Mitch asked.

She looked like he'd slapped her. "No," she said too quickly. "What man? I don't know who stabbed him."

Mitch had said "murdered," not "stabbed."

She was getting upset, and Mitch knew that if she did, Zander would swoop into the room and make him leave. So he quickly changed the subject.

"You and your sister were on the bus together — did both of you get out at the Sandstone Creek station?"

"The bathrooms on that bus are smaller than a broom closet and I needed to use the plumbing," was all she said.

"When you got off, did you see anything … *odd,* out of the ordinary in the bus station?"

"No … not in the station," she said, and he had the

sense that she was mentally skipping over important parts of the narrative. "But when we walked outside, we saw a man getting out of a red pickup truck."

"A man getting out of a red pickup truck — why is that out of the ordinary?"

"Because it was the truck that had been following us."

"A red pickup truck had been following the bus?"

"Yes. I saw him outside Kansas City, but then I decided maybe I was imagining things, but then I'd see him again at other stops, kept getting closer and closer to the bus. Every time we stopped, there was that same red pickup truck."

This was a turn in the story Mitch hadn't been expecting.

"Did you tell the bus driver that somebody was following the bus? Did you report it?"

"We didn't tell anybody, because he wasn't there all the time. So we wouldn't see him for a while and decide it was just coincidence... and then he'd show up again."

She was getting upset again. So he shifted topics.

"So you walked outside with your sister after you used the facilities and you saw a red pickup truck and a man got out of it. Is that right?"

"Yes. And he came toward us and we were scared, and so we ran, split up, I ran one way and Farrah ran the other. And then..." Her voice trailed off and her eyes took on a faraway look again.

Then her eyes suddenly snapped back to his face.

"I don't know what happened after that, okay? I don't remember."

She spoke the words in such a forceful tone, no longer sounding fragile or confused, that Mitch almost took a step back.

"You said you were traveling with your sister Farrah.

Where is she? Where did she go? Nobody came forward after you were stabbed."

"I told you — she ran! We both ran." Her voice grew quieter. "And you won't find her. You'll *never* find Farrah. She can hide right out in plain sight. She's like a ghost, like the wind. She can disappear and it's like she was never there at all."

Micky shook her head.

"And in the woods… she blends in like a deer, just vanishes, catches rabbits without even using snares."

The Sandstone Creek station was right on the edge of the Great Smoky Mountains National Park — eight hundred square miles, more than half a million acres of woods, much of it wilderness.

"Describe her."

"Farrah looks like me, blonde hair, blue eyes. We're very similar. Of course, she's bigger than I am." The girl gestured down at herself as if to make the point that she was especially small. Mitch would have put her at five-four or five-five, but slender, and lying there with bandages on her arms and hands and head, she did appear small.

"What was she wearing?"

"A camo tee and black jeans." The same thing Micky'd been wearing.

"Anything on the front of the shirt — a design, words, a logo?"

"No, just plain camo."

"I'm trying to understand this — why didn't she come out of hiding when she realized you'd been attacked? When it was safe, after the police arrived. Why would she hide?"

"We were scared, okay?" Her voice grew high and reedy thin. "I told you, we were afraid of the man in the pickup."

Apparently, Dr. Dowling had to have been standing just outside the door, listening. When he heard distress in her voice, that's all he needed. He swooped in and took over.

"You're upsetting my patient, Sheriff Webster. You'll have to go now."

"I didn't mean to upset you," Mitch said to the girl in the bed. Then the doctor deliberately stepped between him and his patient as if he planned to tackle Mitch if he spoke to her again.

"I'll be back later when you're feeling better," Mitch said to the person he couldn't see behind the doctor. Then he turned and left the room.

Chapter Nine

AFTER HE LEFT THE YARMOUTH COUNTY HOSPITAL, Mitch drove to the bus station in Collierton to connect with the bus driver who had run the route through the Sandstone Creek station the night before. Deputy Mullins had talked to the man, but Mitch had not, had chosen instead to try to talk to the stabbing victim at the hospital.

The bus driver's name was Harold Gilbert and Mitch found him playing a video game on his phone and chain smoking in the tiny office area of the station.

As Mitch approached, the man stepped to the doorway and called out, "The bus to Cedar Run departs in fifteen minutes. If you have a ticket to Cedar Run, Thomasville, Sander's Landing, or High Rock, you must be seated in the bus five minutes before departure. I will not hold the bus for stragglers."

Then he nodded to Mitch.

"I figure I know why you're here. You want to talk to me about what happened in Sandstone Creek."

Mitch was close enough now that he could smell it —

the distinct aroma of alcohol on the driver's breath. And it wasn't even noon.

"I do."

"Wasted effort. I don't know anything more'n I told your deputy last night. I got no idea what went down."

"What can you tell me about the old man who was killed, Mr. Belcher?"

"Not much. He got on in Granger, a transfer from the 4:45 bus from Nashville, but when we stopped in Harper's Ridge, he started bitching about his walker."

He shrugged. "Hate to speak ill of the dead, but he was a grumpy son of a bitch, if you know what I mean. I'd folded his walker up and put it in the back of the bus, but he started complaining that it had a — he called it a 'saddle bag' — attached to it that had things in it he had to have, absolutely *had* to have. Demanded that I bring him the walker so he could get what he needed. Soon as I brought him the walker, he started demanding that I put it in the seat beside him. There was a young woman sitting there, and she wasn't exactly thrilled to get up and give up her seat to the walker. But the man was pitching such a fit, I told her she needed to move. So she did. Not happily, but she did."

"You assigned her a different seat?"

The driver rolled his eyes.

"*Assigned?* This ain't a big-city bus line. The folks in the back was always shifting around. Wasn't up to me to see who was sitting where. If she didn't like that seat, she coulda got up and moved somewhere else. Bus wasn't full. Lots of empties."

"And when the bus stopped at Sandstone Creek…?"

"Middle of the night, everybody else was sleeping, but the old man was trying to get up out of his seat and having a hard time doing it. And one of the girls that was sitting in the back — there was four or five of them, but I think it was the blonde — reached past him and picked up his walker and put it in the aisle, unfolded it for him, helped him get up and wheel his way out. I was outside, standing in front of the bus."

"Doing what?"

The man scrambled for a beat. "Just stretching, that's all. Your legs will get to cramping if you sit in one spot too long. I helped the old guy down the stairs. He went into the building, then I never saw him again."

"So you didn't see anybody go into the bathroom after he did?"

"I wasn't in the building. I didn't see the bathroom. I was standing out by the bus."

"Did any of the other passengers get off the bus?"

"A few, I 'spose. Maybe. Like I said, I wasn't paying much attention." He seemed to catch himself. "I mean, I was busy, keeping track of the logbooks and such. If they got off, I didn't see. I did see the blonde girl go into the building, but I never saw her again after that either."

"The blonde girl — there was just one blonde girl?"

"How would I know? You think I keep track of what color hair my passengers have?"

"You do know that she was found later, that she had been attacked and stabbed."

"Yeah, that's what they say."

"I spoke to her a little while ago, and she told me she and her sister were traveling from California to Black Bear Forge and—"

"Sister? One of them other girls was her sister?"

"Other girls?"

"Yeah, there was maybe half a dozen 'bout the same age, but I didn't know any of them was related. Ain't two last names the same on the passenger list."

"You sure?"

"Sure, I'm sure. You think I don't know who's on my own bus?"

In truth, Mitch was becoming convinced that the driver likely spent so much time "stretching" that he didn't know much of anything that was going on in his bus.

"When you did a head count of the passengers, didn't you notice if anyone was missing?"

"Head count?"

"You don't do head counts?"

"What for?"

"At each station before you pull out, to make sure nobody got left behind?"

"Hell no, I don't count heads. People get on, people get off — I'm not a babysitter."

"I talked to the young woman who was stabbed, and she said that a red pickup truck had been following the bus all the way from Kansas City."

The man's head snapped up, and he looked at Mitch.

"I don't know nothing about Kansas City, but I think I might have seen that red pickup truck outside Knoxville."

"Tell me about it."

"Well, I just, every now and then I'd look in the rearview mirror, and there was a red pickup truck. And after a while, I got to noticing and it seemed like the same one."

"Did you see who was driving it?"

"Oh no, it never got that close. It's just, every time I looked back, there was a pickup truck."

"So Michaela Hollis didn't tell you that there was a red pickup truck following the bus?"

"Nobody told me nothing about a pickup truck. I seen it my own self."

Mitch then wasted the next twenty minutes questioning the bus driver about each one of the passengers who had been on the bus. The driver had given a list of their names to Deputy Mullins the night before, but knew nothing about any of them, didn't know if they were traveling alone or with one of the other passengers, didn't know where they were seated or if any of them connected in any way to Michaela Hollis or Mr. Belcher. Had protested that you might need a picture ID to get on an airplane but there was no such rule about buses. Mullins had established that none of the passengers were native to Yarmouth County.

The driver was watching the big clock on the wall of the station, getting more and more fidgety. There was plenty of time before the bus was scheduled to depart. Then it dawned on Mitch that the driver was anxious to get his conversation over with so he'd have time to "stretch" before he had to pull out.

"You got any more questions? I got … things to do to get this bus ready, else we'll be late for the pickup in Hoperton."

"That's all the questions I have now," Mitch said. "But I might want to talk to you again later."

"Sure, whatever. You know where you can find me." He shook Mitch's hand. "Right now, I need to use the facilities." Then he practically bolted to the bathroom. Mitch was sure he was smart enough to keep his alcohol intake below the legal limit, so there was no sense trying to bust him, but still he hung around until the driver emerged from the bathroom and watched him to make sure he saw no sign of impairment.

The man yelled out into the lobby of the bus station, "All aboard now. Anybody not in their seat in ten minutes will be left behind." Then he turned to Mitch. "About that red pickup ... I did notice one thing — it had California plates."

Mitch watched the bus pull away, thinking, questioning.

California — that's where Michaela was from. Did she know the driver of the pickup? Was he following the bus because he was following her?

If Michaela Hollis's sister'd also run from the man in the parking lot, did he catch her, perhaps? Kidnap her? Kill her? Was the man in the red pickup truck the person who had killed the old man and stabbed Michaela?

Maybe Rileigh could get more information from the stabbing victim. She had volunteered to take a shot at questioning the girl this afternoon.

Chapter Ten

RILEIGH TOOK MAMA TO HER SEWING CIRCLE AT THE FIRST
Baptist Church before she swung by Yarmouth County
Hospital to have a talk with the stabbing victim, Michaela
Hollis. When she arrived at the hospital, she found Belinda
St. Clair on duty on Michaela's floor. Before she went to
nursing school, Belinda had been a champion skeet
shooter, and Rileigh had envied her prowess, often asked
for her advice before Rileigh became an expert marksman,
courtesy of the training from Uncle Sam.

Rileigh told Belinda why she'd come to the hospital
and asked confidentially if Dr. Dowling was anywhere
around. Belinda rolled her eyes in an appropriate response
to the mention of his name and she said she would let
Rileigh know when he was back on the floor.

Michaela was lying in bed with her eyes closed when
Rileigh went into the room. But her face looked tense.
Surely she wasn't asleep, because faces relaxed in sleep.

"Michaela," she said, and the girl's eyes snapped open
like somebody pulled a window shade down too far and let
it go.

"Name's *Micky*. What do you want with me?"

Rileigh tried to steady her, calm her down.

"I only want to help you. You're not in any trouble. I'm working with the sheriff to investigate your case and the case of the old man who was murdered in the bus station the night you were attacked.

"The old man," she said, shaking her head.

"Did you know him?"

"No, he was just one of the passengers on the bus."

"The bus driver said that you helped him off the bus when he was having trouble getting around."

That was a guess on Rileigh's part. He'd said "the blonde girl" had helped the old man. Micky and her sister Farrah were both blonde, but Rileigh didn't know if they were the only fair-haired passengers.

"Would you mind telling me what you can remember about what happened the night you were stabbed, about who attacked you?"

"I don't know who attacked me. Somebody jumped me out of the dark. I don't know who it was."

"Why did you run away into the woods?"

"I told already told the police — because of the man in the red pickup truck."

"Did he follow you into the woods and attack you?"

"I don't know. Maybe. I just said I didn't see who attacked me. Just somebody leapt out of the dark."

"Tell me about your sister Farrah."

The girl's face slammed shut like Mama's screen door when the hinge was pulled taut. "What about Farrah?"

"Well, for starters, where is she? If the two of you were on the bus together, then where did she go? The bus driver said there was only one bag tagged 'Hollis' in the luggage compartment of the bus — yours. And you were the only Hollis on the passenger list."

"We packed together. We don't have much. And Farrah doesn't go by 'Hollis.'"

"What name does she use?"

"Whatever name suits her at the time. Might decide to be Rumpelstiltskin. She's a free spirit."

A free spirit, or somebody who wants to hide her identity.

"So where is she?"

"I don't know where she is. We both ran."

"We've been looking for her, but there's been no report of a suspicious person, somebody who didn't look like they belonged there, near that bus station. Tell me what she looks like."

"I already told the sheriff. She looks like me. Blonde hair and blue eyes. That's what our parents wanted."

She ground the word "parents" between cinched teeth. There was a story there.

"If you're looking for Farrah, look for somebody who looks like me."

"What was she wearing that day on the bus?" Rileigh knew what Micky'd said her sister was wearing. Mitch had told her.

"A camo tee shirt and black jeans."

"That's what you were wearing, too. Do you always dress alike?"

"It wasn't on purpose or anything like that. Tee shirts are cheap."

The girl reached up and rubbed her temples in the gesture of one who is exhausted. And Rileigh didn't want to tire her out.

"You're not giving us much to go on to find the person who did this to you," Rileigh said.

"I'm giving you everything I've got. I swear, I don't know who it was. I didn't see anybody."

"Did you see who killed the old man in the bathroom?" Rileigh dropped the question unexpectedly on purpose, to watch Micky's reaction.

"No!" she said, too quickly and too forcefully. "I wasn't in the bathroom. I didn't see anything. We just got off the bus and walked out to get some air and saw the man, and he came after us and we ran. That's all I know."

"Your ticket was to Black Bear Forge. Why were you coming here?"

Her face went utterly blank and Rileigh watched her scramble, trying to come up with a good lie. Apparently, the truth wasn't something she wanted to share.

"We just … you know, we wanted to come to the Smoky Mountains. Everybody comes to the Smoky Mountains, and we heard it was beautiful, so we came."

"Do you have relatives here? Did you come to find your family?"

The girl froze as still as a hood ornament.

"Find your family." She repeated what Rileigh said, then fell silent.

"Is that it? Did you and your sister come to visit your family?"

"I'm tired of answering questions. I don't want to just keep telling you I don't know, and I *don't* know. Why can't you stop bothering me?"

"We're bothering you so we can find out what happened to you."

The girl was getting more and more agitated, but Rileigh didn't know why.

"Who are you anyway?" the girl asked, her tone hostile. "You're not wearing a police officer's uniform."

"I was a police officer once — not anymore. But I'm from Yarmouth County, I'm a local, so I help the sheriff on cases when he's short-handed."

She held out her hand. "I'm sorry. I should have introduced myself. My name is Rileigh Bishop."

"Bishop?" The girl coughed out the single word as if it were riding a puff of air that'd just been knocked out of her lungs. "You're Rileigh *Bishop*?"

"Yes. The doctor told us you were mumbling when you were first admitted in the emergency room making odd sounds, and one of them sounded like 'Bishop.' Were you saying Bishop?"

"I don't know. Maybe."

"Does that name mean something to you?"

She didn't answer, so Rileigh plowed ahead. "Actually, what you were mumbling sounded like 'Lily Bishop.'"

"What do you know about Lily Bishop?" Micky Hollis demanded.

"Lily Bishop is my mother. "

"Your *mother*?"

"Why were you coming here to see Mama?"

"I … I wasn't. I mean … I can't…"

"How do you know my mother?"

In strode Dr. Dowling, the nurse who had promised to warn Rileigh trailing behind him. She gave Rileigh an apologetic shrug.

"I'm afraid you'll have to go now, Miss Bishop," Rowling said, sneering at his gotcha. "My patient needs to rest."

"We were just having a conversation."

"Do you want to keep talking to this person?" he asked Micky. She shook her head slightly, then just closed her eyes.

And with that, Rileigh was promptly expelled from the room.

She walked down to the elevator and punched the

down arrow. The man who'd been walking behind her in the hallway punched the up arrow.

"You come to see the babies?" he asked.

"What? No…" Then she remembered. "The maternity ward's on the fifth floor. This is the third."

He cocked a thumb back toward the nurse's station.

"Yeah, that's what they told me."

The elevator arrived — going up — and Rileigh got in. There were only five floors in the building, and this one elevator. She'd ride it up and then back down.

"You visiting somebody sick?" the man asked as the two of them obeyed elevator etiquette and stared at the slowly moving numbers without looking at each other.

"Not sick … injured," Rileigh said.

The elevator doors opened on the fourth floor, but nobody got on. The man reached over and punched the button marked "five," but the doors remained open. He punched again, and they closed.

"In an accident, were they?" the man asked.

"No, it wasn't an accident."

The doors opened on the fifth floor and the man stepped out. You could hear the nearby cry of a newborn and several people stood at the windowed nursery across from the elevator, ogling the babies in cribs.

"Got me a brand-new baby boy," the man said, smiling broadly.

Rileigh looked at him then — an ordinary guy, brown hair and eyes. She noticed his disheveled appearance and his exhaustion, like he hadn't slept in days. Returning his smile, she said, "Congratulations," and the elevator doors closed.

As Rileigh walked out to her car, she rolled around in her mind what Michaela Hollis — who had not been *accidentally* stabbed — had said. And what she hadn't said. She had definitely responded to the words "Lily Bishop." Was she on her way to Black Bear Forge to see Lily Bishop? What possible connection could this strange girl have with Mama?

DANIEL FARLEY WATCHED the elevator doors close, then the smile drained off his face. The maternity ward was the best place in a hospital to go unnoticed. The hallway was always filled with people — fathers, grandmothers, neighbors, friends come to see the new baby.

And since he'd been awake for… what? — three days, maybe, sleeping a few minutes here and a few there when the bus stopped — he fit right in as a new father.

He could get some sleep now, though. He knew where the girl was, and she wasn't going anywhere anytime soon. He'd seen the woman in the elevator come out of her room, so he'd ask around, find out who the woman was, what her connection was to the "injured" girl on the third floor.

Then he'd wait. Bide his time. Daniel Farley was a patient man, and he didn't care how long it took or who he had dispose of along the way. He'd get his hands on the little Hollis bitch sooner or later, and then he'd slit her throat.

Chapter Eleven

MICKY HOLLIS LAY IN HER HOSPITAL BED AFTER THE woman with all the questions left her room — the woman who'd said her mother was "Lily Bishop." She pretended to be sleeping when the doctor wanted to know if she would like for him to block that particular visitor. He could do that, he said, keep her away. All Micky had to do was say the word. She ignored him, said nothing, and eventually he left.

Lily Bishop is my mother. Why were you coming here to see Mama?

The woman's words banged around in Micky's head like an oil drum that had broken its moorings and was pinballing around on the deck of a tanker in a stormy sea.

It had started after she ran away, when the aid worker in the homeless encampment where she'd taken refuge got a crush on her. He'd been intrigued by the lone blonde girl — he called her a "Nordic blonde" in the swarm of South American and Middle Eastern and other nationalities who were streaming unchecked across the U.S.'s southern border.

He'd gently pestered her with questions about how she'd come to be at the shelter, but she'd been reluctant to tell him anything, just said that she had been living with people — not her parents — and it got ugly and she ran. And when he asked her about her family of origin, she shrugged and said she didn't know anything about them. That's when he'd suggested FindYourFamily.com.

"It's a website where you send a sample of your own DNA, and it will look for a match from among the thousands of other people who've also gone there looking for their roots," he tells her. Carson Granger is a very intense young man, with a narrow face and sharp features and a dogged determination she could see in his eyes the first day she met him.

"It doesn't look for a match just … anywhere? Like in criminal or military records?" she asks.

"Nope. Just looks for matches among other people who are also looking for matches," Carson says. He keeps after her, won't let the subject drop. Finally, to shut him up, she lets him swab out her cheek with a Q-tip, seal it up in a Ziplock bag, put it in an envelope with her application, and send it off. What's the harm? A flaming arrow shot out into the darkness that sputters briefly and then goes out.

Days go by in the shelter that's loud and hot, filled to twice its capacity with unruly, undisciplined children, screaming babies, fights, and many very dangerous-looking men who flow in and out of the shelter overnight and are gone.

Then comes the day when Carson runs into the mess hall and snatches her away from lunch.

"Come on, Michaela, they found something."

He takes her outside under the persimmon tree and pulls out of his pocket an official-looking envelope from FindYourFamily.com. In it is a paper that tells her more about herself and where she came from than she has ever known. All she knew were "parents" who abused her and the other children mercilessly. Michaela didn't know how they had arrived in that situation, only knew the cardinal rule: Keep your mouth shut or you'll be sorry. She lived in a little house in the middle of nowhere, where her father and Uncle Dan engaged in unspeakable depravity with the small children in their care. She would still be there, in fact, if it hadn't been for a drunk driver who ran her father's truck off the road. The truck rolled. Michaela was miraculously unharmed, but her father was seriously injured. And as she watched the onlookers try to help him, heard the sirens of ambulances and police that they had called, she suddenly realized this was her chance. She could run. She grabbed what little she had and did just that, ending up with thousands of illegal aliens in a huge facility for the migrants outside Sacramento.

Carson takes the papers out of the envelope and spreads them out on the picnic table in front of them.

"This is the paternal side of your family tree," he says, pointing to the chart on one of the papers. "And this is the maternal."

Carson explains that hers is a very rare case, that the DNA registry had found samples with close familial ties on both sides of her family.

She looks first at the paper that describes her mother's family tree and finds that she is a close match to a woman in Tennessee who had submitted her DNA. Michaela registered a very high match — the woman is either her sister, aunt, mother, or grandmother.

The match on her father's side is equally compelling,

but not as clear and simple. In the space for DNA contributor are the words "group sample # 89."

"What does that mean?"

"You have to read the fine print. That's where it says all the students in an anthropology class at Stanford University provided their DNA to the site. More than 100 people in the class. And you were a very close match to … well, whoever was number 89 in the sample. The person who submitted the DNA could be male or female, it doesn't say."

But it does say that the person is her mother/father, brother/sister, uncle/aunt, or grandmother/grandfather. She stares at the paper, staggered.

"I never thought you'd find anybody," Carson admits. "It was a long shot. You hit the jackpot."

"So, now what?" she says, looking at him in wonder.

"Well, if I were you, I'd go looking for the people you were matched to. Obviously, they're very close family members. And equally obviously, they're out looking for their family just like you are, or they wouldn't have submitted their DNA to FindYourFamily.com."

"So you're saying somebody out there may be looking for me just like I'm looking for them?"

"It's certainly possible."

Carson quickly points out the obvious. Stanford University is about a four-hour drive from the homeless/migrant encampment where Michaela has taken refuge. Tennessee, on the other hand, is all the way across the country — at least 2,500 miles.

"You know what they say — pick the low-hanging fruit first," he says. "I'll take you to San Francisco, if you want to go."

But merely going to Stanford will not provide all the pieces of the puzzle. She must find the class that submitted the sample, and then find the person within that class whose DNA matches her own.

Michaela stares at the pieces of paper — the words on them could transform her whole life. She has been in victim mode for so long, has been a fugitive, living in terror of being dragged back into the hell from which she escaped. She had never spared any attention speculating on what might be out there in the wide world, what might be awaiting a person who is not merely running *from*, but running *to*.

Unlike Farrah, who has always been obsessed with finding her birth mother to vent her rage at being sold like a side of beef, Michaela has kept her focus on the here and now, on playing the cards life has dealt her. But in the space of a handful of minutes, the whole deck of cards has been tossed into the air. Anything is possible now.

Michaela might actually find her mother!

Now she stands outside a closed door in an intimidatingly large, echoing building on the Stanford University campus.

A plaque beside the door identifies the office's occupant: Dr. Phillip McFearson.

"Are you looking for someone?" says a voice from behind her. She turns to see a tall, thin scholarly-looking man.

"Dr. McFearson, my name is Michaela Hollis and I..." she begins. When he nods at her to continue and looks sympathetic, she pours out the whole story... well, most of it — how she submitted her DNA to FindYourFamily.com and discovered that she is a close match to someone in his class.

The man's face breaks into a brilliant smile. He is so excited, he reaches out and grabs her hands.

"You matched to somebody in the class?"

Michaela hands him the results she received from the website. He reads the papers, goes down the class enrollment roster in his iPad, and his smile grows wider.

"A match this close — that's absolutely amazing. Wonderful. And you came here looking for that person, right?"

"Of course. I want to find my family. And the person whose DNA matched mine, they're obviously looking for their family, too."

The professor made a grunting sound in his throat.

"Maybe some of my students are … but that's not why they submitted their DNA. It's a course requirement. This is an anthropology class. We don't do a deep dive into genetics, but they need a basic understanding of how it works to understand some of the more complex concepts later on. These students were surprised to find that they matched others in the class — distant matches. Nothing like yours."

Michaela is rattled.

"You mean … they had to—" she begins, but a bell rings somewhere in the building and the professor tells her the class is starting. The man ushers her into the room and gives her a special seat beside his desk. She looks out over the lecture hall full of students, wondering which one of them she had matched to.

Dr. McFearson calls the class to order and conversation ceases. Then he unexpectedly points to Michaela and explains what she is doing in the class.

"It seems that Michaela Hollis is an incredibly close genetic match to someone in our group sample."

All of the students look at each other with general curiosity.

"Who is it?" Someone calls out.

"Subject number 89," the professor says. He calls up

the roll sheet again on his iPad, then looks up with a smile at a young man two rows back from the front in the audience.

"Ahmad Hussain Khan Al-Saud," the professor says. "The DNA she matched was yours."

"Mine?" The dark-eyed young man with an aristocratic face and black hair cut "high and tight" stares at the professor in disbelief.

"There's some mistake," the student says. "The numbers or samples got mixed up."

With a condescending glance, he continues, "Americans may be unaware of their heritage, but I know my family tree. I know my ancestry back six generations."

Michaela gets it then, understands why the professor was so anxious to bring her into the classroom. He saw the name she'd matched to when she first gave him the papers, and he wanted the opportunity to take this arrogant young man down a few pegs.

"Sorry, Al-Saud, but there's no mistake. I packaged those samples myself. DNA study subject number 89 is you. These results are impressive. The match is so close that you are immediate family — brother, father, uncle. And given her age and yours ... I'd say you're looking at a sister you never knew you had."

Michaela is horrified and embarrassed. She never dreamed the professor would make the "reveal" public! And clearly the young man who is subject number 89 is not happy. The rest of the class titters in amusement.

"Oh, there is a mistake all right, Dr. McFearson and you're the one who made it," the angry young man spits at him. "This is obviously some kind of hoax directed at my family, and you are a part of it. My father's attorneys will be in touch."

The young man gathers his things and storms out of the room.

Michaela sits there shocked, her head spinning, as the professor dismisses the rest of the class.

"Who ... what?" She can't seem to form a coherent question.

"I'm sorry that got ugly," he says. "Guess you hit a nerve. I don't know his exact family connections. I'd have to look up his records to be sure, but I'd say it's a safe bet that his family has more money than God. And he probably thinks you're going to lay claim to some of it."

"I don't want ... I didn't ... I—"

She realizes the professor isn't interested in her explanations, doesn't care that she had come looking for what she thought perhaps was a father or brother — someone who was equally interested in finding her.

Michaela leaves the classroom after it has emptied and walks dejectedly down the big echoing hallway of the classroom building. Suddenly, the young man named Al-Something steps out of a recessed doorway and confronts her.

"Who the hell are you and what do you want?" he demands.

Michaela just looks at him, too shocked to speak.

"Let me see that!" He snatches the papers from FindYourFamily.com out of her hands and scans down them, his rage evident in his trembling hands. They are alone in the hallway, but surely someone would come if she cried for help.

"It could be a simple mistake," he says after he has read through the papers. "Dr. McFearson screwed up the numbers and you really do match somebody in the class — just not me." He glares at her. "I don't believe that, though. I believe you're a con artist, a stupid one if you think I'd fall for this. I ought to call the police."

Michaela can't breathe. The police! They'd drag her back ... no, she's over 18, they can't ... but they'd tell her parents, her father, where she is!

"I don't want anything from you," she says, then turns and runs down the hallway to the door. She is already outside before she realizes that the angry young man still has the papers he snatched out of her hands. She has to get them back. She starts back into the building and freezes. The young man is standing in the empty hallway, using his phone to take pictures of the documents, and then he continues an angry conversation on the phone — in a mixture of English and some other language she doesn't understand.

She catches fragments.

"... DNA match ... impersonating ... is it true... sister?"

He pauses, listens, and obviously is soothed by whatever the person on the other end of the line says because he calms down. She catches one more word in English before he ends the call. "Papa."

The young man wads up the papers, walks to a trash basket in the middle of the hallway, and tosses them into it. Michaela waits until he has left the building before she goes back inside and retrieves the pages.

Smoothing out the wadded paper, she can still see the name of the maternal match clearly.

"Lily Bishop. Black Bear Forge, Tennessee."

Chapter Twelve

RILEIGH WAS PONDERING THE CONUNDRUM OF MICKY Hollis as she headed toward the First Baptist Church of Black Bear Forge to pick up Mama from her sewing circle. Nothing about Micky Hollis made any sense. Why in the world was she so reluctant to provide the kind of information that would help Rileigh and Mitch find out who had stabbed her? Who doesn't want to catch the person who stabbed them?

But that wasn't the only strangeness about the girl with the pale blonde hair who looked so very fragile and pale lying on those white sheets in the hospital.

What was going on with her sister? If indeed there really was a sister. They only had Micky's word for that, after all. If her sister was a stowaway on the bus, the driver didn't know it. Of course, Mitch'd said that wasn't unlikely given what he'd observed of the bus and its driver.

Still, why had her sister not come forward when she realized that Micky had been hurt? Why had she just kept running from the man in the red pickup truck? And why had nobody seen her since? It had been more than twenty-four hours, and she hadn't turned up anywhere. People in Black Bear Forge noticed when a stranger was wandering up and down the streets or the highways. So where was she?

Rileigh pulled into her usual spot, put the car in park, and turned off the engine. The sewing circle had officially ended fifteen minutes ago. But of course that didn't mean anything. If the women decided to keep talking, they could go on and on for hours. Rileigh was prepared to wait. Going to that sewing circle was one of Mama's favorite activities. She'd been doing it for Rileigh's entire life. The sewing circle was called Bestowing Sewing. Rileigh shortened the name in her head to simply BS, and she suspected most others did the same. But not out loud — you couldn't call a group of old ladies making booties and other things for people in need *BS*. And if there was a disaster, you could be sure that Bestowing Sewing had gotten together to make blankets, or quilts, or socks, or gloves, or wool caps, or whatever might be needed by the survivors of whatever catastrophe had struck.

All of Mama's friends were in the sewing circle, including her best friend Mildred, who usually came by and picked Mama up so that Rileigh didn't have to offer to take her, which she always did. Because if Millie wasn't around to provide transportation, that meant Mama would drive her own car, and Rileigh avoided that happening at all costs. She would soon be having the "Mama, I need your car keys" conversation, but she was putting it off. And so long as she provided transportation to the few places Mama wanted to go, it hadn't become an issue.

The side doors of the fellowship hall of the church opened, and a stream of elderly women moved slowly outside.

There was Mrs. Higginbotham, who, at almost six feet

tall, had been an all-state basketball champion way back in the day, a center who could jam the ball back in the days when there weren't many people, certainly not many white women, who could accomplish that task.

She was followed by Thelma Reynolds and Betty Whitaker, both chattering as they walked together toward their separate cars. A car pulled up and parked beside Rileigh's then. It was Ramona Cargile, who had come to pick up her mother and her mother's friend to take them home. Apparently, she'd already had the "Mama, I need your car keys" conversation with her mother.

Lily emerged then, walking beside Paula Crandall, a sweet old woman who had worked at Farmer's State Bank for most of Rileigh's life. Rileigh had taken her weekly babysitting money to put in her savings account to Thelma at the bank every Friday. And every time she handed over the money, Thelma had winked at her and told her, "Just like the good book says — you only get to spend eighty percent of what you earn. The first ten percent goes to the Lord as a tithe, and the next ten percent into savings. You're a good girl, Rileigh Bishop."

Mama said goodbye to Thelma, opened the car door, and slid in beside Rileigh.

"Where have you been, dear?" she asked.

"Remember, Mama? I said I was going to talk to the woman who got stabbed the other night at the bus station."

"Oh, that's right. I remember. What was her name again?"

"Micky Hollis," Rileigh said, and was about to tell Mama about her conversation with Micky when Mama held up her hand.

"I don't s'pose you're in the mood for a milkshake, are you?" Mama said, her eyes glittering. Rileigh didn't bother to point out that they were going home to fix supper, and the last thing either one of them needed was a vanilla milk-shake to spoil their appetites.

She just nodded and said, "I'll take you to get one and I'll wait in the car. I'm not thirsty."

Rileigh sat in the car outside the Red-Eye Gravy diner while Mama went in. Her mother'd become addicted to vanilla milkshakes at the diner as soon as it re-opened with a new cook, Junie Thomas, and now she went to get one at least a couple of times a week.

Rileigh looked at her watch. There weren't very many customers in the diner, only a few cars in the parking lot. So what was taking Mama so long?

She peered through the windshield and through the diner's windows and could see her mother talking animat-edly with Big John behind the counter. Big John didn't usually have a whole lot to say. He was the strong silent type, so to speak. But he certainly seemed to have plenty to say tonight to Mama.

Mama finally appeared at the door with *two* milk-shakes. So much for "I'm not thirsty." Mama went to the passenger side door, set the milkshakes on top of the car, opened the door, then picked up the unrequested milk-shake she'd gotten for Rileigh and handed it to her.

"I couldn't decide whether to get you strawberry or chocolate. I picked chocolate. Will that do?"

Rileigh liked vanilla milkshakes just like Mama liked vanilla milkshakes. She never got any other flavor, but Mama didn't remember that.

"Either one is fine with me."

Mama picked up Rileigh's milkshake off the top of the car, leaned in, and handed it to her. Rileigh set it in the cup holder in the console between the seats.

"I got something real important to tell you," Mama said. "Big John told me all about it while Susie was making our milkshakes." She straightened and picked up her own milkshake and started to get into the car with it as she continued. "He told me that the other day there were—"

But that's as far as she got before she either momentarily lost her balance or clipped the side of the door with the edge of the milkshake cup. Rileigh didn't know for sure which it was, but for some reason, the milkshake bobbled in Mama's hands. Rileigh leaned over to help steady her. Wrong move. When she leaned, Rileigh tipped her own milkshake sideways, and the mixture of brown chocolate flowed out the side of her cup and down onto the console.

Before Rileigh had time to be upset by the spill, Mama made it the lesser of *two spills* by dumping the entire contents of her own milkshake into the passenger side seat.

"Oh, I'm so sorry!" Mama cried, flustered. "I'll clean it up."

"No, it's okay, Mama. I—" Rileigh reached down to set her own half-full cup upright, but it was so sticky and slimy that it slid out of her hand, dumping the rest of the chocolate milkshake into the floorboard.

From that moment forward, everything else in life took a backseat to cleaning two milkshakes out of the front seats of Mama's car.

Rileigh hurried into Red-Eye Gravy and flagged down a waitress, explaining that she needed some paper towels. A lot of paper towels.

Big John was in conversation with someone else and merely lifted his eyebrows and waved, and she waved back. Armed with paper towels — and wash cloths, towels, and basins of water — Rileigh went back out to the car to clean up the mess. Two full milkshakes dumped into the car was a sticky catastrophe now but would become a worse catastrophe if they didn't clean up all the mess. If they left even a small amount of milkshake in the car, in a few days the whole car would stink of sour milk.

Susie the waitress came out of the building when she saw what Rileigh and Mama were doing, and she brought out more sopping wet cloths — and paper towels. Half an hour later, Mama and Rileigh sat down on big pieces of paper Susie'd brought out to put on the seats so they wouldn't ruin their clothes with the milkshake mess, though both of them were as splattered with it as if they'd been trying to paint the walls with milkshakes. Both of them went inside to wash their hands to get as much sticky off as they could before they left. Rileigh looked for Big John to wave at him, but he must have been in the kitchen because she didn't see him.

When they headed for home, Rileigh turned on the AC and blasted it to cool the interior and delay the onset of the rotten milk smell she was sure was in their future no matter how hard they'd tried to prevent it. Mama was babbling her apologies for making the mess. And Rileigh was reassuring her that everybody dropped things now and then. In an effort to change the subject, she asked how the sewing circle had gone, and that sent Mama's thoughts off in an entirely different direction. For the remainder of the trip home, she bubbled about somebody's granddaughter who was now expecting triplets and somebody's son-in-law who had just joined the Marines.

When Rileigh pulled up in front of the house, Mama got an odd look on her face.

"Wait!" she said, "There's something I'm supposed to tell you. Big John said—"

But Rileigh didn't have time for more babble. She needed to go into the house for upholstery and carpet cleaner and get busy on the seats and floorboard.

"Not now, Mama. Tell me later."

"No, this is important. It was something Big John told me, and he said I had to tell you soon's I could."

"Later, Mama," Rileigh said and closed the door, then hurried up the steps into the house for cleaning supplies.

Mama was standing beside the passenger side door, her brow crinkled in concentration as if she were trying to remember something important, when Jillian hurried out with a cloth and a can of spray-on upholstery cleaner.

Lily stopped her daughter and said, "Big John told me to tell Rileigh something important."

Jillian stood still and listened.

"What?"

But Lily Bishop couldn't for the life of her remember what it was.

Chapter Thirteen

MAMA FILLED UP A BIG BOWL WITH SOAPY WARM WATER, then she and Rileigh went to work on the floorboards of Mama's car while Jillian worked on the upholstery. They scrubbed the seats and the side panels of the doors. They were able to clean up the console, but between the console and the seats was a very narrow space. Vanilla milkshake had drained down one side of it and chocolate down the other. Try as they might, Rileigh didn't think they'd been able to clean it all up, and she had a sinking feeling that in a couple of days the milkshake disaster was going to return and bite her in the butt.

Jillian had been preparing pinto beans and cornbread for supper. When the three women finally sat down at the dinner table almost two hours later than normal, they were famished. Mama hadn't gotten more than a couple of slurps of her milkshake. Rileigh hadn't gotten a single drop.

"You know, I was going to volunteer to take Mama to sewing circle tonight," Jillian said, "but looks like I picked a good night to stay home and tend to the beans and corn-bread." Rileigh nodded, then saw her mother's face fall and realized that Mama still felt guilty about the mess, so she quickly tried to think of a change of subject. "While Mama was at Bestowing Sewing, I was at the hospital talking to that stabbing victim," she said.

Jillian's face grew serious. "What did she tell you?"

"Not a whole lot." Then Rileigh described what the young woman had told Mitch earlier in the day, that she had been traveling with her sister, which was a surprise given that that nobody had seen her sister anywhere around after she was stabbed.

"Well, how come her sister didn't go to the hospital with her?" Mama asked.

Rileigh shrugged. "You got me. I couldn't tell you. I also couldn't tell you why she seems so damn reluctant to offer any kind of information to Mitch and me. We're trying to find out who stabbed her, for crying out loud, but that doesn't appear to matter much to her."

"We got more information from what was in her purse, or rather what *wasn't in* it, than we did from the girl," Rileigh said.

"And that was… or wasn't?" Jillian said.

"No cell phone."

"You're kidding me."

Rileigh raised her hand in the traditional mountain *if I'm lying, I'm dying* gesture.

"Nobody under the age of thirty in the whole country walks around without a cell phone," Jillian said. "How old did you say she was?"

"Twenty." Rileigh paused. "Well, not quite twenty." Then Rileigh cocked her head to the side. "Maybe we could use that to get her to open up."

"Use what?" Jillian asked.

"Her birthday is next week, September 18th. Says so on the ID that was in her purse."

Rileigh saw Jillian go very still.

"The eighteenth of September?"

"Yeah. She'll be twenty. So I'm thinking maybe if we made her an early birthday cake, took it to her, sing Happy Birthday or whatever, we could convince her we're not the bad guys. And maybe she'd talk to us."

"A birthday cake," Jillian said with an odd look on her face.

"I'm glad to make her a cake," Mama said. "We can make them little roses out of icing, the ones you make by squirting icing through a tube of wax paper. It'd cheer her up even if it don't make her more talkative." Mama turned to Jillian. "You're better'n I am at making them little roses."

Jillian said nothing, acted like she hadn't heard.

"You don't think it's a good idea?" Mama pressed.

"Whatever," Jillian said dismissively, then turned to Rileigh.

"You said she had a ticket to Black Bear Forge, so she was on her way here?"

"Black Bear Forge was her final destination."

"Why was she coming here?"

"That's yet another question that I asked and she didn't answer."

"She wouldn't tell you why she was coming here?" Mama said.

"Oh, she had a lame explanation. Said everybody comes to the Smoky Mountains. I asked if she had come to find her family, and she wouldn't say."

"I don't mind sayin' — I done it," Mama said.

"Done ... did what?" Rileigh asked.

"I done that," Mama said, reaching for the butter and

slathering some on her piece of cornbread. "Find your family. I done that."

Jillian and Rileigh looked at each other and looked at Mama.

"Oh, come on, you know that website," Mama prodded. "Find Your Family dot com."

"What is it?"

"It's one of them things where you send them your DNA and they'll find your family for you."

What possible reason could Mama have to go searching on some obscure website with her DNA to find out her roots when she could trace her ancestry back to the Mayflower? Rileigh was about to ask that question when Mama held up her hand.

"I know, I know, it ain't like I don't know what my roots are. I wasn't looking for them. I was looking to see if they could track down the roots of my *former* lives."

"Former..." Rileigh began.

"...lives," Jillian finished for her.

"Yeah, you know. Back when the Dalai Lama was here. You remember him. He was such a nice fella. I never did understand why he walked around in a bathrobe."

"Mama, it wasn't a bathrobe," Rileigh said, smiling at Jillian.

Jillian didn't return the smile. She was staring intently at Mama. "So you went on that website to see if you could find your past lives?" Jillian asked.

"You do know, don't you, Mama," Rileigh pointed out, "that websites like that — ancestry.com, findyourroots.com — can only connect you to people who also have sent their DNA off to that particular website. Not to just anybody."

"Yeah. I know that now. But I hadn't figured that part out when I sent it off. And besides, I don't think you can send off your DNA and find out who you was in a past life.

You know, who you was before you died and come back who you are now."

"Mama, you don't believe that," Rileigh said.

"I didn't say I believed it." She smiled innocently. "The Dalai Lama does, though. He told me all about it, said he will be immediately reborn into the body of a baby born at the moment he dies."

Rileigh rolled her eyes, wondering where in the world her mother came up with such creative and colorful delusions. She never should have taught her how to use Google.

"So you sent your DNA off to findyourfamily.com. Is that right?" Jillian asked quietly.

"Yeah, that's what I done."

"Did you find any matches?"

"Nah. I don't figure any of the people I used to be sent their DNA off to that website."

Jillian relaxed back into her chair. "So there were no matches?

"Oh, I don't know if there was matches or not."

"How could you not know?"

"I got stuff back a couple of times, but I'd got to thinking by then that I was probably better off not knowing I was Joan of Arc or Pocahontas or Mamie Eisenhower in a previous life. So I threw everything they sent me in the trash with the rest of the junk mail. Will you pass me the cornbread, Jillian honey?"

Jillian rose to her feet. "I'm really not feeling well," she said.

"You sick?" Mama was instantly concerned.

"No, just… I'm getting a headache. I'll be fine." She dropped her napkin onto her plate and hurried out of the dining room to the stairs and up to her room.

"If she wasn't feeling well, she hadn't ought to have

been out there helping us clean that milkshake mess out of the car," Mama said. "I bet that's what made her sick."

Rileigh looked at the empty chair where her sister had been sitting, wondering.

"Yeah," she said. "That was probably it."

Chapter Fourteen

MICKY HEARD THE DOOR TO HER HOSPITAL ROOM SLIDE open. It was almost silent, but she had very acute hearing and her eyes popped open. And what she saw was Farrah silently crossing the room toward the bed. She was shocked but not surprised that her sister has managed to sneak into her room unnoticed. That's just how Farrah rolled. Farrah always seemed to be a step ahead of her. She always got there faster, wherever or whatever "there" was.

"I admit I never thought this would work," Farrah said, "but appears I'm wrong. You're close, actually close to finding *her*?"

Apparently, Farrah noticed Micky's body language, how she was cringing back against the pillow. Micky's fear amused her. Gesturing to her healing knife wounds, she said, "Your own fault, kiddo — appearing suddenly like that, startling me. You can't just show up out of nowhere. For all your whining, you're not hurt bad. Suck it up. You're tougher than you give yourself credit for. I'm proud of you."

Micky knew that at any moment Farrah could pull a

knife and plunge it into her heart, and that she might do just that. After what Papa did to her while Micky was away … Farrah was capable of anything. She had always been an enigma to Micky, a paradox of contradictions impossible to understand — smiling and pleasant one moment, hate-filled and raging the next. She could turn on a dime. Now it was clear that where Farrah was concerned, there were no rules, no boundaries anymore. Farrah would get her way, would force Micky to do whatever she wanted her to do. Independent thought was not an option.

"Just don't screw this up. Play along. We have to catch the spider before we can kill it, pull its legs off one at a time. Watch it squirm."

Micky knew exactly what Farrah was talking about and the thought of it dropped a cold, hard rock deep into the pit of her stomach.

"You need to—"

Farrah froze at the sound of the door opening slowly. The sisters stared at each other for a moment before Farrah blended into the dark shadows of the room and was gone.

A machine rolled through the door, pushed ahead of a small orderly with a thin mustache and two or three days' growth of beard that was a hygiene statement rather than a fashion statement.

He shoved the machine up against the far wall in the room and then approached her bedside. She closed her eyes, pretending to be asleep. He just stood there saying nothing. She opened her eyes enough that she could peer out at him through a forest of eyelashes, not understanding why he was still just standing there. He had delivered the piece of equipment. Why didn't he leave?

"You're a right pretty young lady," he said softly.

And Micky recognized that tone of voice. Oh dear

God in *heaven* did she recognize it. She would recognize that tone in a man's voice anywhere. It was a slimy tone. When her father and her uncle spoke to her that way, she always imagined that their words were slathered with some kind of stinky sludge that smelled bad and would stick to your hands if you touched it.

She held her breath, didn't open her eyes, willed him to go away, but he didn't. He reached out his hand and very slowly, tenderly, wiped a tendril of hair off her forehead and hooked it behind her ear. She had managed not to cringe at his touch. That was one of Micky's life skills, developed over years of practice. She could feel a man's touch on her just about anywhere without flinching, without grinding her teeth, without showing any kind of recognition at all.

She remembered that years before when he came during the night to her room to get her. She'd cry, even tried to pull away a time or two, which resulted in being slapped. She learned quickly that she was not allowed to protest, that what was happening to her was totally out of her control. And she taught herself not to flinch and withdraw. After a while, she saw that as her own small protest, that when they touched her, she went to that place where she didn't care, silently pulling up around her a suit of armor that couldn't protect her body from the ravages of what they did. But it did protect her mind and her soul.

She learned to make no physical response that anybody could see. Inside the fortress where Micky lived, she slammed all the doors, closed all the windows, locked them, pulled the shades, and sat down in the dark in the middle of the room, secure there, safe from harm, while whatever happened to her on the outside couldn't touch her.

The orderly continued to talk to her softly in his slimy

voice, telling her she was pretty, telling her that her skin was soft, that he had longed to touch it. Just talking now, not touching her, just talking. But that would come, she knew, the touching would. It always did. So she lay there frozen, her breathing regular, as if she was sound asleep and not feeling a thing as his fingers roamed over her skin, slid under her hospital gown to touch her in those places that men always touched her, the places that were private and hers, that they violated without caring.

She barely heard what he was saying, realized that he had produced a knife, not some big butcher knife, but a knife that he said he would use on her if she told anyone what he had done. He waved it in front of her face. She saw it through the forest of eyelashes. And she knew how bad it hurt to be stabbed by a knife, and she didn't want to give this man any excuse to hurt her. Let him touch her all he wanted. She was used to that.

But when he pricked her skin under her ear with the pointed end of the knife, she felt a little dribble of blood slide down her neck. And that made her angry.

What happened after that was dreamlike.

The man with the knife…

The blood on her neck …

Then Farrah suddenly appeared and grabbed the man's hand and shoved the knife back toward him. He was caught off balance. Micky saw the surprise on his face that the knife he'd used to threaten her had been plunged into his own chest.

He stood there looking surprised for a moment.

And Micky had time to be thrilled, to be grateful that Farrah had protected her as she had done so often in the past. Micky smiled in gratitude as she stared into her sister's eyes, aware of the bond that horror had forged between them, stronger than any blood tie could ever be.

The man reached out and grabbed Micky's arm as he fell, dragging her off the bed on top of him. He was making strange sounds as his breath bubbled in and out between his lips. She felt the blood from his wound, felt the warmth of it on her skin. But his grip on her quickly loosened. She squirmed out of it, crawled on her hands and knees to the corner of the room, curled up in a ball, and stayed there, crying.

Chapter Fifteen

MITCH'S CELL PHONE JANGLED ON THE CHARGER BESIDE HIS bed in the middle of the night and jarred him from sleep. He squinted at the dial on the digital clock: 4:30.

"This is Mitch," he said into the phone, rubbing his eyes and trying to get his bearings.

"I thought you'd want to hear about this one," said a voice he recognized — Sylvia, the dispatcher. "That girl you found in the woods, stabbed ... we just got a call that one of the hospital orderlies was found dead in her room."

Mitch leapt out of bed and into his uniform. Didn't shave. Just raced out to his cruiser and made for the Yarmouth County Hospital. The place was suitably lit up with three different deputies' cars. Mitch went inside and saw Deputy Beau Mullins talking to a woman in scrubs.

Beau had been pulling extra duty ever since Deputies Jeb Rawlings had come down with COVID, and Deputy Tony Hadley had been attacked in the woods by bloodthirsty poison ivy. But Rawlings was supposed to be back on full duty tomorrow, so Beau would be given a well-deserved day off. Of course, Mitch deserved a day off as much or more than Beau did but he wouldn't be getting it. Such were the privileges of leadership.

Mullins was definitely rising to the occasion with all this extra work. He'd done a good job at the scene of the stabbing the other night, and as he began to speak, Mitch realized he had been just as thorough here.

"The deceased is James Roscoe Hurkel, 37, lives out on Whistler's Pike next to the Pendleton County line. He was found by one of the nurses." He flipped ahead in his notes. "Name's Ellen Pembroke. She said she went into Miss Hollis's room to check her vital signs and found the deceased on the floor with a knife sticking out of his chest. We haven't moved the body so you can see for yourself."

"What about Michaela Hollis? Was she hurt?"

"Not injured, but totally freaked out. Why she didn't scream is anybody's guess."

"Have you spoken to her?"

"No sir. I figured you'd want that privilege."

Mitch headed down the hallway where he could see a bevy of activity outside one of the rooms.

"Are you Ellen Pembroke?" he asked the nurse who seemed to be in charge.

"Yes, I am."

"You were the one who found the body?"

"Yes, I came in this morning just, you know, to take the patient's vital signs, and there was Jim, laying on the floor with a blade in his chest."

"And the patient, Michaela Hollis?"

"She was curled up in the corner crying. Pulled all her IVs out and some of her stitches. The IV pole and bag were on the floor. She was covered in blood."

Mitch went into the hospital room and found the scene just as Beau and the nurse had described it. A man lay on his back on the floor with a scalpel stuck into his chest.

Mitch leaned closer for a better look. The murder weapon, the blade in the orderly's chest, was a scalpel. A search of the woods outside the bus station where Michaela'd been attacked had revealed a bloody switchblade.

The last attempt on her life, the killer'd at least brought along a weapon. Why would he show up again unarmed and have to snatch a scalpel to commit the crime?

Mitch walked around the body, careful not to step in the puddle of blood. The room was in disarray. The bed was on wheels, and it had been shoved all the way over against the wall. The water pitcher and other things from the bedside table were strewn across the floor. And the patient who was supposed to be in that bed was nowhere to be seen.

Turning to nurse Pembroke, Mitch asked her where he could find Michaela Hollis.

"She's just down the hall in another room, but she's been sedated, so you won't likely get much out of her if you talk to her."

Mitch hadn't been able to get much out of her when he talked to her before when she wasn't sedated. But he went down the hallway anyway, pushed the door open, and peeked inside. Michaela was in a fresh hospital gown lying on clean, crisp white sheets in a hospital bed.

Mitch went into the room and stood beside the bed and said quietly, "Miss Hollis ... uh, Micky, it's Sheriff Webster. I'd like to talk to you if I could."

She opened her eyes and looked at him quizzically. Then realization dawned on her face, and she knew who he was.

"Can you tell me what happened to the orderly in your room?"

She looked at him as if she hadn't understood the question, then shook her head.

"Who killed him?" Mitch pressed.

"I … I don't know."

"It wasn't too dark to see, like it was in the woods. You *saw* who it was. Tell me."

"I don't—" She'd been going to say she didn't know but gave up on it. "It was …" She hesitated, took a deep breath, then continued. "It was … *him* — the man in the red pickup truck. That's who did it. He killed the orderly."

"The man you saw the night you were stabbed? He came *here?*"

"Yes. He came for me. He … he came here to kill me."

Came to kill her … and brought a surgical scalpel as his murder weapon?

Then the words flowed out of her in a torrent, a semi-hysterical babble, like she wanted to say it fast to get it over with.

"He had a knife and I opened my mouth to scream, but I couldn't. I couldn't make a sound. I just froze. I was so scared. I thought he was going to kill me and I didn't want to die, but I couldn't breathe, couldn't get my breath, couldn't find the air to scream, and then the orderly came into the room."

She pointed to a machine of some kind up against the wall in the room.

"He was just bringing that in and before he could say anything, do anything, the man with the knife attacked him and they fought and they knocked things off the bedside table and I jumped out of the bed and I tried to run, but they were between me and the door, so I just, I just … I curled up in the corner."

Tears filled her eyes as she spoke and spilled down her cheeks.

Zero to sixty. The girl had gone from monosyllabic-grunt answers to a stream-of-consciousness babble. It was the medication they'd given her, making her woozy, lowering her defenses.

"So this was the man in the red pickup?"

She swallowed. "Yes. My Uncle Dan."

"Uncle Dan. So you *knew* the man in the pickup truck?"

"Yes, I knew who he was. I didn't tell you because I was afraid. He's ... very powerful where we come from."

Mitch held on to his surprise response, didn't want to jolt her.

"And where is that?"

Micky just shook her head.

"Somewhere in California, right?"

"No."

"No what?"

She wouldn't say, just shook her head and clamped her mouth shut. Why wouldn't she tell him where she was from?

"He had been following us for miles, maybe ever since we left. I don't know how he found us," she said.

"Why would your Uncle Dan be following along behind you? Did you run away?"

"He didn't chase us to take us home. He wanted to kill us."

"Why?"

Either she didn't hear him or pretended she didn't.

"What does your Uncle Dan look like?"

"Ordinary. About six feet tall, brown hair, brown eyes. Unmemorable."

"So tell me about him. His name ... was it *Daniel* Hollis?"

"Not Hollis. He was my mother's brother, her real

brother. But my mother wasn't my real mother. Neither was my father."

She didn't answer his question, didn't tell him her uncle's name, but what she did say caused a sensation like cold water dripping down Mitch's spine from one vertebra to the next.

"The people you and your sister lived with were not your parents?"

"Not our real parents. They bought us when we were little."

"*Bought* you?"

She nodded her head but wouldn't look at him as she spoke.

"Farrah was the oldest. I was next, barely a year younger."

"Who did they buy you from?"

"I don't know. We overheard them talking about buying us when they were getting ready to buy Elyssa."

"Elyssa?"

"Elyssa was our little sister."

"When you and Farrah ran away from the people who bought you, why didn't Elyssa go with you?"

Micky looked momentarily stricken.

"She died. Then there were just the two of us, then. Me and Farrah."

Mitch could see that she was getting drowsier and drowsier.

"How did you get away?"

"Papa was in a wreck and I was with him. He was hurt, knocked out, bleeding. But I was fine. And I suddenly realized that I could run, that he was unconscious, he couldn't stop me. I backed up, blended back into the crowd, and then … I *ran!*"

"What about Farrah?"

"I went back for her."

"How did your Uncle Dan find you?"

She shook her head. "I don't know. But we knew he'd come after us, that he'd never let us go after I went back for Farrah and…"

"And what?"

The girl shook her head violently.

"We got away. I don't want to talk about it." She was getting agitated.

Mitch didn't press any longer, fearful that her agitation would draw the attention of the nurses. He circled back to what appeared to be a safer topic.

"So when you saw him the night the old man was murdered, you knew who he was."

She nodded. "We knew who he was and what he wanted. That's why we ran."

"Did your Uncle Dan kill the old man in the bathroom?"

She shrugged. "Maybe … I don't know."

"But it was your Uncle Dan who stabbed *you*. He caught you in the woods and tried to kill you?"

She shook her head, almost sadly it seemed. "I told you, it was too dark to see. I couldn't tell who it was."

He tried to kill her tonight, but he wasn't the person who'd inflicted the stab wounds that had brought her to the hospital in the first place? That didn't make any sense at all. She seemed to be unplugging from reality, so he changed topics again.

"How did you get the identification that was in your purse?"

"At the shelter," she said.

"What shelter? Where?"

He could see her sliding away from the here and now, the sedative beginning to take hold.

"…everything at the shelter … all I needed … but I couldn't leave her, I had to go back for Farrah… my big sister, Farrah…"

Mitch was losing her.

"What happened when you went back for Farrah?"

Her head shook again, mumbling, "No … no… I won't tell…"

The door to the room opened then and in walked Dr. Dowling.

"Are you in here upsetting my patient again?" Dowling asked Mitch.

"I'm just trying to find out what happened to her."

"Well, clearly she doesn't want to talk to you right now. You need to leave."

Mitch nodded in acquiescence, then turned and left. He was short-handed, but he couldn't leave this girl unprotected after somebody had tried to kill her, and obviously hospital security wasn't up to the task. He glanced out a window at light slowly returning to the world as the sun peeked over the horizon somewhere out there on the flat. He'd have to station a deputy at her door. So much for Beau Mullins's day off.

Chapter Sixteen

SUNRISE HAD LONG SINCE MOVED UP AND OVER TUCKER Mountain by the time Rileigh pulled up in front of Georgia's double-wide trailer house.

Rileigh knocked, opened the door, and stuck her head in. "Yo, Georgia."

"Coffee's on. Just made a fresh pot." Georgia said.

Georgia had already accomplished a day's work, had shipped off Liam, Eli, and Conner to school, Mason to preschool, and farmed out Mayella to her Granny Pauline's. Then she had covered the kitchen floor with a drop cloth and had a lone kitchen chair taken apart, the screws removed, the legs lying on the kitchen table. It looked a little like she was performing an autopsy on it.

Georgia's five kids put a lot of wear and tear on everything she owned, and there was no piece of furniture in her whole house that hadn't been banged up, dented, and scratched. But her kitchen furniture had taken the biggest hit. It hadn't been expensive furniture to begin with. It might have belonged to her older sister, or perhaps Georgia got it at a garage sale. Rileigh wasn't sure which.

But it had taken a huge amount of abuse over the years, and the chairs were all wobbly now. Rileigh had suggested the last time she was at Georgia's that they could take the chairs apart, re-glue the legs, and put them back together again to make them sturdier. And Georgia had been all over that.

"Looks like you're on top of things," Rileigh told Georgia.

"Need to finish up before Mama brings Mayella home at noon."

"Surely, we can get these chairs re-glued by then."

Georgia grimaced. "They're harder to take apart than I thought they'd be."

The legs to the chairs were screwed on, and they were wobbly because the screws had wallowed out the holes. Georgia had armed herself with Gorilla Snot wood glue, and she and Rileigh planned to take each chair leg off, put some glue into the holes, and then reassemble the chairs.

"So what's the problem?" Rileigh asked.

"The screw heads are screwed up," Georgia said, pushing a lock of her curly butter-colored hair out of her eyes. "It didn't occur to me that perhaps somebody else before I got them had taken the legs off and tried to fit them on more snug. And whoever it was, stripped the screws so they're really hard to get out."

"Goody," Rileigh said. She crossed Georgia's kitchen to the coffee pot, poured herself a cup, doctored it up with her signature amount of creamer and sugar, and took a big drink.

"Mitch called me this morning, early," she said as she leaned over to watch Georgia wrestle with the final screw in the final leg on the first chair.

"That's never a good thing," Georgia said. "Or is it? Did he just call to tell you how much he missed you?"

"No, he called to tell me that an orderly was murdered at the hospital last night."

"Holy shit," Georgia said. "Murdered in a hospital room?"

"Oh, not just any hospital room," Rileigh said. "The room of the victim of the stabbing we investigated Saturday night. Mitch and I tried to talk to her then, but that didn't work out, and Mitch went back yesterday morning, and I followed up yesterday afternoon."

"Well, tell me everything. Ouch!" She dropped the screw and stuck her finger in her mouth. "Pinched my finger," she said, sucking on it. "Come on, tell me the whole thing. We've got all morning."

They quickly developed a system. Rileigh, who was smaller but much stronger than Georgia, removed the screws and the legs. Georgia came along behind with the snot and filled up the holes where the screws had wallowed out, and then put the legs back on. When a chair was done, Georgia set it upside down on the kitchen table to let the glue set.

Rileigh had only spoken to Georgia briefly on Monday morning. All she'd had to tell her at that point was the story of her aborted date with Mitch Saturday night, finding an old man stabbed to death in the bus station bathroom and a surviving victim in the woods — and their equally aborted efforts to talk to the stabbing victim at the hospital.

There was much more to report about the case now, and Georgia gobbled up every morsel. But not to gossip. She wasn't a gossip like Mama, who poured out everything she knew to everyone she knew as soon as possible after she knew it. Georgia just found the details of Rileigh's cases interesting, and spending all day every day talking only to children made her eager for adult conversation —

even if the topics often included violence, blood, and danger.

"Mitch got past the hospital gatekeeper briefly yesterday morning," Rileigh said, grunting as she put her weight into leaning on the screw as she was struggling to remove. "Damn it, I hate it when somebody wallows out the head of a Phillips head screw."

Obviously, somebody had tried to remove the screw at some time in the chair's checkered past and had difficulty getting it out, had pushed too hard and scooped out the top of the screw.

"What was Mitch able to find out?" Georgia asked as she squirted glue into the holes where Rileigh had already removed the screws from the first chair.

"Well, he went in armed with a little bit of information," Rileigh said. "Beau Mullins brought in her purse and suitcase to the sheriff's office, so Mitch picked them up on his way to talk to the girl."

"So he'd already gone through her belongings. What did he find?"

"What was more interesting was what he didn't find."

Georgia lifted an eyebrow.

"She just had a small carry-on bag, and there was nothing interesting or enlightening in it, just clothing and a few toiletries. But she had a purse, and there was ID in the purse."

"So you know who she is?"

"Bare minimum. Her name is Michaela Marie Hollis, said to call her Micky. She'll turn 20 in three days. I suggested we bake her a birthday cake and take it to her to get her to open up, but Jillian did *not* like that idea."

"Why not?"

Rileigh shrugged. "You got me."

"So now Mitch has the girl's address?"

"He doesn't, because she didn't have a driver's license, just one of those official stamped IDs with a picture on it, and all those provide is name and date of birth."

"Well, that's more than you had going in," Georgia said.

Rileigh was silent, and Georgia looked up.

"What? Did I miss something?"

"Well, you didn't ask about her cell phone."

"What about her cell phone?"

"There wasn't one."

That got Georgia's attention. "No phone. Who doesn't have a cell phone?"

"The same person who's not particularly interested in finding out who stabbed her," Rileigh said. "All she told Mitch was that she and her sister were on the bus, got off in the middle of the night to go to the bathroom, and then saw a man getting out of a red pickup in the parking lot — the same red pickup that had been following the bus since Albuquerque. They got scared and ran away."

"So it was the guy in the red pickup who stabbed her?"

"She didn't say that. She didn't want to talk about being stabbed."

"Some guy in a red pickup chases her and her sister, she gets stabbed, but we don't know if it was that guy who stabbed her? Who the hell else would have been at the Sandstone Creek Bus station in the middle of the night?"

Georgia accidentally dropped a gob of glue on the floor and had to rush around with paper towels to get it up before it hardened to become a permanent fixture in her kitchen.

"So, can we fast forward to the phone call you got from Mitch this morning about somebody being murdered in her hospital room last night?" Georgia asked as she tried to get the sticky substance off the floor.

"She told Mitch that the mysterious man in the red pickup truck — you know, the one she *didn't* say stabbed her in the woods — tried to kill her and the orderly was wrong place, wrong time, and got killed. And the guy got away."

"But she still wouldn't say it was the red pickup dude who tried to kill her in the woods?"

"Nope. But she did say that red pickup dude was her Uncle Dan. Except he wasn't really her uncle."

"Okay…"

"Because his brother, her father, wasn't really her father. Her 'parents' purchased her and her sister from the black market when they were babies."

"You have *got* to be kidding me. That is the craziest story I ever heard."

"I'll drink to that," Rileigh said. "No, actually, I won't. That's really not the craziest story I ever heard."

"Well the craziest you've heard in the last week."

"No, not even that. The craziest story of all is what Mama told Jillian and me at supper last night. Remember when Mama was dating the Dalai Lama?"

"Was that before or after the guy who landed on the moon and Rhett Butler?"

"Rhett Butler was before Neil Armstrong. The Dalai Lama was after."

"Glad we got that straight. What about the Dalai Lama?"

"While she was hanging out with him, Mama decided she wanted to know about who she might have been in a past life."

"I thought it was Hindus who believed you could be reborn as a turnip."

"Maybe he didn't tell Mama he was a Buddhist.

Anyway, she got so curious about reincarnation, she decided to find out who she might once have been."

"How can you find out a thing like that?"

"Well duh, you send your DNA off to FindYourFamily.com."

Georgia burst out laughing, dropping the screw she was trying to fit into the hole where she'd just poured Gorilla Snot.

"I suppose in Mama World that makes some kind of sense. What did she find out?"

"She doesn't know. She got some responses, but she threw them in the trash, decided there were some things in life you're better off not knowing."

"Ever noticed how none of those ancestry things ever find ordinary people in your lineage?" Georgia pointed out. "It's never like, 'your great, great, great, great, great uncle Cletus was the village idiot.'"

"Jillian must have feared Mama had a village idiot uncle lurking in the family tree."

Georgia looked at her questioningly.

"She didn't think Mama's ancestry snooping was humorous. It gave her a headache, and she went to bed."

The two of them worked on the chair legs for the next couple of hours, positing first one explanation about what was going on with Micky Hollis and then another, never coming up with anything that made any sense. They finally paused after they had finished half the chair legs and sat down for a cup of coffee.

"So this girl, you say her name is Michaela Hollis, has blonde hair that looks like Jillian's, at least that's what Whitley Jefferson said."

"Yep. And she says her sister looks a lot like her. We're looking for her sister — Mitch put out a BOLO. But we've found no trace of her. Maybe she's like Mama's Dalai Lama. Maybe this girl made her up."

"So why was she coming to Black Bear Forge?"

"Oh, I forgot that part."

"Ooh. Tell me, tell me."

"Well, Mitch asked, and all he got out of her was she was looking for her family."

"Okay, what family?"

"She never said. And when we talked to Dr. Asshole at the hospital the night of the stabbing, he said that all she had said to him was mashed-up syllables, something that sounded like, well Mitch thought it sounded like Billie Eilish. But I thought it sounded more like Lily Bishop."

"Lily Bishop?"

"Yeah."

"Why would she have said Lily Bishop?"

"Why would she have said Billie Eilish? Why would you come to Black Bear Forge, Tennessee looking for a rock star? And maybe that's not what she said at all. Jillian thought that was interesting. She wasn't interested in making a birthday cake, though. As soon as Mama suggested we make a birthday cake for the girl's birthday, Jillian got up and left the table, and she did *not* look good."

"Hmm," Georgia said. "So there's a girl who has blonde hair like Jillian's, who was on her way to Black Bear Forge to find her family, who mentioned the name Lily Bishop. And when you told Jillian what the girl's birthday was, Jillian got upset."

"Uh huh," Rileigh acknowledged distractedly. She'd finished off her coffee, went back for more, and found that the pot was empty. "Want me to start another pot?"

"Don't you get it?" Georgia asked.

Rileigh turned to her. "Get what?"

"Oh, come on, Rileigh, you're sharper than that."

"What? What am I missing?"

Georgia paused, then spoke slowly. "Your mother filled out that FindYourFamily form and sent off her DNA. Maybe this girl sent her DNA off to that website, too. And maybe when the results came back, she discovered she was related to Lily Bishop … who is *Jillian Bishop's mother*."

Georgia drew in a breath.

"Your sister was gone for thirty years, Rileigh. Think about that. *Thirty. Years.*"

Rileigh froze at those words and couldn't think of anything else to say.

Chapter Seventeen

MICKY HOLLIS FLOATED SOMEWHERE BETWEEN SLEEP AND wakefulness — aware of her surroundings, the crisp white hospital sheets and the muffled steps of nurses in the hallway outside her door. But she was unwilling yet to plug back in. When she did, she would have to have her wits about her, not get tripped up by all the questions. They can't *force* her to tell them where she's from. They can't *make* her tell them Uncle Dan's name. But she has to be careful, because just one slip ... if they traced Uncle Dan, they'd find out *why* he was trying to kill them. And then she'd be blamed for all of it.

Farrah's visit in the middle of the night had shaken her to the core, but still she shied away from the reality of it. The reality of Farrah — not the little girl she'd grown up with, the one who had cowered with her in the dark, the one who had suffered untold indignities with her. The Farrah she found at the farm when she went back to save her was someone else entirely.

"You have to go to the police, Michaela," Carson says. "When the two of you tell them what's been going on, the police will help you."

"No! You don't understand, Carson."

She has told him only a little of her story, leaving out the true horror, too ashamed to admit that … her own father. Uncle Dan is a sheriff's deputy, respected and admired, next in line for the job when the current sheriff steps down. Nobody will take her word and Farrah's over his in the small, isolated northern California county. Their mother and father are pillars of the community. Papa is a church deacon, Mama is president of the church's women's auxiliary. They both show up to feed the homeless every Thanksgiving and Christmas. They've made it impossible to stand up to them. The town would never allow two teenagers to "smear the Hollis's good name." If Michaela and her sister try to fight, they will lose — all they can do is run.

"If you won't help me get her out of there, I'll go alone," Michaela tells him, knowing there's no way she can pull it off without him, and also knowing he's too smitten with her to allow her to try.

How can she explain to him the bond their shared misery has forged between them, a connection beyond the genetics of real blood sisters? All they'd had was each other. As she grew older, Michaela'd watched helplessly as the evil around them consumed Farrah, filled her with an acidic rage that ate through her soul from the inside, hollowing her out, leaving a husk of the little girl who'd always tried to protect them both, and always failed.

If she cannot get her sister away from that nightmare soon, there'll be nothing left of who Farrah is to save. And now, with a future that actually holds promise, she can offer her sister a life to run to, not just an existence to run from.

"Will you help me or not?" she challenges Carson and watches his defenses fold up. She doesn't know what she will do about Carson, about his feelings for her, but that's a problem for another day. On this day, she will bring her big sister out of the darkness of captivity ... just as she promised she would.

Michaela had gone to the isolated old farmhouse armed with a bolt cutter to snap off the padlock that seals shut the old coal chute into a basement fortress where she and Farrah were locked up every night of their childhoods. During her months of freedom, Michaela considered and planned. The fortress had been painstakingly designed to keep its captives inside, making a breakout impossible. But no one gave any thought to preventing a break-in, and it's simple for her to slip down the coal chute from the outside.

Farrah is sitting on the edge of her bed and Michaela rushes to embrace her. It's like hugging a flagpole.

"I told you I'd come back for you," Michaela says.

She had called the day she ran away — before she destroyed her cell phone. Farrah had begged her not to run, but Michaela'd had no choice.

"What took you so long, Micky?" Farrah asks, her voice as cold as the bottom of an Arctic sea.

Micky is what Farrah calls Michaela. When Farrah was little, she struggled to say "Michaela," and it came out "Micky." But when she was older and able to pronounce the word, she still clung to the mispronunciation, and when Michaela asked why that was, her younger sister grew very serious.

"Everyone thinks you're Michaela, but you're not."

She'd pointed to her own chest. "In here, in my heart — I know better. You're Micky."

Now Farrah sneers. "What's the matter? Did you get so busy having fun out there, you forgot all about me?"

"No. It just took me a long time to set it up. I couldn't do it alone. I had to have help and transportation."

"Transportation?"

"Yes, Carson Granger. He's waiting outside in the car."

"Your boyfriend?"

This conversation is not going as Michaela envisioned. Why isn't Farrah desperate to leave, terrified they'll be caught? Farrah seems in no hurry to go anywhere.

"We have to get out of here!" Michaela urges.

"So you can rush back into the arms of your boyfriend?"

He is more or less her boyfriend, she supposes. At least she lets him think he is. Without Carson, she would never have survived.

"Later … can we talk about that later?" Michaela looks at the door, fearing Papa will come barging through it any second. "We need to go now."

"Go where?"

"We have a place, there's hope…"

"Hope?"

"My birth mother, I think I may have found her on one of those ancestry websites. I may have located—"

She realizes too late that wasn't the best thing to say. Farrah almost … snarls.

Her rage has warped and twisted her mind with virulent hatred for all the people who have abused her and Michaela. But she has reserved her greatest hatred for those who should have protected them but betrayed them instead, the "Judases," the highest-ranking war criminals of all — the mothers who sold her and Michaela on the black market, the women who got paid to deliver their own children, their helpless newborns into the hands of monsters. Farrah has sworn vengeance on all the abusers. She lives for the day of "retribution," the day she can make them pay, Mama and Papa and Uncle Dan … and the other men they invited to the party — and, of course, the Judases.

Michaela tries to walk it back.

"I don't know for sure. Just genetic matches — strong DNA matches."

"To the parents that sold you to the highest bidder!"

"Farrah, please — not now."

There is no time now for Farrah's rage.

"How? How did you find them? Tell me."

"Not—"

"Now! Tell me everything, everything you've done since you abandoned me here."

Farrah is holding Michaela's wrist, squeezing so hard it is painful.

"Tell me now!"

"All right. Will you come with me then, after I tell you?"

"All of it. Don't leave out even the smallest detail."

Michaela tells her story, talking in a harsh whisper as fast as she can, gives Farrah a blow by blow of how she'd lived, survived on the street and in the shelter, everything she'd done since the day she disappeared in a crowd gathered around a wreck. Farrah listens to it stone-faced, no emotional reaction of any kind. She asks questions, though, wants specific details. The name of the college student at Stanford. The town where the maternal match lives. She wants to see Michaela's ID and asks about Carson.

When Michaela finally finishes the story to Farrah's satisfaction, Farrah looks at her with dead eyes and asks,

"Aren't you going to ask what I've been doing since you left?"

"Of course, I want to know. But we need to go — now!"

"You think you know what happened to me after you left? But you're wrong. Oh, my, yes, you are so wrong."

Farrah's words come out in a hoarse whisper. Unlike Michaela, it's not because she's trying to be quiet — she doesn't seem to care if they are heard. Her voice is low and ragged with fury.

"Without you here, there was just me. Did you think about that when you left? Did you think about what it would mean if there was only one of us?"

Michaela says nothing.

"Papa was hurt bad in that wreck you walked away from. He still can't breathe right, and it messed with his … manhood. Since he couldn't … 'participate' anymore, he brought in other men to do what he couldn't — while he watched. Uncle Dan brought friends, too, handed me from one to another like a party favor. They all watched and laughed and applauded."

"I'm so, so sorry," Michaela says. Farrah merely stares at her.

"And then I got pregnant."

"You…what?"

"Pregnant. Yeah, pregnant."

"But the IUD, they took us in and made us both get them."

"Apparently, those things aren't foolproof. Maybe they don't work when there's multiple partners."

"What did you…? Where did you…?"

There is the venom of a thousand rattlesnakes in her voice when she speaks the word. "Abortion."

"They took you to get an abortion?"

"I didn't say that."

"You said—"

"They didn't take me anywhere."

"You mean they brought an abortionist here?"

"No. I mean Papa did it himself."

Michaela looks like Farrah has slapped her. "How did—?"

"They tied me down first."

Michaela can't breathe, starts crying and can't stop. It's all too awful, too monstrous. She is becoming hysterical until Farrah slaps her. Hard.

"Please, Farrah," she sobs out the words, "we can get away now. But it's time to go."

"Oh, it's time alright," Farrah says, and she actually smiles. "Now that there's somewhere to go, it is definitely time."

FARRAH LOOKS at her pathetic little sister, crying and sniveling like a baby. Farrah doesn't cry. Not ever.

"You can come with me, or you can wait here," Farrah says. "Your choice."

"With you … where?"

Farrah feels her smile getting bigger but never allows it to reach her eyes. "Payback's a bitch!"

The door to the bedroom is padlocked on the outside, and the lock is always secured, snapped shut every night. But tonight, Farrah can get out — the way Micky came in, down the coal chute. As soon as she gets outside, she turns toward the back of the house instead of heading for the road, where she can just make out the shape of a parked car.

"Where are you going?" whispers Micky.

"It's time," is all she says. Farrah quickly finds the window in the laundry room where the latch is broken, and climbs back into the house — free now, not locked in her room.

What happens after that has a quality of déjà vu to it because she has imagined it so many times. Farrah goes to the wooden block on the countertop in the kitchen where all the knives are stored. She picks the biggest one. She knows it's the sharpest. She turns and sees that Micky has followed her into the house. That's good, she supposes. When she's finished here, she won't have to go looking for her sister.

Farrah moves as silent as a wraith down the hallway and into the first bedroom. It had been the guest bedroom before, but now Mama is asleep in the big four-poster bed. Michaela stands at the doorway watching, a look of horror and disbelief on her face. Farrah goes to the bedside, lifts the knife high in the air above Mama, and then whispers, "Mama, wake up. It's me."

Her mother's eyes pop open. Farrah pauses, waits for recognition. Then fear. When she sees terror transform Mama's ugly face, she slams the blade of the knife down into Mama's chest. Mama makes a gurgling, coughing sound, struggles, tries to get away, but Farrah stabs her again in the throat. Then over and over and over, doesn't stop stabbing until she's panting, splattered with blood.

Getting to her feet, she shoves past Micky in the doorway and goes to Papa's room. The old man now has some kind of machine by his bedside, with a tube that leads to a mask on his face. The machine makes so much noise, Farrah approaches his bed without bothering to be silent.

"Papa, wake up, it's me!" she cries. And when he opens his eyes, Farrah draws the blade of the razor-sharp butcher knife in a slashing motion across his neck, sending blood gushing in a torrent out of the gaping wound onto his pajamas. His eyes are wild. He tries to talk, but there are just more bubbles of blood.

Farrah laughs at his effort, throws her head back and bays in triumphant laughter. Then she uses the knife on Papa, cuts pieces off Papa's body, leaves him totally unrecognizable.

Farrah finally finishes, stands up drenched in blood but feeling so very alive, more alive than she's ever felt. It's the beginning of a whole new life for Farrah. She turns to her sister standing in the doorway. The look of horror stamped on her features surprises Farrah. What, did she think Farrah would just leave, run away and let them get away with what they did?

"Payback's a bitch," Farrah says and smiles a cheerless smile at her little sister, her Micky.

Chapter Eighteen

RILEIGH GOT INTO HER CAR AT GEORGIA'S HOUSE AND immediately got back out of it at Mama's house, and she had absolutely no memory of any time in between. She was there, and then she was here, and her thoughts had bubbled and boiled the whole time like storm clouds. A big storm. Hurricane Katrina had been blowing through Rileigh's mind between Georgia's house and Mama's house as she contemplated the possibility that her sister had had a child. A child.

Rileigh walked slowly up the sidewalk to the porch and up the steps, wondering what on earth she could say. It had felt like puzzle pieces falling together when Georgia pointed out what had seemed obvious to her but had not crossed Rileigh's mind. Or maybe it had. Maybe she had put it together herself but just flat out wouldn't face it because it was too — yeah, right, too what? Awful? Too strange? Too …just too.

She could hear Mama call to Jillian when she opened the front door. "I'm gonna be feeding the chickens," she said. "I left that meatloaf at 350. Don't believe you need to look in on it, but if you want to, that'd be fine."

Rileigh opened the squalling screen door and went into the living room, through the living room and the dining room and into the kitchen, where Jillian was chopping up lettuce for a salad for supper tonight.

Jillian glanced over her shoulder when she heard Rileigh come into the room. "Mama's out feeding the chickens, and I'm making salad. If you want to cut up some red potatoes, we could have roasted potatoes with Mama's meatloaf."

Rileigh opened her mouth to speak and found she couldn't make words come out. She just stood there looking at Jillian's back. When she didn't respond, Jillian glanced over her shoulder, saw the look on Rileigh's face, and turned around to face her.

"What?"

And then her face registered something like shock and …recognition, maybe? Perhaps that's what it was, and then it closed up tight. It was like you could see doors slam and drapes drawn over windows, shutters closing tight. She turned back around immediately and furiously began cutting up the lettuce.

"Mama said maybe we could have corn on the cob, too. If you want some, you need to go pick it and shuck it. If you don't want corn, that's fine with me. I don't care."

Jillian kept talking, and Rileigh heard the sounds, and they were words. She recognized that they were words, but none of them fit together in a sentence that made any sense to Rileigh. And she wondered if they made any sense to Jillian either. Rileigh simply stood where she was while Jillian babbled with her back turned, frantically chopping lettuce, and then she stopped. Her shoulders slumped, and she turned back toward Rileigh.

"What is it?" she said, and there was a dead quality to her voice. Rileigh didn't know how to respond. "Come on. What is it? What's wrong?"

"I was at Georgia's telling her about — about…" Then Rileigh lost the air to speak. She pulled in another lungful. "About Mitch and I and the stabbing … you know, the stabbing that happened, and I—" She stumbled again and couldn't speak.

"Come on, girl, out with it," Jillian said.

Rileigh drew in another breath. "It's just that Georgia put together in her head things that — I didn't think about. I mean, she made connections that—"

"What connections?" Jillian was staring at Rileigh with no look of any kind on her face.

"Well, she put it together, you know. She — she thought about that girl, that girl, Michaela, and how, you know, how…" She drew in another breath. "How she had blonde hair, you know, like yours, and — and—" She looked to Jillian for help, hoping her sister would form the words for her so she didn't have to, but her sister crossed her arms across her chest, leaned back against the cabinet, and didn't say a word.

"And it just kind of seemed to me that when — when Mama thought, suggested that we make a birthday cake for, you know, the girl, so maybe if we took her a birthday cake, she would — she would open up and talk, you know, maybe and—"

Rileigh could hear herself babbling and couldn't seem to stifle the words. She let out a breath, drew in another one, lifted her eyes to Jillian's, and focused on her face. She stilled her turmoil.

"It just seemed to me that when Mitch said she would be twenty years old on September eighteenth, you looked —" She let the words tangle.

"Looked what?"

"Looked, I don't know, surprised or — no, not surprised, shocked, like…"

Rileigh let out a breath. "Oh, come on, Jillian, like the date meant something to you. Does it? Do you see where I'm going with this?"

"As a matter of fact, I do," Jillian said.

She tossed the paring knife that she'd been using to cut up the lettuce into the sink and untied the apron she always borrowed from Mama.

"Yeah, I see where you're going with this, and I don't appreciate it one damned bit."

With that, she threw the apron onto the table, turned, and stormed out the back door. She crossed the back porch and headed out across the backyard.

"Where are you going, sweetheart?" Mama called after her. "It ain't gonna be long 'til dinner."

Jillian said nothing, just marched across the backyard to the trail up into the woods. Rileigh and her mother both watched Jillian climb the trail up the hill until she was gone.

Chapter Nineteen

JILLIAN STARTED UP THE TRAIL INTO THE WOODS, MADE IT as far as the trees and the first turn before she began to run. She raced up the mountainside, felt her cheeks wetten, and realized that perhaps she was crying and didn't care. She ran as fast as she could, leaping from rock to rock along the craggy trail. When she reached the overlook on Tucker Mountain, she was gasping for breath. Leaning over, she put her hands on her knees and stood, nauseous from the exertion, swallowing down her lunch that was threatening to go flying out onto the rocks.

Slowly, the nausea receded, and she could catch her breath. She looked around then as if she was surprised at where she was, like she didn't even remember running up the mountain, but of course she had.

She let out a huge sigh, lifted her face to the sky, and wanted to scream. She didn't. Instead, she made her way to the sitting rock. As she sat down, she wondered, as she'd wondered often in the past, if the rock had been worn smooth by all the backsides that had plopped down on it to rest after climbing up the mountainside.

Then she sat staring out over the most beautiful vista she'd ever seen.

And in her strange life, Jillian Bishop had seen a lot of beautiful vistas. She had seen the sun set over the Mediterranean Ocean in a blaze of red and gold. She'd seen snow-capped Alps, villages in the Italian countryside, and the deep blue of the Indian Ocean off the coast of Madagascar.

Every time she'd seen something beautiful like that — a Parisian gala with women in fancy dresses dancing as if they were monarchs out of some nineteenth century romance novel — she'd think about sitting here looking out over the Smoky Mountains from Tucker Ridge. And every time she compared whatever she was looking at to the view she was looking at now, this view always won. Hands down. This was the most beautiful sight Jillian Bishop had ever seen.

She sat here now, staring out at a beauty God had created, a beauty that was unequaled by anything she had ever seen, and wanted to cry. Or scream. She wasn't sure which would have made her feel better and realized that neither would.

If Georgia McGinnis, no, Georgia *Stump* had put two and two together and come up with five, and Jillian's little sister had added the same two and two together and also came up with five, then Jillian's own addition probably wasn't too far wrong.

Now here she sat staring out at God's beauty and considering that maybe the girl who had been on her way to "find her family" in Black Bear Forge, Tennessee, had come looking for *her*.

Maybe the answer that the girl named Michaela Hollis was seeking was Jillian herself.

Maybe the girl who was lying on a hospital bed right

now not fifteen miles away from where Jillian Bishop sat with her butt on a rock was the baby that Jillian had stared at in revulsion and disgust and ... and *wonder* twenty years ago.

What in the hell she was supposed to do now?

Jillian threw her head back and let out a primeval cry as wild and Jurassic as she had done two decades ago when she was in labor with the baby a monstrous man had planted inside her. Not a child of rape. Worse than that. A child of prostitution, conceived as the accidental byproduct of a financial transaction.

Sitting on top of the world for the rest of the afternoon, Jillian cried and railed and pounded her fists. When all of the emotion was spent, she sat there as the cool breeze of early evening caressed the dampness of her tear-streaked cheeks and made some kind of peace with the reality that the little baby she'd given life all those years ago had found her.

Jillian had wiped all memory of her baby daughter out of her mind. Had never even told Dr. Al-Masri about it. It was different from the other awful things that had happened to her because she didn't know what to feel — hadn't known at the time and didn't know now, two decades later.

She'd never countenanced the possibility that she'd ever see the child again. The girl had obviously gone looking for her *mother*, her *family*. Was that what Jillian was — her mother? Just because she'd given birth to her in another world, another whole life, did that make Jillian her mother?

Yeah, she supposed it did.

Shaking her head, Jillian rose slowly to her feet, her butt completely numb from sitting on that lumpy rock for how long? Jillian didn't even know. It was hours or maybe years or centuries or geologic epochs. But there was a reality to be faced, and there was nothing for it but to do exactly that. She had to go talk to Rileigh.

When Jillian came down out of the trees, she could see the lights shining out of Mama's house, glowing warm and welcoming. She walked slowly down the end of the trail and across the backyard and took a deep breath. Rileigh and Mama would be waiting inside. And it was time now to tell them ... the rest of her story.

Jillian stepped up on the back porch and was relieved to see that Mama was not in the kitchen, and neither was Rileigh. But she could smell dinner and knew that neither of them had eaten yet, that they had waited for her. She wished they hadn't. She certainly wasn't hungry. But they probably weren't either. She wondered what Rileigh might have said to Mama. But it didn't matter. They both had to know now anyway.

She opened the back door, went into the kitchen, through it to the dining room and the living room and the front porch, where, as she suspected, she found Mama and Rileigh sitting outside. She pushed open the screen door, and it squawked in protest, and their conversation stopped in mid-sentence. Mama leapt to her feet, ran to Jillian, and threw her arms around her.

"Are you okay, Sugar?"

Rileigh quickly interjected. "I told Mama what happened. You know, how you had something like a PTSD episode and needed to go be by yourself."

Relief washed over Jillian. Thank God she was spared having to tell Mama. At least not yet.

"I'm fine, Mama. I'm really fine."

"Well, I worry about you all the time, sweetheart. Now let's go on in the house and have supper. I kept it warm for you."

"I smelled it in the kitchen. It smells wonderful."

Jillian locked eyes with her younger sister over Mama's head and nodded gratefully.

Rileigh understood the nod.

Jillian pushed food around on her plate, kept it moving sufficiently that Mama didn't notice she really didn't eat any of it. Rileigh managed to keep pleasant conversation going through dinner, kept Mama engaged so she wouldn't notice how distant Jillian was.

"I was thinking I'd like to go to Gatlinburg to that shoe store out on the bypass," Rileigh suddenly said. "I saw some sandals there I liked. Would you come with me, Jillian, and help me pick?"

"Sure," Jillian said and nodded, grateful that Rileigh was carrying all the conversational weight.

They got into Rileigh's car and drove down the driveway onto the road. The two were silent as they drove. Rileigh pulled off at the first overlook, killed the engine, pushed the seat back, and looked at Jillian.

"You don't have to tell me about this," she said.

"Yeah, I do," Jillian said,

"No, you don't. This isn't any of my business."

"It's everybody's business now," Jillian said. "The whole family is involved, and you know it."

Rileigh nodded. "But you don't have to go into detail," she said.

Yeah, Jillian thought. Yeah, I do.

Chapter Twenty

JILLIAN BISHOP LEANED HER HEAD BACK ON THE SEAT, closed her eyes, and tried to think what she could say that would capture the events of twenty years ago. How could she take Rileigh back there and show her, just by tacking words onto the experience?

AT FIRST, Jillian doesn't believe it. She's missed her period. And is concerned. But just concerned. Nothing more. After all, how likely is it? They all had been fitted for IUDs, and Jillian's, as far as she knew, was still in place. Then there was the extra precaution of daily birth control pills. Jillian had not missed a single one. How can she possibly be pregnant? The weeks pass, but still no period.

Of course, perhaps it's something worse than being pregnant. One of the scary words. The C word, or something worse. But in Jillian's view, there is really nothing worse than the possibility of being pregnant. She'd far rather have cervical cancer or uterine cancer or any other kind of cancer than find out she is carrying the child of Hussain Amir Al-Saud. If she is pregnant, he is the father. She has been living as a part-time servant, full-time bed partner in his house for six months while his wife and young children are in the United Arab Emirates, where her mother has undergone double-hip replacement and is not doing well.

When she finally tells Omar her fears, he takes the news with equanimity. This isn't his first rodeo. He quickly makes an appointment for her with a gynecologist. Omar takes good care of his girls. They have to be in top physical condition to fetch the prices he charges for them. And he makes sure that they are healthy, that they have bright, shiny, white teeth, and balanced diets and clear complexions. Omar's girls use only the finest beauty products and exercise regularly — get plenty of fresh air — though not in the hot sun. Their blonde hair and fair complexions, are, after all, why they are in such high demand.

Omar sits in the waiting room while Jillian is examined. And when the doctor confirms her worst fears, she somehow manages not to burst into tears.

"But how…? I have an IUD. And I take birth control pills."

"Nothing is perfect," the doctor says. "Well, except abstinence." He looks her up and down. "Which in your case clearly is not an option."

Leaving her in the examining room, the doctor goes to consult with Omar in his office.

Jillian sits naked except for the stupid wrap-around garment that hides absolutely nothing, a one-size-fits-all that doesn't. She strains to hear the voices coming under the exam room door.

"Of course, abortion is your best option," the doctor's

voice says, "but it will leave her unable to … for some time afterward."

"I'm thinking about letting her have the baby," Omar says. Jillian almost cries out, bites the inside of her lip so hard it bleeds bled to keep from making a sound. "The black market pays well for blonde babies."

"Are you sure you want her to go through nine months of pregnancy?" the doctor inquires. "There will be irreversible changes to her body as a result."

"I know, but she's getting a little old anyway — 28. There are still certain, customers who request her, though. I won't let her gain more than twenty pounds and … we'll see."

Omar informs her that she will be put on a strict diet and continue to work for the next couple of months.

"Then, I have a place for you as a house servant and nanny, where you can work until you deliver."

"What about the baby?" Jillian asks. She can't stop herself. She didn't mean to form the words, didn't intend for them to come out of her mouth.

"We'll take care of the baby. That's none of your concern."

Jillian climbs back down into that part of herself where she lives that shows no emotional response to anything going on around her. And she stays there until she is back in her room in the master suite of apartments where she lives with three of the other girls. She tells them she is pregnant, see the looks of compassion on their faces, and she sits up all night pondering the thought of having a baby whose father had raped her.

No, not rape. She no longer thought of it as rape. Rape was when you protested. She didn't protest. Rape was when you had something to lose. And she had nothing to lose. She feels her belly that is still flat and wonders what it will be like to feel a child moving inside her, and what she will feel about that child.

~

JILLIAN CAME BACK from those thoughts, sitting in the car with Rileigh, who was waiting patiently for her to say something.

"At least I knew who it was," Jillian started, "though I don't know that it would have made any difference if I hadn't. He owned an import-export business, was rich and getting richer by the day."

She paused then and looked at Rileigh, knowing Rileigh had a million questions that she wasn't asking.

"What was he like, the baby's father?" she finally said.

"Amir was tall and dark like most Arabs, had a really prominent, maybe almost Roman nose. High cheekbones and dark black hair. His children were beautiful, but they looked like their mother. After I knew I was pregnant, I studied his face and wondered what he had looked like as a child."

"Did he know ... did your boss tell him you were pregnant?"

"He did. I think Amir was glad, no, not glad... proud. You know, that somehow it demonstrated how macho he was."

"Did they take her from you as soon as she was born?"

Jillian shook her head. "I wish they had, but they didn't. She was born jaundiced, and they needed to keep her under a bilirubin light, and I needed to nurse her. After all, who wants to buy a baby that isn't healthy? So they left her with me ... I had her for four days."

~

JILLIAN IS SCREAMING, shrieking. The pain is unbelievable. She's being torn apart by this thing coming out of her, and now she can scream. So she lets go then and screams for the pain of childbirth. Screams for the agony of rape. Screams for the debasement of being owned. She screams for all the times she wanted to scream and couldn't. By the time the little wiggling, squirming infant is placed sticky in her arms and she looks down at it, she has no voice left at all.

They take her back to her room in the small, remote hospital, clean the baby up, and then bring it to her. Wheel it into her room in a bassinet and leave it there. Jillian ignores the child, just stares straight ahead until the baby starts to cry. And she feels the ache in her breasts as her milk lets down. And even though her emotions are as snarled as tangled sewing thread, she picks the baby up, holds her to her breast, and nurses her.

And looks down at the child in stunned wonder.

Jillian does not name the baby, because to name it is to acknowledge how much it means to her. And she can't do that. To name it is to acknowledge that it is hers. At least partly hers. And she can't do that either. To name it is to lay some claim on the child. And she has to be able to give it up as she has given up every other thing in her life since she was eighteen. Refuse to do what you're told and you die. Retribution is swift and totally merciless. That's the overriding principle of Jillian Bishop's whole existence.

She holds the little girl tight to her chest on the final morning before they come for her, nurses her a final time, looks at her perfect little body. Well, not completely perfect. She had examined her from the tip of her head to the bottom of her feet, did what every other mother on the planet has ever done, which is count her baby's toes.

One, two, three, four, five, six, seven, eight, nine.

Nine.

There are supposed to be ten. Then she realizes that the big toe on the baby's right foot and the toe next to it were grown together to form only one toe

Jillian has not allowed herself to show affection to the baby, but now she wants to shower the baby's tiny face with kisses. But she doesn't, merely wets the baby's cheeks with her tears. She grabs hold of her emotions before they come for her, releases the baby into the arms of the nurse one final time. And then stares straight ahead. She doesn't cry. She doesn't cry that night. She doesn't cry the next day. She doesn't cry for weeks. And then one day she hears a newborn baby crying in the distance, and it hits her like a piano dropped on her head. And she collapses to her knees during her morning workout and sobs, gut-wrenching, heart-tearing sobs that rip out of her chest.

When she got her emotions under control that day, she sealed them up. Locked them tight. And she never again thinks about or mourns the baby she has lost.

"SHE WASN'T PERFECT," Jillian told Rileigh, who was seated behind the steering wheel, waiting patiently for Jillian to say whatever it was she wanted to say. "Her right big toe and the toe next to it were grown together. So she only had nine toes, technically. I'm sure it was repaired, simple to separate. But when she was born, she only had nine toes."

She paused.

"And I never gave her a name. It helped not to have anything to call her in my head, just 'the baby.'"

"You don't have to explain, Jillian. I understand," Rileigh said, then stopped. "No, that's glib and absurd. I'm sorry. I *don't* understand. There's nowhere inside me that understands this, nowhere that understands all the horror that has happened to you and how any human being could survive it and remain sane. But you have. I don't know what you're going through right now. Nobody knows what you're going through. I just … I care. You know, I just, I wish I could make it better."

~

RILEIGH WATCHED HER SISTER SOB, held her hand, and squeezed it tight, and wanted to cry with her for all that she'd lost. Jillian looked up at her and smiled through her tears.

"And now I don't know what to think," she said, then sniffled and sat back up in the seat. "I know how to keep myself from feeling anything for her. I didn't give her a name, because to give her a name was to make her mine, and I couldn't make her mine. And besides, I didn't know if I wanted to make her mine. I mean, she was my child, but she was also the child of my *customer.*"

It was amazing how much loathing Jillian managed to slather on that ordinary word.

"How could I care anything about a child when her father bought me? But I was her mother. How could I *not* feel anything about my own baby girl?" She shook her head. "It was too long ago, and the feelings were buried deep, and there's no sense in dredging them all up. I would never have thought about this again for the rest of my life if…" She paused and let out a sigh. Then she fixed Rileigh with a concentrated look. "What do you think? Do you think that girl, Michaela Hollis … do you think she's my daughter?"

Rileigh refused to tell her what she knew she wanted to

hear — the easy reassurance. The painful truth was harder. And better.

"From all the evidence … my opinion? Yeah, I think she must be."

Jillian sat back against the seat. "Now what?" she said, "What do I do now?"

"No, it's what do *we* do now?"

"This girl who may be my child, the little baby I gave up twenty years ago — God only knows what kind of life she's had. I mean, she was bought on the black market. The kind of person who'd buy a baby on the black market is probably not someone who'd be featured on the cover of *Parents Weekly*. Who knows what she lived through. It must have been really ugly — she ran away to come here. Somebody tried to kill her."

"And that somebody is still out there somewhere."

"I don't know how she has been wounded, but emotional pain is emotional pain, and I can relate. This is a young woman who has been damaged, and I suspect she's looking for a mommy to kiss it and make it well." She paused. "And Mommy is me."

"*Maybe* is you."

"*Probably* is me."

"I think we need to talk to Mitch about this. Get together with him and figure this out."

"And what about David?" Jillian said, and Rileigh thought she heard despair in her voice then for the first time. Jillian was just beginning to find a real life, have a real relationship, just beginning … and now this.

"You certainly don't need to tell David anything until there's something to tell him *for sure*. Just like with Mama — let's find out the facts before we do anything."

Rileigh picked up her cell phone and called Mitch.

"What's going on in your world?" he asked cheerily as soon as he heard her voice.

"You have no idea."

"I don't like the sound of that."

"You're going to like the sound of it even less when I tell you about it. Can you come over tonight? You and I and Jillian need to talk … about Micky Hollis."

"Micky Hollis? What do we have to talk about Micky Hollis?"

Rileigh took a big breath. "Maybe, nothing for sure but maybe … no, it's very *likely* Micky Hollis is Jillian's daughter."

There was such profound silence on the other end of the line that Rileigh said, "Mitch, Mitch, are you still there?"

"I'm still here. Knocked on my ass, but still here. Okay, I'll be over as soon as I finish up this paperwork, probably half an hour."

"Wait," Rileigh said before he could hang up. "On your way, would you mind stopping by and getting Mama a vanilla milkshake? She and I got milkshakes yesterday and she didn't get to drink hers."

"Why not?"

"Because her milkshake is currently soaking into the front seat of her car. No, not anymore, we got it out. She spilled it and … never mind. Would you please stop by and pick her up a milkshake on your way here?"

"I'll get you and Jillian milkshakes, too."

Chapter Twenty-One

RILEIGH'S WORDS BANGED AROUND IN MITCH'S SKULL LIKE a bowling ball in an oil drum. What in the world? How could…? The questions raged as he slapped his signature on a couple of arrest warrants and told Sheila he'd be leaving early today.

Then he got into his cruiser and drove to Red-Eye Gravy. As he drove along, he tried to put the pieces together and discovered that he could make some sense of them. Some of them fit: the words "Lily Bishop," the odd look on Jillian's face when he told her about the girl with hair like hers whose birthday was in two days. And when you put that together with Mama sending her DNA off to that website, yeah, some of the pieces fit. And Rileigh wouldn't have called him over there unless she believed there was something to it.

He pulled his cruiser up in front of the diner, hopped out, and went inside. Big John was behind the counter, moving the rag around in precise circles.

"How's it going, Big John?" said Mitch as he sat down on a stool.

"Can't complain."

"You can complain, just won't do no good."

"What can I do for you?"

"I need three vanilla milkshakes."

"Let me guess, one for Rileigh, one for Mama, and one for Jillian."

Big John turned to Susie and told her to make three vanilla milkshakes with a little added vanilla, and to be sure to put whipped cream and a cherry on top and set them in a carrier for Mitch. While she worked, he turned back to Mitch.

"So, what did you think about what I told Lily the other day?"

"What was that?"

Big John looked surprised.

"I figured you'd know. I told Lily to be sure to tell Rileigh."

"If you want Lily to deliver a message to Rileigh, you'd be better off putting it in the beak of an owl, like on Harry Potter."

"I saw those movies, those owls were pretty efficient." Then Big John shook his head, "But I didn't think about, you know, how Lily is. I told her to tell Rileigh about something that's important. It happened Sunday morning. There were two men seated at a table, and they were pumping Turnip Smothers with questions."

"Questions about what?"

"About Lily Bishop."

Mitch's eyes opened wide.

Big John continued, "I sidled over to eavesdrop on the conversation, and when I realized who they were getting information about, I sent Turnip packing and sent the men on a wild goose chase."

Mitch sat very still.

"They were Middle Easterners, heavily muscled." Big John leaned on his elbows on the counter toward Mitch and spoke softly. "And both of them were packing."

Mitch felt his blood run cold. They were looking for Lily Bishop.

"So you sent them on some kind of wild goose chase?"

"Yeah, I sent them looking for Miss Lillian Bichon in Nashville to throw them off the scent for a while so I'd have time to warn Lily."

"So that was Sunday morning."

"Uh-huh."

"And now it's Tuesday evening."

Big John nodded. "The Lily Bichon ruse has probably run its course by now, and if they're really looking for Lily Bishop, they're back in Yarmouth County."

"If they're not here now, they soon will be," Mitch said.

"You got any idea why they're looking for Lily?"

Mitch had made it a practice not to share the private information he had about what had happened to Jillian while she was gone. If she wanted people to know, she could tell them herself.

"Just kind of a family matter," Mitch said.

Big John nodded. "Okay, I get it. Has to do with Jillian and where she was for thirty years, right?"

Before Mitch could protest, Big John held up his hand. "Ain't none of my business. I don't want to know, but those guys," the big man hissed a breath between his teeth, "I should have made sure Rileigh got the message. Those guys looked dangerous."

When Mitch parked in front of Rileigh's mother's house, he saw the three Bishop women sitting together on the front porch. Lily leapt to her feet when she saw him.

"Well, I didn't know you were coming over tonight, Sheriff. If I'd known, I'd have a held supper for you."

"I've eaten already, Lily," he said, "and you're putting weight on me." He patted his absolutely flat abdomen. "Too much fried chicken and mashed potatoes. I have to spend hours in the gym working it off."

He leaned back into his cruiser and picked up the carrier with the three milkshakes Susie had set carefully in it, all with whipped cream and cherries on top.

"Why, you brought me a milkshake," Mama said, her face lighting up. "Ain't you the sweetest thing ever."

Mitch turned to Rileigh and then to Jillian, "I couldn't very well bring Mama one and not bring you two anything."

Rileigh pasted a pretty good imitation of a smile on her face, while Jillian just nodded.

They made small talk for a little while as Mama slurped on her milkshake, Rileigh sipped hers, and Jillian didn't take a single swallow.

When Mama was finished with her milkshake, Rileigh asked Lily for a favor.

"What's that, sweetheart?"

"What I want is for you to find that box of all the things you knitted years ago. You know the box I'm talking about. You stored it somewhere, but I don't know where it is."

"Why? What do you want that box for?"

"There's something in it I want to give to Mitch."

Mama rose to her feet. "I think I know where it is, and if it ain't there, I'll look somewheres else. I'll find it." She turned on her heel and went through the squawking screen door into the living room. As soon as the three of them were alone, Mitch turned to Jillian.

"Why don't you tell me what this is all about," he said.

Jillian let out a long breath, and when she pulled it back in, her eyes were no longer in a thousand-yard stare.

"Not complicated. I had a baby on September the 18th, 2004, a little girl. She was taken away from me and sold on the black market."

Mitch couldn't help the gasp that escaped his lips.

"And you think Michaela Hollis is—" he began.

"Same hair, same birthdate, and Mama sent her DNA off to that website. Yeah, I think Michaela Hollis is that child. It seems reasonable to me."

"I think that should be our first order of business," Rileigh said. "We need to establish for lead-pipe certain that Michaela Hollis is the baby that Jillian gave up twenty years ago."

"And it sounds to me like you have a plan to do that."

Rileigh's eyes went to the front door where Mama had just gone into the house.

"I do, and Mama's going to help me."

Then she turned the full force of her gaze on Mitch. "Okay, out with it, what's wrong?" Mitch was momentarily surprised. Rileigh pressed. "I could see it on your face as soon as you got out of the car. Something's wrong, what is it?"

"When I stopped by Red-Eyed Gravy tonight to get the milkshakes, I had a talk with Big John."

"Did he tell you what a mess we made in Mama's car with milkshakes the other day?"

"No, that's not what we talked about." Mitch paused. "He did tell me, however, that he had given some information to Mama and told her to be sure to tell you about it."

Rileigh's eyebrows went up. "Mama did say Big John told her to tell me something, but we spilled the milkshakes, and I never found out what it was. What did he want Mama to tell me?"

Mitch took in a deep breath; this was going to knock the slats out from under Jillian's and Rileigh's worlds.

"He said that on Sunday morning, there were some men in Red-Eye Gravy asking questions about Lily Bishop."

Rileigh and Jillian froze with identical looks of horror on their faces.

"I'm sorry, Jillian. Big John said they were Middle Eastern men, suits and ties, heavily muscled, and both of them were armed."

Jillian couldn't stop herself; she cried out a squeak of terror and put her hand over her mouth.

Rileigh's face went as white as a new gym sock.

"Oh dear god, no," she said. "What…? Tell us about it."

"Big John sent them on a wild goose chase to Nashville, but they've likely run that to ground by now. I suspect they're already back in Yarmouth County."

"Oh god, what am I going to do?" Jillian looked like a lost rabbit, and Mitch had no way to comfort her.

"It was Mama sending off that DNA, wasn't it," Rileigh suddenly said, and Mitch nodded.

"That's what I figure. If it hooked that girl up to Mama, then it must have hooked her up to—"

"Her father's side of the family," Jillian interrupted, sounding like a robot. "That's why those men have come looking for Lily Bishop … to lead them to me. And to her, to that girl, Michaela, if her DNA sample matched and he found out about it."

"It would be pretty brazen to go after Michaela in the hospital, and I've already stationed a deputy outside her door," Mitch said.

"But here," Jillian said, "they could come here. What can I do? Should I — should I run?"

"For starters," Mitch said, "I've got my go-bag in the car. I'm spending the night here. As soon as Mama goes to bed, we need to talk about what to do going forward. We need to map out a plan."

Jillian nodded, then set back in the rocker, the thousand-mile stare taking over her eyes again. She might not even have known she was whispering, "Oh God, Oh God, no."

The protesting screen door squawked, then Mama came out on the porch carrying a cardboard box.

"Is this what you was looking for?" she asked, setting it on the coffee table. The box was filled with scarves and caps, booties and mittens, all hand-knit by Mama. "Indian summer's just getting started," she said, fanning her face with her hand. "What could you possibly use these for?"

Chapter Twenty-Two

"Now why is it again that you're spending the night here, Mitch?" Mama asked, her head cocked to the side, a quizzical look on her face. "Not that I mind, you understand. You're certainly welcome anytime, and I'll make a really good breakfast in the morning. You'll like it. I make strawberry waffles. I got the strawberries already."

"Well, Lily, there are some things about this case that we're working on that Rileigh and I need to talk about tonight," Mitch stammered, "and I just don't feel like making the drive back home."

That was so lame. A four-year-old could have seen through it, but Mama bought it, smiled cheerily, and went off to bed. Rileigh let out a huge sigh of relief as soon as her mother was gone.

"I don't know how much longer I could have kept up the cheeriness," she said.

"You were great," Mitch said, patting her hand.

Then Rileigh went upstairs to bring Jillian back downstairs so the three of them could talk. Jillian had gone upstairs as soon as Mama brought the cardboard

159

box out onto the porch, and she'd been up there a long time. Rileigh couldn't imagine what she'd been doing … crying, sobbing… What do you do? How do you react when you discover that the monsters who kidnapped you and kept you as a slave for thirty years are looking for you again? What's the proper response to a horror like that?

But Jillian had her emotional duck's beak to tail feathers better when she came back downstairs. She was still pale and shaky, but the panic had left her eyes, at least temporarily.

Rileigh sat down on the porch swing with Jillian next to her and Mitch in the rocking chair across from them. The porch light was on. So was the light in the living room. Mitch wanted anybody who happened to pass down the road to see that his cruiser was parked in front of the house, and anybody who got any nosier than that couldn't miss his uniform and his badge as he sat on the porch.

"It's her," Jillian said. "It has to be. That girl, Michaela Hollis, sent off her DNA to findyourfamily.com and that hooked her up to Mama, and it must have hooked her up to Amir too, somehow."

"The only DNA that's available on that website is DNA somebody volunteered to put there," Rileigh said. "Is there any reason why someone in his family… the man, Amir… would have done that?"

"Who knows?" Jillian said. "I didn't put my DNA up there voluntarily. It was Mama's, so it could be somebody else in his family did it. He has two children, at least he did when I was there. Maybe one of them did, or his brother, a nephew, who knows. And I can't imagine any reason why." She paused and then spoke more quietly. "But they would not have sent out a team after me unless Amir went to Omar."

Mitch stopped rocking, leaned over in the rocker, and put his elbows on his knees.

"I don't need gory gruesome details, Jillian, but could you explain to me how this operation works?"

Jillian let out a sigh. "A man named Omar was in charge of a group of us girls. We serviced the men who paid him handsomely for our services, and there was no possibility of escape, not then anyway. I mean, we were blonde. All of us were blonde. That's what the Arabs liked, the blondes with blue eyes. One of the girls, Sheila, was a natural redhead, and she was in high demand, too." Jillian pointed up to her own pale blonde hair. "But so was this pale, pale blonde. It was unique and different."

"Are you sure? I mean, how do you know for sure who the father — I mean, how could you…?"

Mitch was stumbling.

"Let's not be awkward about this," Jillian said. "We all know what we're talking about. I know it's hard for you to ask questions, and it's hard for me to answer them, but let's just do it. The reason I'm sure who the father is, is because that particular summer, I was living in the house of Hussein Amir Al-Saud as a part-time servant and full-time bed partner. His wife and young children were in the United Arab Emirates, where her mother had double hip replacement surgery or something like that, and she wasn't doing well. She wanted her daughter and her grandchildren around her, so Amir packed them off and moved me in. He ran an import-export business and had more money than God. He lived in a palatial house in the suburbs, and he was the only man in my life when I got pregnant. He had to be the father."

"Who is this Omar person?"

"I don't know his last name. I don't know that anybody does. He was just Omar. He was in charge."

Jillian went back to talking about Michaela.

"The only way I can make this work in my head is that Michaela sent off her DNA to the website, and so did Mama, and so did somebody in Amir's family, because Michaela must have gotten in touch with him. She must have tried to connect to her father's side of the family, and that raised the alarm."

"How would they know about Lily Bishop?" Mitch asked.

"It had to come from Michaela. I don't know what the results look like when they send you them. I do know you're notified when there's a match, and if she was matched to Amir and Mama, somehow Amir found out about Mama, and he immediately got in touch with Omar, told him to handle it."

"So obviously this Amir guy doesn't want..." He stopped there, stumbling, trying to find the right word.

"Go ahead and say it, Mitch. Some bastard daughter suddenly rearing her head up in his life? I'm sure he didn't like it. He wanted it taken care of. He wanted her eliminated, and since they finally knew where I was, I'm sure Omar ordered the team to simply clean up the whole mess."

"Was that like standard operating procedure?" Mitch asked.

"There is no standard operating procedure. These people operate outside the law. The law of the land, the law of God, the law of morality — they recognize none of them. There is nothing that prevents them from doing whatever they want. If you are a Muslim in the United Arab Emirates, or Saudi Arabia, or Sudan, or, or any of those places, Sharia law allows you to have slaves just so long as they are not other Muslims, so long as they're 'infidels' ... like me."

Mitch sat back in the rocker. "I didn't know that."

"And if you are wealthy and prominent, it's almost expected. There's certainly nowhere for a slave to run to and find anybody who would be willing to help them get away." She pointed to her blonde hair and blue eyes.

"Then how did you ever escape?"

Jillian sighed. "Look, I don't mind telling you the whole story, anything you want to know, but that's not the point now. That's a story for another time, and it's a big, long, complicated story. I think we need to stick to the business at hand…" Her voice trailed off.

"Which is keeping you and Mama and Rileigh safe."

"And Michaela," Jillian put in.

"And Michaela."

"And how exactly do you plan to do that?" Jillian asked. "These people are animals. They operate outside of every authority. International law, American law, they don't care. They do whatever they have been hired to do, and if they've been hired to eliminate us, they won't stop until they finish the job."

"No," Rileigh said. She ground her teeth and said again, "Let me change that. No way in *hell* are these bastards going to lay a finger on anybody in my family."

"I second that motion," Mitch said. "We just have to figure out how to pull it off."

There was silence then until Mitch spoke again. "Obviously, we have to get Jillian and Michaela and Mama out of here. In this house, they're sitting ducks. They don't need Turnip to tell them where to find Lily Bishop. They can ask anybody in town."

"There's something we have to do before that," Jillian said.

"And that is?" Mitch said.

"We have to make sure she is who she purports to be. I

mean, we have to know, absolutely know, that she is, that she is my child."

"I've got that covered," Rileigh said. "Well, Mama and I have that covered. Let me handle it." There was the hint of a smile on her face.

"All right then, we'll leave that to you," Mitch said. "And as soon as we find out whatever there is to find out, we have to find somewhere for Jillian and Lily and Micky to go, somewhere nobody knows about, someplace that would be safe for them." He paused. "And I already have a place in mind."

Rileigh looked at him quizzically, but he only smiled.

"First, you need to go work your magic on Micky Hollis."

"Check," Rileigh said.

Mitch sat back in the rocker. "There's nothing we can do until tomorrow morning, so you guys need to get some sleep."

"You take the first watch," Rileigh said, lifting her tee to reveal her UWB holster holding her Glock close to her side. "I'll take the second watch."

Mitch raised his hand as if to protest, but Rileigh shook him off.

"This isn't my first rodeo. I've been on guard duty a time or two in my checkered past. I'll be fine."

Mitch nodded. "I'm sure you will."

Chapter Twenty-Three

RILEIGH, JILLIAN, AND MITCH SHOWED UP EARLY AT Yarmouth County Hospital on Wednesday morning. Rileigh went directly to Micky Hollis's room, leaving Mitch and Jillian to wait in the hospital lobby.

Micky had recovered so quickly and well that Dr. Asshole didn't bother to claim that she and Mitch were disturbing his patient and had to leave when he said to. It was Micky Hollis's decision who she talked to and who she didn't now.

Rileigh spoke briefly to Deputy Rawlings, who was stifling a yawn. He had stayed up all night too, guarding Micky Hollis. Rileigh at least had gone to bed. She hadn't slept much, but she'd gone to bed, set her alarm for 4 a.m., and when it went off, she went out to where Mitch sat on the front porch swing.

"I'll take it from here. You know where to find the guest room."

Mitch didn't bother to argue with her, not just because he was being polite, but because as an acknowledgement that he knew she was as competent as he was to stand

165

guard, and she appreciated that. Before he went into the house, he pulled her into his arms, held her tight and close, and she realized she was suddenly close to tears again.

She had firmed up her resolve as she lay in the dark, trying to go to sleep. She and Mitch would keep her sister and mother and maybe her niece safe from harm. She didn't know how, but they'd figure it out *some way.* No matter how powerful and untouchable the Arab men might be in their native country, they were in the Smoky Mountains of Tennessee now, and they absolutely did not call the shots here.

Mitch kissed the top of her head, then she pulled out of his embrace.

"I got this," she said.

"I know."

He leaned over and kissed her tenderly, his lips soft and warm on hers, and she melted into his embrace.

Her life right now was better than it had ever been. There was so much promise, so much joy to be had for the taking, and she was damned if she was going to let some bastards from the other side of the world screw it up.

Rileigh knocked on Micky's hospital room door and then slowly opened it, where she found the girl sitting up in bed eating breakfast off the tray that was set in front of her. She had suffered multiple stab wounds, but none of them had been serious. A knife can slice through all kinds of vital organs, but she'd been fortunate that the killer had missed all of hers.

"Good morning," Rileigh said.

Micky nodded. "Good morning."

Clearly the girl was not happy to see Rileigh and wasn't looking forward to talking to her. Maybe the gift that Rileigh had brought would grease the skids.

"How are you feeling?"

"I'm ready to get out of here," Micky said.

"And do what?" Rileigh asked. "Where will you go when you leave the hospital?"

"I'll go and find my sister."

"Her name's Farrah, right?"

"Yes, Farrah."

"You and she were traveling together."

"Yes, we were."

"But no one has seen her."

Micky's voice was firm. "Look, you don't know Farrah. She's different, okay? She doesn't do people or crowds or social interactions, or," she looked at Rileigh, "being questioned by the police."

"So you're saying she's hiding?"

"Hell yes, she's hiding. What else would she be doing after the police descended on that bus station Saturday night like storm troopers?"

That spark of anger was more energy than Rileigh'd seen out of the girl since she met her.

"Then how will you find her?"

"I'll find her. I know how. Look, what is it you want from me? I've answered every question you've asked. The answers may not have suited you, but they're the only answers I have."

Rileigh thought about the questions they didn't ask. Why was she looking for Lily Bishop? And who else had she gone looking for? But now wasn't the time to ask questions that would get her agitated. Rileigh didn't want to get kicked out of her room, at least not yet.

"I come with a peace offering," she said, and smiled her very brightest smile.

"Peace offering?"

"Yeah, I brought you something."

Rileigh fished around in her bag and brought out a

small box with a ribbon tied around it in a bow. "This is from my Mama."

The girl's eyes snapped to Rileigh's. She'd made the connection. She'd remembered what Rileigh had said, that her mother was Lily Bishop, but Micky didn't comment on it.

"Why did she send me a gift?"

"Because that's just who she is. My mama is the single sweetest human being on the planet, beloved by every man, woman, and child in Yarmouth County. She's thoughtful, she's compassionate, she's generous." Rileigh paused for a beat. "And she has dementia."

"Dementia?"

"It's the charming kind, if there is such a thing. She's forgetful but in a sort of entertaining way. She mixes up people's names. She has imaginary friends, you know, like a little kid. Except her friends are not the kind of friends a little kid would have. For instance, Mama thought at one time she was dating Rhett Butler."

A smile flirted with the corners of Micky's mouth, but she kept it down.

"Seriously?"

"Oh yeah, he came to dinner often. And so did Neil Armstrong, the guy who walked on the moon."

The girl couldn't fight the smile now.

"He told Mama all about it."

The smile was small but real. Now Rileigh was about to make the smile disappear.

"And her latest boyfriend, well, she says she wasn't dating him because monks don't date, was the Dalai Lama."

"Your mother is dating the Dalai Lama."

"And he apparently convinced her she'd had several previous lives."

The girl shook her head. "I thought Hindus believed in reincarnation, not Buddhists."

"That's what I said. But apparently Mama didn't get the distinction. So she went looking for her past lives."

Rileigh paused for a beat before she continued. "She sent her DNA off to findyourfamily.com to see if maybe she'd been Joan of Arc in a previous life."

Micky Hollis looked like she was about to choke. The color drained out of her face, and she just stared at Rileigh. Rileigh let it sit for a couple of beats in silence. Then she hurried on. "I think it's more likely she was Pancho Villa. Or maybe Attila the Hun — she was one strict mama when I was a little girl. But she didn't find out anything."

Micky said nothing.

"Maybe she matched with someone, maybe not. She doesn't know. She threw away all the information that was sent to her."

Rileigh let that sit for another beat. Micky picked up the conversational ball then and tried to take it in a different direction.

"Why do you investigate crimes?" she asked.

"I was a police officer in a former life. Not the kind of former life Mama was looking for, but one several years ago. And the sheriff needs all the help he can get in this rural county with a shortage of manpower. So that's why I pitch in."

Rileigh pointed to the box in Micky's hands.

"Go ahead. Open the present."

"So your mother sent me a present because she's a sweet little old lady. That's why?"

"Go on. You'll be glad you opened it."

The girl untied the pink satin bow and let the ribbon fall away. She lifted the lid off the box, and now there was a real smile on her face. She picked up first one and then another of the soft hand-knit booties from the box. They were from back in the day when Mama still knew how to knit rather than just turn strange balls of yarn into nothing at all.

"Hospitals are the coldest places on the planet," Rileigh said. "Trust me. I've been in them often."

The girl cocked her head at that but didn't ask.

"And Mama always brought me booties to wear, so she sent these to you. Would you like me to help you put them on?"

"No, that's all right."

But Rileigh was not to be deterred. She lifted the sheet up at the foot of the girl's bed and held her hand out for the booties in the box the girl had just opened. Michaela handed Rileigh the first one, pink and fuzzy, and Rileigh fitted onto her left foot, careful not to make it obvious that she was examining her toes. She lifted the other foot then. This was the money shot, and Rileigh's heart began to pound. She examined Michaela's foot. Five distinct toes. Nothing was grown together. There were five of them. A big toe and all the others lined up beside it in a row.

Rileigh didn't allow her face to show her disappointment, just fit the bootie onto Michaela's foot and pulled the sheet and blanket back over them.

"There, that's better. Isn't that warmer?"

"Yes, it's warmer. Please tell your mother thank you for the booties." She smiled a little bit of a smile. "I always wanted a…" She stopped then, and Rileigh was sure she almost said grandmother but didn't. "…a person in my life, somebody who'd knit things for me. I always thought that was sweet."

"So you didn't have grandmothers or aunts around to do that for you?" Rileigh asked.

"Ours wasn't a very touchy-feely kind of family. If you're working on this case with the sheriff, then he told you what I said. We were purchased. Farrah and me were bought. All three of us."

"Three?"

"Farrah was the oldest. I came next. Alyssa came along when Farrah was about four years old. Cutest little kid you ever saw … blonde hair and blue eyes, just like mine and Farrah's."

"So your sister Alyssa is how old now?"

"She died." The girl said simply. "When she was eight years old, she died."

"I'm sorry," Rileigh said. "I know what it feels like to lose a sister."

The girl cocked her eyebrow at her. "You lost a sister?"

"But I got her back. She didn't die, and I got her back."

Rileigh wanted to ask all manner of other questions of the girl, who now seemed relaxed enough and willing enough to talk, but she'd found out what she came here to find out and she needed to go back and tell Jillian and Mitch. Then the three of them needed to make some kind of plan. Needed to put their heads together and figure out what their next move was.

"I just came by to drop off Mama's present. Hope you're feeling better." She paused. "You know, most people who are the victims of a violent crime are curious about the investigation. They want to know what law enforcement has done to find the person who hurt them."

"And I'm not curious enough, right?" Micky said.

"It's just surprising to me that you never ask."

"I never ask because I don't believe you're ever going to find who stabbed me and because I don't have any information I can give you about what happened to that old man. So the results of your investigation aren't that important to me."

"Well, I hope you have a good day."

Rileigh turned and started out the door, but when she opened it, she looked back. Micky had lifted her foot up out from under the blanket and was holding it in the air, wiggling her toes inside the booty.

"These are so soft, and they fit perfectly," she said with a genuine smile. "They probably wouldn't have fit as well when I was a little girl. My big toe and the one next to it were grown together until a doctor separated them when I was in first grade. I remember it hurt."

Rileigh was glad she was standing at the door when Micky said that so she could merely nod and step outside without Micky seeing the look on her face. She headed down the hallway at something resembling a run. Deputy Rawlings spoke to her, but she missed it, in a hurry to get to the elevator before the doors closed. If she'd missed the elevator, she'd have taken the stairs, but she got there in time, leapt in, and listened to her heart banging as the elevator went down.

Rileigh had left Jillian and Mitch sitting in the lobby of the hospital, waiting for her to come with a report of what she'd been able to find out with her pair of fuzzy booties. They were seated in chairs opposite the elevator, and when the doors opened, both of them looked at her with matching quizzical expressions on their faces. They must have read on her face what the response was, because Jillian's eyes grew huge and her hand went up to cover her mouth.

Rileigh crossed the distance between them, and as Jillian got to her feet, Rileigh wrapped her arms around her.

"Tell me," Jillian said so softly Rileigh could barely hear her.

"She had ten toes, and they were all separate." Rileigh felt her sister stiffen. "But then she said that her big toe and the toe next it had been grown together since she was little, and a doctor had them separated."

Jillian gasped and then simply stood with Rileigh's arms around her. She was shaking, but she wasn't crying. Rileigh looked at Mitch over Jillian's shoulder and shook her head sadly, conveying that she didn't know if this was the good news or the bad news ... but it was definitely *the* news. If there'd been doubt, it was gone now. The young woman lying with healing stab wounds on a hospital bed on the third floor was the baby that Jillian Bishop had mothered for just three days twenty years ago.

Jillian finally got control of herself and stepped back, looking into Rileigh's face.

"I guess it's my turn now, isn't it?"

"You sure you want to do this, Jillian?" Mitch asked.

Jillian barked out a grunt of laughter. "Like I've got a choice. Yes, I need to do this. I *want* to do this."

Rileigh didn't bother to ask how Jillian felt about it. It didn't really matter how she felt. She had to go up to the third floor and talk to the girl lying in the hospital bed.

And then whatever was about to happen would, well, happen.

Chapter Twenty-Four

JILLIAN STEPPED OUT OF THE ELEVATOR AND WALKED slowly toward the door at the far end of the hallway. She had that sense you get sometimes in nightmares when you're walking down a long hallway with doors on either side. And no matter how far you go, you never seem to get to the end of the hallway. Only this time it was in reverse. This time it seemed to Jillian that she took one step away from the elevator, then suddenly she was standing next to the deputy who'd been stationed outside Michaela's room. Jillian said nothing, she just offered him the scraps of a pathetic smile. She rapped quietly on the door, heard no response, but pushed it slowly inward anyway.

The girl looked up at her quizzically when she stepped into the room.

Jillian stopped just inside the door, then found she couldn't speak. She couldn't find any words. All she could do was stare at the face of the young girl with pale blonde hair lying on the hospital bed. She kept superimposing upon that face, the face of the baby she'd held so briefly, trying to make it fit together, trying to do that thing they do with artificial intelligence where they age a baby to see what it will look like as a grown-up. Her mind wasn't able to pull it off. She saw the baby and she saw the adult, but she couldn't make any connection between the two. Then she realized that the girl was talking, and she tuned in to what she was saying.

"…don't understand what you're doing here."

"My name is Jillian," she said, "and you're Michaela—"

"I'm *Micky!* Who are you?"

"My sister, Rileigh, was here a few minutes ago."

"Rileigh Bishop is your *sister?*"

Jillian nodded and watched the girl try to make the connections. Jillian hadn't practiced what she would say. Her mind had been ping-ponging around as she tried to figure out what she *should* say. She thought maybe she could ought to explain why she'd given her up, or explain why she'd given birth to her to begin with, or explain or maybe not explain anything at all, maybe just ask questions. Ask Michaela why she'd seen sent off her DNA, what she was looking for, why she was searching for Lily Bishop. All of those things had run around in circles in her mind all night, and she hadn't settled on any of them.

As she stood there looking at the young woman, her mind went almost blank.

"You're Jillian Bishop," the young woman said. "Rileigh Bishop's sister." She paused for another beat. "Lily Bishop's daughter."

When Jillian spoke, her voice was very soft. "And you are the young woman who came here looking for your family. Looking for Lily Bishop because you were connected to her by the DNA sample you sent off to findyourfamily.com. Isn't that right?" The girl's eyes grew huge,

Jillian could see that suddenly she was breathing faster like she'd been running.

Jillian looked at the young woman in the bed, and the young woman looked back at her. And after a period of time which might have been a few seconds or a few minutes or who knew, it was as if their gazes connected somewhere in the middle. And it was no longer Jillian looking at the girl, or the girl looking at Jillian. It was a connected gaze that went from Jillian to the girl on the bed and back to Jillian in a continuous connected loop. And Jillian found her voice then, found herself speaking. Words came unbidden to her lips, and she was not only powerless but unwilling to stop them. She let the words flow the same way the connection flowed.

"The night before I got married — I was eighteen years old — the wedding was all set. But that afternoon I came home and found my father molesting my little sister Rileigh's best friend." The girl sucked in a gasp, covered her mouth with her hands in a gesture that felt familiar to Jillian, but she wasn't sure why.

"I won't tell you the whole ugly story of what happened after that. It was a story worse than anything you ever saw in a horror movie. The monster in the story was my Aunt Daisy, and she did to me when I was eighteen years old what Omar did to *you* when you were four days old."

The girl's eyes had grown huge.

"My Aunt Daisy *sold* me. And the next thing I knew, I was a prisoner." She let out a breath. "I'll tell you about it someday, if you want to hear it. But right now, I'll fast forward through the nightmare to 2004, when I was 28 years old. At that time, I was a very high-paid sex slave owned by a man named Omar, who had the very finest of clients all over the Middle East — Yemen, Saudi Arabia,

Kuwait, Sudan. I've been to all those places. There was no way to run away. No way not to stand out, a blonde in that culture, a woman where women have no rights, an American where Americans are hated. A slave in that culture, where slavery is the right of any Muslim man so long as the slave is an infidel. I've done a little research since. If slavery were a state, it would have the population of California and the economic output of Texas. The largest number of sex slaves is in Saudi Arabia, and I spent a lot of time there. I was there in 2008 when I found out I was pregnant."

She had been slowly moving across the room as she spoke, and now she was next to the bed, and she held Micky's hand, but she didn't know whether the girl had grasped her hand or whether she reached for the girl's hand. But either way, they were connected now, and the physical connection was hands clasped so tight it was almost painful.

"It wasn't supposed to happen. I took every precaution that there was, but I got pregnant anyway." She shook her head. "What happened then wasn't up to me. Decisions weren't up to me. It wasn't like anybody asked what I wanted. The only thing that mattered was what was most commercially relevant."

Jillian looked up at the ceiling and realized she was about to cry, and she took several deep breaths and then looked back down at the girl whose eyes she was sure had never left her face. And if it was possible, the girl was squeezing her hand even tighter.

"I listened to the doctor talking to Omar. I listened to them talk about *me*. I was … *property*. I was used to being property, but somehow this was harder. I don't know why. I'd been property since I was eighteen years old. Very, very valuable property. Property that got the very best possible treatment, because I had to look good, had to be in top physical condition for my customers. And the doctor told Omar that his best move was for me to have an abortion."

She looked deep into the girl's blue eyes that looked so much like the eyes that looked back at her from the mirror every morning. "Nobody asked me what mattered to me or what I wanted. I heard Omar say he wanted me to have the baby because…" Her voice began to tremble. She couldn't control it. It was hard to speak, but she forced words out through it. "Because blonde, blue-eyed babies commanded a really high price on the black market."

The girl gasped. And then it seemed to Jillian that maybe the girl was crying too. She didn't know. All she knew was she was standing there and the two of them were holding on to each other and she was explaining about the decision that she was to have the baby and about the night the baby was born.

The girl spoke then, softly. "On September eighteenth."

"Yes," Jillian said. "You were born right before sunrise. I was in labor for days. I was lying there, panting. When it was finally over, I was lying there, panting, drenched in sweat, and I glanced out the window and saw a sunrise. Sunrises in the Middle East are beautiful because there's always some some sand from sandstorms in the air, and the sand refracts different colors, so every sunrise has streaks of yellow and gold and red." Jillian was quiet for a moment, looking at the girl, their connectedness putting them in a bubble that included only them and nothing else in the world. The two of them, all alone together.

"The first time I heard you cry, I was looking at a breathtakingly beautiful sunrise. And you had a set of lungs on you. Oh my gosh, could you cry." Jillian threw back her head and laughed.

The girl laughed with her.

"You had jaundice, and so you needed to spend time under a bilirubin light to make the yellowness in your skin to go away. Omar couldn't put you on the market until you were perfect, a little pink and white baby with blue eyes and blonde hair that Omar could make a lot of money on. And so they let me keep you for the next four days."

Jillian smiled ruefully.

"They just left you there, figured since I was your mother, I'd know how to take care of you, but I was totally clueless, and there was nobody for me to ask. I didn't know what it meant that when a baby cries, no, when *your* baby cries, your milk lets down. What was that about? All I knew was when *you* cried, suddenly there were wet spots on the front of my gown because milk was dripping out. And so I nursed you." Jillian paused. "And when I did, you were mine, the only thing that was truly mine in ten years. It wasn't that I owned you the way they owned me. It was that you *belonged* to me, you were *mine* in a way that nothing they did could change."

The girl lying on the bed and squeezing Jillian's hand so tight that it hurt was crying. Jillian reached out her hand and pushed the girl's pale blonde hair back off of her face and gently wiped away her tears.

"When you were a baby and you cried, I sang to you the only song I knew."

Jillian took a breath and she began to sing "Puff the Magic Dragon."

As she sang, the girl on the bed began to sob. Her sobs racked her body like seizures, and Jillian continued to sing and hold her hand and wipe her hair out of her face and wipe her tears away until the girl finally stopped crying.

"I never named you," Jillian said. "I knew they were

going to take you away. And I knew it would hurt worse if I made you even more real by giving you a name."

Jillian didn't tell her how conflicted she was about the fact that her baby was a child of rape. How conflicted she felt about the baby that she didn't want to love — but did whether she liked it or not — and had refused to name and who was ripped out of her arms as soon as she was marketable.

"I heard the nurses outside the door say that the bilirubin light had done the trick. I looked down at you and saw the truth — you weren't jaundiced anymore. You were a beautiful, round, chubby little baby, and they were going to take you from me that day. And so I nursed you and I held you so close. I wouldn't let myself kiss you though, because to kiss you was to love you, and to love you when I was going to lose you… it would have broken me. And so I never named you and I never kissed you. But I knew you were mine."

Then Jillian brushed the girl's hair back away from her face and kissed her tenderly on her forehead.

Chapter Twenty-Five

Jillian came back to where Mitch and Rileigh were waiting in the lobby of the hospital, her eyes wet. She grabbed Rileigh in a bear hug.

"It's her. It's true."

Rileigh and Mitch had been talking about next steps as they waited for Jillian to come back down from her visit with Micky in her hospital room. Rileigh'd told Mitch that Jillian had said she didn't know how to feel about the baby during that little bit of time she was allowed to be with her daughter, how to reconcile that the girl was the child of rape. She'd been conflicted and torn then, but from the look on her face now, the conflict was gone. Jillian had found the baby girl she gave up twenty years ago, and it was clear from her face that she had no reservations.

Now they just had to figure out what was next. The three of them filed into Micky's hospital room and found her sitting up in bed, beaming.

Jillian went automatically to stand beside Micky's bed, and Rileigh watched Micky reach out and grab her hand and give it a squeeze.

"We still have no leads at all on whoever it was who stabbed you in the woods on Sunday night," Mitch began, and Micky's face remained emotionless. "But whoever did it is still out there."

"Still out there," she said quietly. "Yeah, the person who stabbed me is still out there."

"And we've had no luck locating your Uncle Dan, the man who came into your hospital room and killed the orderly." He paused, then fired a hopeless shot over the bow. "If you'd tell us more about him than a description—"

The hospital was old and had to be retrofitted with surveillance cameras. But all those showed were the front and back entrances and the parking lot. It would have been easy to sneak into the hospital without being recorded.

Still, Micky said nothing. Offered no hints, no help, no further information, just silence. Mitch looked at Rileigh, back at Jillian, and continued. "But there's more than that going on here."

Micky showed some interest then.

"What?" she asked. "What more?"

"When you put your DNA sample on that website — what happened? Would you mind telling us the whole story? We need to know the details."

"It really wasn't even my idea. It was Carson's."

"Who's Carson?"

"He was working at the homeless shelter where I was hiding." She shook her head. "It's a long story."

"We want to hear the story, to hear your whole story. What we need to hear right now is what you did with the results you got back."

Micky told them about matching to someone in a group sample, about going to Stanford and what happened there.

"The student in the group sample, the one you matched with ... what was his name?"

Jillian's question stopped Micky in the middle of her narrative, then Micky said, "Ahmad Hussain Khan Al-Saud."

Jillian looked like somebody'd kicked her in the belly. She turned to Rileigh. "The man I told you about, the man I was working for when ... his name was Hussain Amir Al-Saud." Jillian's voice was airless. "He had children, two little girls ... and a *six-month-old son.*"

There was a beat or two of silence as the import of that sunk in. Then Mitch got Micky to continue. She described the embarrassing scene in the classroom and her confrontation with the young man in the hallway.

"So you saw him take a picture of the paperwork?" Mitch confirmed. Micky nodded.

"He called his father," Jillian said. "You know he did. He sent his father a picture of the information from the website. And Amir..." She wasn't trembling, but her voice was shaky. "I'm sure he reassured his son that everything was all right, that he'd handle it. Then Amir called Omar. Pitched a fit with Omar. Told him about the girl whose DNA matched Amir's son ... and also matched a woman named Lily Bishop in Tennessee. And Omar never..." She spoke the last words in a whisper. "He never *ever* left a customer dissatisfied, certainly not one as rich and powerful as Amir Al-Saud."

"What are you talking about? What's going on?" Micky asked, looking from one to the other.

"There were some Middle Eastern men here in Black Bear Forge a few days ago," Mitch said. "They were asking around about Lily Bishop."

Micky still didn't understand the implications.

"What does that mean?"

"It means that Omar — who is a soulless monster — sent somebody to fix Amir's problem."

"Fix it? Fix it how?"

None of them answered her question. She looked from one face to another and back, and when it suddenly dawned on her what "fix it" must mean, her face became a rictus of fear.

She began to shake her head slowly, back and forth, mouthing "no, no, no" without actually speaking the words.

Then she suddenly grabbed Jillian's hand and burst into tears. Sobbing, she begged, "Mommy! Mommy, don't let the bad man hurt me. Please, Mommy. I'm scared."

It was so odd and jarring that Jillian and Rileigh shot looks at each other, eyebrows raised.

And then it was over as fast as it had begun. Micky stopped crying, shook her head, and then lowered her gaze, obviously embarrassed by her own outburst. She took a deep breath, leaned back on the pillow, and wiped her eyes.

"So, what am I supposed to do? If they're looking for me—"

"And me," Jillian put in.

"We have to assume for Mama, too," Rileigh said.

"If there are men out there who want to … eliminate us, what can we do?"

"We've talked about that," Mitch said, "and I have some thoughts I want to discuss."

Mitch noticed that Jillian's attention was fixed on Micky. She was holding both her hands in hers, squeezing tight.

"It'll be fine," she whispered to the girl in the hospital bed. "We can figure this out."

Mitch looked from the two of them to Rileigh. He said nothing but nodded his reassurance to her. His look said, "We got this."

Chapter Twenty-Six

MITCH WAS HAVING TROUBLE SHAKING THE IMAGE OF Micky Hollis sobbing and calling Jillian "Mommy." It was so striking, it was hard to get his concentration back.

"We have to do whatever it takes to keep you," he was looking at Micky when he said it, then he looked to Jillian and forced the words out, "and your *mother* safe."

"Which means we can't stay at Mama's," Jillian said. "Where will we go?"

"I've been thinking about where you could hide for a few days."

Jillian shook her head. "It's going to take more than a few days. Hiding for a few days isn't good enough. Micky and I need to do what I did. We need to disappear. To become other people so they can't find us."

Jillian went on before anyone could contradict her, words tumbling over each other as they came out. "I did it before. I can do it again." She stopped. "But then I was in a world where that kind of thing was possible. A world where if you had enough money, you could make anything happen. And I had enough money."

Jɪʟʟɪᴀɴ ᴇᴀsᴇs ᴏᴘᴇɴ the door of the bedroom and walks as quietly as a night breeze to the dresser and opens the jewelry box. There are diamonds, rubies, sapphires, and emeralds. Hundreds of thousands of dollars' worth of jewelry. But she can only take one small thing. Some little ring or small bracelet that won't be missed. The lady of the house will assume she left it somewhere or dropped it somewhere if it's a small thing.

Jillian stares at the jewelry, deciding, picking. Finally, she selects a set of diamond earrings and takes only one. The diamond is huge, worth a fortune. But people lose one earring all the time. The mistress of the house won't be surprised when it's missing. She slips what she has stolen into the pocket that she has sewn into her bra. She leaves the room and closes the door behind her, then hurries back through the bathroom to the bedroom, where she emerges tranquil and peaceful and smiling.

Jillian had begun stealing jewelry from the wives of the men she serviced two years ago. It was a dangerous business. If she got caught, there would be only one suitable punishment. She would vanish just like every other girl who didn't play by the rules. But the older she got, the more she came to understand that she was stuck in that life until she rescued herself. It weighed on her until finally she forced herself to act, knowing nobody was going to come riding up on a white horse and save her.

The first piece of jewelry she ever took was an emerald ring, and she hadn't taken it from the jewelry box of the mistress of the house. She'd sneaked into their daughter's room, a young teenager with clothes thrown everywhere, everything in disarray, and she had taken one piece of jewelry because she knew the girl would never miss it. And then she lived in terror for days waiting for the axe to fall. It hadn't.

She found a place where she could keep her stolen items, hollowed it out in the bottom of the suitcases the girls carried from one place to another. She'd removed the backing on the inside of the suitcase and hollowed out a space. Very small, but pieces of jewelry didn't take up a lot of space.

After that, Jillian looked for every opportunity she was presented with to slip something small away. Months passed, then years, and her stash grew. Now, she looks down at it and decides that she finally has more than enough to barter with, and she begins to plan how she will enlist the aid of Omar's chauffeur. Akeem is a man Omar believes is utterly loyal and trustworthy. Omar does not know that he makes advances toward the girls every time Omar is out of sight and has managed to rape two of them when Omar was out of town. He would never help her unless he had to.

In a daring move, she gets another girl to film the chauffeur making advances on Jillian. The video shows her trying to push him off, and eventually his strength overpowers her and he rapes her. When Jillian goes to him with the video, she is afraid that he will kill her on the spot, but he doesn't dare. Jillian is valuable property, and Omar would not take it lightly if that property were damaged. So now she has an ally, unwilling but dependable. And Akeem knows everybody who lives in the shadow world under the rocks. With the money from the sales of her cache of jewelry, Akeem is able to purchase for Jillian a whole new life, an identity, a passport, and everything else she will need to start over. And then, in an incredible stroke of good fortune, Akeem is killed in a barroom brawl, and Jillian's secret dies with him.

BUT HERE IN AMERICA, there were actually laws that most people, anyway, actually obeyed, and she didn't know any of those kinds of people, the under a rock people. She was able to buy a new identity in the Middle East, but she had no idea how to start the process here. She had enough money. She had gotten more brazen in the last year of her captivity and had secured for herself a fortune. It never ceased to amaze her that no one ever missed anything she took. Why would they miss a few jewels out of a jewelry box worth millions?

But that was then, and this was now. Jillian looked at Mitch in despair.

"I know how to run." She stopped and let out a sigh. "But I don't know how to escape. If we just run, they'll catch us. Eventually, they'll catch us."

"We've talked about that," Mitch said, casting a look at Rileigh, "and it has to end here and now, or you and Micky going to spend the rest of your lives running and looking over your shoulders, and eventually your luck will run out."

"What else can we do?"

"We can stop them here. We can set a trap for them here and smoke them out."

"But if we find them, say we catch these men, you and Rileigh, and I don't know how you do it, but say you catch this particular team. Omar will just send out another one. He's the ultimate deep pocket. He has millions, and his reputation is on the line. There's nothing and nobody he can't buy. He'll just keep sending out one team after another until…"

"We've considered that too," Mitch said, "and we have a plan." He stopped, gathered himself. "Look, we need to take this one step at a time, and the first step is that we need to get Micky checked out of the hospital and take her home."

"And at Mama's," Rileigh added, "we'll pack up Mama and move the three of you to a safe place."

"Where? Where's a safe place?" Jillian asked.

Mitch smiled at that.

"I think I know just the place. Not many people even know it exists, and only a handful know how to get to it. It's certainly a place nobody would suspect you would go. It belonged to a man named Jeremiah Johnson, a mountain man. He was killed a few months ago, and the cabin, as far as I know, is just sitting empty. He has no heirs, so eventually it will become the county's property to pay the real estate taxes, and they'll auction it off, but right now it's just sitting there locked up. I'm going to move you two and Mama into his cabin, and then Rileigh and I are going to see what we can do to flush the quail out of the bushes so we can shoot them."

"There's someone else you're not thinking about," Jillian said. "David. I can't just vanish in a puff of smoke and not tell him where I'm going."

"We thought about that, and I'm hoping I can enlist David's help. I'm hoping he'd be willing to stand guard over the three of you at the cabin while Rileigh and I set our trap."

Micky spoke for the first time since she'd cried out for her mommy.

"Who's David?" she asked Jillian.

"Remember I told you that I disappeared on the night before my wedding? The man I was supposed to marry is David Hicks." She smiled a little then. "And in a wonder of wonders, in a world that sometimes grants you way more than you expect or deserve, when I came back, he still loved me, and now…"

She stopped then and didn't finish the sentence.

Mitch knew she was stopping short of saying they were going to get married again, but he was sure that was the case.

"How's he going to feel about finding out about me?" Micky asked.

Jillian's face tightened. "I suppose I'm going to have to find out."

Chapter Twenty-Seven

RILEIGH WAS THE BEST STRATEGIST OF THE GROUP, AND SHE had figured out they needed to divide and conquer to pull off the grand plan. Her job would be to go downstairs to the billing office of the hospital and get Michaela checked out, whatever that involved. She certainly had no insurance, and Rileigh didn't know what they did about such things, but she'd figure it out. Hospital security had been engaged to keep watch on Micky's room. It was broad daylight, and Mitch needed all his deputies working to locate Uncle Dan.

Rileigh's next stop would be Jeremiah Johnson's cabin to see what was there and what wasn't. Mitch had described it to her once, but she'd never been there, and she couldn't imagine that a mountain man like Jeremiah Johnson lived in a spacious, airy, well-equipped cabin. It made more sense to her that Jeremiah lived as simply as he possibly could and that what she would find was nothing but the bare essentials. Mitch had said there was indoor plumbing, that Jeremiah had run water to the house from a spring on the side of the mountain. But beyond that, all bets were off. Rileigh would check that out, and then she would go to the grocery store and buy enough supplies for Jillian, Micky, and Mama for what they hoped would be only a few days.

The accommodations would be jammed, but the cabin was the safest place that Mitch could think of.

While Mitch and his deputies beat the bushes trying to capture Uncle Dan, Jillian would go home and tell Mama what was about to happen … and then tell David.

When Rileigh thought about it, she decided she would rather have her job than either Mitch's or Jillian's.

Jillian left Micky Hollis's room with her emotions a complete dumpster fire. She took out her cell from her purse and called David as she waited for the elevator, watching the little red-headed nurse flirt with the security guard who was leaning over the counter at the nurse's station a few feet away.

"What's up, Jillie?" David asked.

"I need to talk to you."

David picked up on the distress in her voice and immediately asked, "What's wrong? What happened?"

"It's not something we can talk about over the phone. Can you come to lunch today?"

"Sure, of course. I'll be there. But what's going on?"

The elevator doors opened then.

"Really, I can't talk about it now. I promise I'll tell you everything as soon as I see you."

Jillian clicked off the call, got into the elevator, and watched the doors close in front of her.

FARRAH HOLLIS HAD BEEN DOING what she did best, using one of her "superpowers." Hiding in plain sight was easy if you didn't move, didn't do anything to call attention to yourself, didn't do anything that raised suspicion. All you had to do was keep your head down, and nobody would ever notice you were there.

She had watched the goings-on in Micky's hospital room since the parade of people first began marching through there this morning. It was fascinating to observe, all the different people and their different reactions. Very entertaining.

Now that Micky was finally alone, Farrah stole silently into the room and confronted her sister.

"That was her, wasn't it?" she said. Micky jumped at her words, hadn't known she was anywhere near. "I can see the 'family resemblance' — the hair, facial features. She's the one, isn't she?"

Farrah knew Micky didn't share her feelings about the betrayer she'd unearthed, the new "family" she'd found. She wanted to sit around a campfire with them, roasting marshmallows and singing Kumbaya.

Micky believed their explanations and excuses, didn't want to remember that every pain, every disgusting touch, every indignity, every abomination they had suffered in the past two decades was because that precious *family of hers* had sold her to the highest bidder as soon as she was born.

Well, Farrah hadn't forgotten. She had kept a mental score card so that when life finally afforded her the chance, she could make all the betrayers pay for every moment of the suffering they'd caused.

"We're in this together, just like we always have been," she told her sister. "Don't worry, when the time comes for payback, I'll be right there beside you. I won't let you falter and go all soft on them. When the time comes to *kill that bitch*, I'll keep you strong. I'll hold your hand and we'll do it together."

Farrah looked into Micky's eyes, waited. Finally, Micky nodded her head.

"Together," Micky said.

JILLIAN FELT REALLY bad about being mysterious with David, but there wasn't any way around it. She couldn't very well tell him what she had to say over the phone. And besides, she needed to see his reaction with her own eyes. She needed to be able to read him.

Mitch had agreed to send Deputy Mullins out to Mama's house to park his cruiser literally at the bottom of the hill by the mailbox. It would only be a few hours while Jillian talked to her mother and David and gathered up their things before they left for Jeremiah Johnson's cabin.

Jillian pulled up into the driveway of her mother's house and saw Deputy Mullins coming down Bent Twigg Road from the other direction. He waved at her, pulled his cruiser crossways in her driveway, and smiled. He'd have to move aside to let David through, which would sound every alarm in David's psyche. And she couldn't blame him, but there was nothing else she could do.

She went into the house and could hear Mama talking to somebody in the kitchen. There was no car parked outside. And she'd come to recognize that particular tone of voice as the one that Mama used when she was talking to people who weren't really listening to what she had to say.

She walked into the kitchen and Mama was sitting at the table.

"Jillian, honey," Mama said in greeting. "You want some coffee or some lemonade?"

"No, Mama, I'm fine."

"Look who's dropped by for a visit."

Mama gestured toward the empty chair at the head of the table. "Don't you recognize him?"

"No, Mama, I don't. You're just going to have to tell me."

"Why it's Prince Harry. The red-headed, freckle-faced one? You know, Princess Diana's second son. The one who calls himself The Spare."

Jillian turned obediently to the empty chair and said, "Hello, Prince Harry."

"Ain't you going to speak to his wife?" Mama gestured to the empty chair beside the first empty chair.

"Sure I am, Mama. What's her name again?"

"It's Meghan."

"Hello, Meghan, it's good to meet you."

"They didn't bring the children, but I told them they needed to next time. And you could get Georgia to come over with her younguns, and they could all play together in the backyard."

"Sounds like a good time, Mama."

Jillian paused, re-centered herself, and let out a breath.

"Mama, I need to talk to you about something important. Would you mind coming out and sitting on the front porch with me?"

"Why, sure, darlin'."

Mama looked at the people who weren't there. "I won't be but a few minutes. If you need any more lemonade, there's a cold pitcher of it in the icebox. Just make yourselves to home."

Jillian seated herself in the silent swing, and Mama sat

down in a rocking chair across from her. Jillian got right to the point.

"I haven't talked a whole lot about where I was after I left and was gone for all those years."

Mama's face looked like Jillian had slapped her. "You ain't told me, and I don't need to know. It don't matter to me one way or another where you was and what you was doing. All that matters to me is that you's home now."

"Thank you, Mama. But you need to remember that I was gone for a long time, and while I was gone, I…" She stopped there, gearing herself up before she went on, "I got pregnant."

"Pregnant?" Mama's face was the definition of shock and surprise. She reached out and grabbed Jillian's hand. "Oh, I'm so sorry that happened to you when you wasn't around family."

Mama stopped for a minute, then started again. "You was pregnant, and you had a baby." She was trying to put it all together in her head. "Was it a boy or a girl?"

"It was a baby girl, Mama, and I was forced to give her up for adoption."

"You give your own baby up for adoption?" Mama's eyes filled with tears. "Oh, no, sugar, you didn't. You gave my grandbaby away?"

"It wasn't my fault, Mama," Jillian said. "It wasn't up to me. Other people were making all the decisions in my life, and I couldn't do anything about it."

Mama shook her head. "A baby girl."

"There's more to the story."

"What more?"

"You know how we've been talking about the young woman who was stabbed the other night? Mitch and Rileigh had to leave their big date and go to the bus station where the crime was committed?"

"Uh-huh," Mama said. But you could tell by the look on her face she had absolutely no memory of it.

"Well, that girl came to Black Bear Forge looking for Lily Bishop. Remember we said that?"

"Now, why would she have come here looking for me?"

"Her name is Michaela Hollis. She goes by Micky. And the reason she was asking for Lily Bishop was that she sent her DNA off to findyourfamily.com."

"Oh, I sent mine off to that site, too. You remember? I told you all about it. I wanted to find out who I'd been in past lives."

"I remember, Mama. Well, when Micky sent off her DNA, she found a match. Found some members of her family."

"Well, ain't that nice. I don't know if I matched up to anybody. I just threw all that stuff away when they sent it to me."

"Mama, the reason she was looking for Lily Bishop was because that was who she matched to. Her DNA matched Lily Bishop."

"What are you saying, sugar?"

"I'm saying that Micky Hollis's DNA matched the sample of DNA that you sent off."

Mama stopped cold, and Jillian could see the cogs turning in the old lady's head. "What are you telling me, Jillian?"

"I'm telling you, Mama, that the DNA of the girl, Michaela Hollis, matched your DNA because you're *my* mother." She paused for a beat. "And I am *her* mother."

Mama was having trouble putting it all together.

"The daughter that I had all those years ago, the baby girl I had to give away — Michaela Hollis is that girl." Jillian watched connections firm up in Mama's head before she started to squeal.

"Your baby daughter?" She leapt out of her chair, flung her arms around Jillian, and cried out, "You got a baby daughter!"

"Mama, she's not a baby anymore. That was twenty years ago."

"And I got a granddaughter!"

Mama was squealing, practically jumping up and down in the kitchen.

"Oh, sugar, that's the most wonderful news... the most... I ain't never heard no gooder news than I got a granddaughter."

Mama finally saw the more somber look on Jillian's face and asked, "What's the matter? Something's wrong. What is it?"

"We're in danger, Mama, my daughter and me... and *you*. There are some very bad people out there who are looking for us and who want to harm us."

"Well, whatever for?"

"It doesn't matter why, Mama. All that matters is that you understand somebody wants to hurt us. So we have to go away somewhere and hide."

"You are not making a lick of sense," Mama said. "Go away and hide? From who? Go where?"

"We've got that all worked out, Mama. We know where a safe place is, and we're going to go there. You and me and Micky are going to go there until Mitch is able to find the dangerous men and stop them."

"Whoa … let's haul this wagon back to the barn and load it all over again. You saying that me and you and my brand-new granddaughter is going to go off somewhere together, just the three of us?"

She might as well have told Mama that the sky had opened up and diamonds were raining down on her head.

"That's right, Mama. Rileigh's going to bring Micky

here, pick you and me up, and we're going to a cabin up in the mountains."

Mama's eyes filled with tears, and she stood there smiling as broad as Jillian had ever seen her smile, laughing and crying at the same time.

"I got me a brand-new granddaughter! I'll go anywhere you want and stay anywhere you say just to be with her."

Chapter Twenty-Eight

JILLIAN SAT DOWN HARD ON THE SILENT SWING AND LOOKED at the spot at the bottom of the driveway where the deputy sheriff's vehicle sat blocking the entrance. She could hear Mama packing. God only knew what she was throwing into a suitcase.

She shook her head. Her life had been returning to something that approached normal, or at least as normal as Jillian Bishop's life was ever likely to be. She and David had discussed the possibility of setting a date for another wedding that they would *both* show up for this time, and she had felt almost as excited as any girl who was getting married because she wanted to, because she loved the guy.

Jillian had never told David that she'd been getting a little panicky that last day, a little freaky, but she'd kept telling herself that it was too late to back out now, it's not like she had any choice, but if she did, she wouldn't go through with it. That all had been bullshit. The truth was she would have gone through with it. She would have married David Hicks that day, if only...

Jillian had learned a long time ago not to let her mind go past that point. She couldn't entertain thoughts of what life would have been like if she hadn't come home early that afternoon and found her father with Georgia.

But the turbulent waters of Jillian Bishop's life had smoothed out. Oh, her life would never be normal, not like other people's lives. She'd be seeing the shrink probably for the rest of her life. She'd be suffering from horrifying nightmares probably for the rest of her life. She'd probably even suffer from violent flashbacks and PTSD for the rest of her life. And the place she and David had never gone, literally, was still an unknown to them both. They had not slept together. They hadn't had sex before their first wedding that didn't happen. David had thought it was because Jillian wanted to be a virgin on her wedding night, but that wasn't it at all. Jillian had been putting off the inevitability of explaining to him why she wasn't one. Oh, she'd had no intention of telling him the truth. She had a story all concocted about a boy at summer camp he never met, but now there weren't any made-up stories between her and David. Her husband-to-be knew that his wife had since had sex with hundreds of other men, but David had made peace with that. He said it was a physical act that didn't mean anything unless you gave meaning to it. She had been forced into that physical act, and it didn't matter. He and Jillian would give meaning to it, and then it would be what it was supposed to be: making love.

Jillian barked out a bleat of laughter as she heard a car turn off the main road into the driveway. That had been the biggest worry she'd had until Sunday, when Mitch and Rileigh had told her about the young woman whose name was Michaela Hollis.

She watched as David stopped by Beau Mullins's

cruiser, rolled his window down, and spoke to him, certainly asking what the hell he was doing there. Then David pulled the rest of the way up the driveway, performing the driving acrobatics required not to go flying through the fence after the bump at the top. He got out and walked up the sidewalk. Jillian watched him and wondered if this would be the final straw. She wondered if when she told him this, it would really be over this time, over for good.

"Hey, Jilly," he said, but there was no smile on his face or in his voice. "What is it? What's going on? I asked Beau why he was sitting down there. He shrugged his shoulders and said that the sheriff had told him to, and he was a guy who followed orders. Why is there a sheriff's deputy posted by the road?"

"So whoever drives by will see the cruiser."

"But why?"

"Have a seat," Jillian said. David sat down beside her on the swing and took her hand in his.

"Tell me what's going on," he said, the words so kind she wanted to cry.

"I don't know where to start."

"How about the beginning?" he said, which everybody always said, as if there were always a discernible beginning to a story. This one seemed to have no beginning and no end.

And so she told him, watching his face as she spoke the words. He'd been at dinner on Sunday and had heard Mitch talk about the girl who'd been stabbed in the woods outside the Sandstone Creek bus station. So that part didn't surprise him. But as she continued speaking, she watched his eyes grow bigger and felt his hands on hers go cold.

She used very short sentences, didn't elaborate, just told him the facts. She'd had a baby years ago, and that baby had grown up to be Michaela Hollis.

"It's all so sudden, David. I'm sorry. I didn't even know myself, at least not for sure, until this morning."

David sat back abruptly in the swing and let out a big breath. "Well, I'll be damned," he said. He tried to put a smile on his face, couldn't manage it, and gave up. "You have a daughter," he said, the words "a daughter" in wonder.

That's as far as she had gotten in the story. She hadn't told him what the implications were. She thought she needed to let the first bit of information settle first.

"How do you feel about it?" he finally asked. "How can you feel about it? And the girl, somebody tried to kill her, didn't they?"

"That's the rest of the story that you need to hear," she said. And so she told him that part. About the man in the red pickup truck who was still out there somewhere. About the mysterious sister, Farrah, who was still out there somewhere, too. And then she told him the story of the men Big John had seen at Red-Eye Gravy Sunday morning. His jaw clenched when she explained who those men were. And the only reason they could possibly have to be looking for Lily Bishop.

David stood up abruptly, dropping her hand. He paced to the porch railing and looked down to where Deputy Mullins had parked his cruiser. Then he turned back around. "Those men have come here for you and the girl, Michaela," he said. It wasn't a question, but she answered it anyway.

"Yeah, that's right."

David reached down and took Jillian's shoulders and pulled her to her feet and spoke into her face. "Ever since you came back. I've thought about it — every day for months. I wanted nothing more than to kill the bastards who had held you captive. And now maybe I'm going to get the chance."

"David, you don't understand. These men are trained killers."

"I don't care if they're the whole damn Russian army. Bring it on. All I want is to get my hands around their throats and choke the life out of them."

"But do you get the implications of what I'm saying?"

"Hell, yeah, I understand. You and Michaela are in danger from more than one front."

"That's why Mama's packing." Jillian sat back down on the swing, but David remained standing in front of her, holding both her hands.

She looked up into his face. "Mitch doesn't want us to stay here. And I think he's probably right. Those guys are bound to be here soon. It won't be hard to find the house of Lily Bishop, not in Yarmouth County."

"Where are you going?"

"You remember Jeremiah Johnson?"

"Yeah, well, he was that old mountain man, the one who was killed by the people who were looking for—" He paused for only a beat and then went resolutely on. "The FBI agent who was staying at your house."

"Jeremiah Johnson has a cabin way up in the mountains. Nobody even knows it's there. And it's empty. Mitch says he thinks it would be a good place for us to go."

Jillian let out of breath. "Mitch and Rileigh have some kind of plan that I haven't heard about yet. I've had plenty to think about without that."

"Are you telling me Mitch is planning to send you and Michaela up there by yourselves?"

"No, Mama has to go too. Mama can't stay here in this house."

David shook his head. "Fine then, the three of you up there by yourselves?"

"We'll be heavily armed," Jillian said. Then she paused. "He wants somebody to stay up there with us to help us defend ourselves." Jillian squeezed David's hand. "He's hoping you might be willing to do it."

"Mitch wants me to go up and hide out in Jeremiah Johnson's cabin. For how long?"

Jillian shrugged her shoulders. "Who knows?"

David sat back down. "Of course you don't know. There's no way you can know. Well, hell yeah, I'll help. I'll need to make some arrangements. Hand some things off to some other people, but that won't take long. And I guess I need to throw some clothes together. Sure, I can be ready. When are we going?"

Jillian sat looking at him, at his earnest face, and tears welled up in her eyes and fell down her cheeks before she could control them. He reached up without saying a word and wiped them tenderly away.

Taking a calming breath, she said, "Rileigh's going by the hospital to pick up Michaela and bring her here. We're going to make some final plans. And then we'll go."

David reached out and hooked a straw of her blonde hair behind her ear.

"I'm so sorry all this has happened," he said. Then his face hardened. "But maybe I'll get an opportunity I wouldn't otherwise have had. Maybe I'll get the chance to kill one of the bastards. That would be very, very satisfying."

Mama came barreling out the screen door then like her hair was on fire.

"David, I seen your car out there. Did Jillian tell you?

Did she tell you? She's got a little girl. Did she tell you? She has a baby girl. I got a grandbaby. Did she tell you? Did she?"

Her words all ran together into a single sound of joy and delight. And Jillian did smile then. At least there was someone in the family for whom the events of this past week weren't the worst news they'd ever gotten.

Chapter Twenty-Nine

WELL, IT WAS A LEAD PIPE CINCH. IF YOU DIDN'T KNOW these mountains like the back of your hand, you'd never find Jeremiah Johnson's cabin.

Rileigh had to backtrack twice, had taken the wrong road. "Road" defined as tire tracks that might have been reasonably visible when Jeremiah Johnson was living in the cabin and used that road but were now merely shadows in grass that was rapidly growing up to disguise their existence forever.

She pulled up in front of the cabin, which was set on a rise. And the driveway, if you could call it that, stopped at the bottom of the rise, meaning you had to climb the hill to get there. She suspected, knowing Jeremiah Johnson, that that had been intentional. He did everything he could to drop out of society. And he certainly didn't want society dropping in on him.

She climbed up the rise and onto his porch. and when she did, she realized that it stretched the whole length of the front of the cabin. And the cabin was a whole lot bigger than she thought it was. There was the debris from a "junk tree" in the yard all over the porch. Black walnut trees served no useful purpose unless you wanted to wait 150 years and cut them down for timber. In the meantime, they were pain in the ass trees that constantly dropped off pieces of crap. There was a black walnut tree beside the porch of Georgia's mother's house, and Pauline McGinnis had to go out every morning and sweep the trash off the porch.

Rileigh stepped up onto the first step of the porch and it was as solid as if it had been made of concrete. The steps were made of oak, either white oak or red oak, she couldn't tell which. Once on the porch, she noticed that all the corners were square, the slats firmly in place, nothing shaky or flimsy.

Easing the door slowly inward, she was greeted with the smell common to all unused places — attics and closed-up houses that hadn't been inhabited for a time. Mitch had said there was no electricity. Rileigh had brought a kerosene lantern with her, wondering if that's what Jeremiah Johnson used or if he used candles

The kerosene lantern barely lit the semi-darkness around her, and she squinted in the gloom, surprised to see what appeared to be the lumps of furniture in the rooms. She hadn't known what she expected, what she thought the man might have hauled up to this cabin over the years to make himself comfortable. But she was surprised that there were curtains on all the windows, and they were drawn. Turning to the window beside the front door, she pulled back the curtains, moved to the window on the other side, and did the same, then turned back toward the room and gasped.

The sunlight illuminated a dim space where everything was in shades of red and gold. The furniture was big and blocky, handmade, certainly by Jeremiah Johnson himself.

And all the wood she could see was either golden — probably oak — or cherry. The two colors blended together in a red-gold pattern that was absolutely beautiful.

Rileigh walked around the room slowly, gobsmacked, more surprised with every step. There were tables and chairs, a couch, and footstools, and sitting on the tables were kerosene lamps — functional, but also beautiful.

One wall had a huge floor-to-ceiling bookcase jammed with books. She went to it and ran her fingers along the spines. Classics: *Huckleberry Finn* and *Tom Sawyer* and *The Great Gatsby*. Hemingway. Faulkner. Steinbeck. *To Kill a Mockingbird* beside copies of the whole *Lord of the Rings* trilogy.

Rileigh was more surprised with every step. The room where she stood was a combination kitchen and dining room, one big open space with the kitchen in one corner that featured an island of glowing cherry wood with a fine sheen of dust on it. She blew the dust off, ran her hand over the surface, and saw the shine. She was sure every piece of furniture in the place was shined up as well.

Turning in a circle, she looked over the cabinets and stove. She'd never seen one but thought it might be a wood-burning cooking stove. That was old school.

The woodworking surrounding her was not fine artistic craftsmanship. Jeremiah Johnson was a man who created functional pieces but made them beautiful with the wood he selected and the care with which he built it. She turned toward the back of the room and saw doors on the back wall and a couple on the sides of the room. She went to one of the doors and found a bathroom with a toilet seat sitting on a bench, the waste below to be composted. She reached out and turned on the tap on the sink. Water ran out, brown at first but then clear.

She left the bathroom and went to the other doors to

examine the rest of the house and was staggered again by just how much work the man had put in to make his simple house functional and yet beautiful.

One of the doors lead to a spacious bedroom with a big four-poster bed with hand carved posts. Another door revealed a similar bedroom, only there were two small, smaller beds in it. She wondered what possible use Jeremiah Johnson could have had for a guest bedroom with two small beds. Who did he expect to visit him? There was so much about Jeremiah Johnson that nobody had known about.

She found a room that appeared to be a closet but was instead a tiny windowless office with a desk and dresser with paper drawers, something like a credenza against one wall. There were papers scattered about the desk, and she was sure that there were private papers in the drawers that someone needed to go through — not to be nosy, but to see if they could find out if there were any heirs. As far as anyone knew, Jeremiah Johnson had never married. His parents and brothers were all deceased or had moved away, and nobody knew where they were now.

Rileigh walked back into the center of the spacious open room, assured that Mama, Jillian, and Micky could live here comfortably — and David Hicks, if he was willing to. If not, then she and Mitch and some deputies would trade off duty here. The big couch in the open room looked very comfortable. In fact, all the furniture looked comfortable.

She went to the door in the back of the kitchen that opened onto another wide porch with an unobstructed view of the woods. The mountain man had obviously cleared out the undergrowth so that the trees were tall and rose up straight out of the ground. It even appeared that maybe he had planted some flowers around the edge of the porch, but they were dead now with nobody to water them.

When she opened the side door on the west side of the house, she spotted something in the rocks near the back porch steps. Jeremiah Johnson had rigged what passed for a *refrigerator* there! God only knew how long it had taken him to hollow out the rocks around a natural spring so he could fit a huge cooler as snugly as a foot in a shoe. The frigid spring water flowing over the cooler would keep whatever was in it good for several days. No freezer, but she doubted Jeremiah Johnson kept meat long enough to freeze it.

Rileigh's mind felt easier now that it was clear there was a good place for her family to go to ground. To hide. The word "hide" grated against her psyche, made her angry.

How dare those bastards show up here. How dare some asshole decide that Jillian's and Micky's existence didn't suit him, was an inconvenience that needed to be terminated.

Rileigh had to let go of her anger, or it would consume her.

There was a gun rack on the wall but no guns in it. She looked at the bars. There was space there for four rifles. Mitch had recovered one rifle out of the yard that Jeremiah Johnson had had on him. But what had happened to the other three, she didn't know. Everyone knew the man was a hunter and trapper. It would occur to a lot of people that he probably had some serious guns in his place. And the few people who actually knew where the cabin was and how to get to it might have decided to avail themselves of the weaponry. But as far as Rileigh could tell, they hadn't taken anything else.

She walked out of the cabin and closed the door

behind her, turning her thoughts to the next task on her to-do list. She needed to go to the grocery store and stock up on supplies, basics for Jillian, Mama, Micky, and David. Mama would want to cook on that stove, and it wouldn't surprise Rileigh at all to find that she knew how to use it.

Chapter Thirty

RILEIGH MOVED SLOWLY UP AND DOWN THE AISLES OF THE Buy Low Grocery Store, the store where her mother had shopped for groceries when she was a little girl. The store where she knew the location of every item. And the store where, on at least one occasion, she had walked out with a basket full of groceries that she didn't pay for because she'd forgotten her purse. The man working the cash register had told her just to bring him the money the next time she came in.

She smiled at Mr. Jenkins, who smiled back, and then she began to load up her cart. Just basics: flour and sugar and salt and pepper, bread and canned goods, crackers, eggs, coffee, tea. By the time she was finished, the grocery cart was filled all the way up to the top, and it was almost hard to maneuver down the aisles.

The aisles were smaller than the aisles in the big supermarket in Gatlinburg, but Rileigh liked the fact that these aisles contained only a small selection of items. She'd always stood in consternation at the toothpaste aisle in Walmart. Toothpaste as far as you could see. There was toothpaste to keep you from getting cavities. Toothpaste to make your teeth shine. Toothpaste to clean the plaque off your teeth. Toothpaste for sensitive teeth. There was mint flavored and peppermint and spearmint. There was green toothpaste, white toothpaste, and blue toothpaste, and at least one brand where when you squeeze the tube, it squirted out red and green side by side.

In the Buy Low, there was a rack with toothpaste. Three or four different brands, and that was it. If you couldn't find what you wanted there, then your teeth would just have to rot in your mouth.

When she pushed the heavily loaded cart up to the counter, Emilio Ruiz, who had worked the counter there when she first came home on leave from Afghanistan, looked at her haul and whistled.

"Holy shit Rileigh, what do you need all this stuff for?"

She knew he would be asking, and she had prepared an answer.

"Well, we've decided that we're going to take a little vacation to a cabin in the mountains way up above Gatlinburg on Ruby Falls. You know the place?"

"Oh, it's beautiful up there, but those cabins." He whistled again. "Those babies cost an arm and a leg."

"We've decided to splurge. We need a vacation."

He nodded at the basket full of supplies. "Doesn't look like a vacation to me if you've got to cook."

"Shut your mouth, Emilio," she said and shook her head. "We're talking Lily Bishop here."

Emilio rolled with it. "Oh, well, yeah that's right. It wouldn't be a vacation for her if she couldn't cook."

It took two trips to carry all the bags out and stick them in the back seat of her car and in the trunk. Then she headed to the Quick Stop Convenience Store owned by Sundeep Singh for gasoline and to get caramel bugles. The

Quick Stop was the only place in town that sold caramel bugles. They were tourist food, but Rileigh had gotten addicted to them when she was in the military, and anytime she was anywhere near Sundeep's store, she went inside to buy a bag. She didn't pay for her gas at the pump, just went into the store, down the familiar aisle, snatched up four bags of caramel bugles, and handed them to Sundeep.

When Sundeep saw her, he rolled his eyes. "Oh man, you just missed them."

"Missed who?"

"The guys who were in here just a few minutes ago asking for directions to Bent Twigg Road."

Rileigh's gut tied into a knot.

"Any particular address on the road?"

"No, just wanted directions to Bent Twigg." GPS signals were notoriously unreliable in the mountains. "If you'd been here, you could have told them how to find whoever they were looking for. That's your neighborhood, isn't it?"

Rileigh nodded. "Who were they?"

"Only one of them came in, the other waited in the car. Tall guy, dark hair, dark eyes, accent, wearing a suit and tie, which you don't see that often in Black Bear Forge."

Rileigh's gut tightened into a bigger knot.

"An accent, you say? Did you recognize it?"

"It wasn't Hispanic. If I'd had to guess, I'd say Middle Eastern, Arabic maybe. I don't know."

Rileigh stood speechless for a moment, and Sundeep picked up on her distress.

"Hey, what's wrong?"

She found she couldn't come up with a convenient lie. "What kind of car were they driving?"

"A rental, looked like, black, maybe a Lexus. I don't know. Expensive. What's the matter, Rileigh? I told you about those guys, and the color drained out of your face like somebody pulled the plug."

No sense in not telling him at least some of it. In fact, it might be a good idea to tell him.

"There are some bad people looking for Jillian," she said and watched his eyes grow wide. Everyone in town knew Jillian had been AWOL from her life for thirty years, and word had circulated when she returned that she hadn't gone wherever she had gone willingly. Most people knew that something bad had happened to Jillian Bishop. Something bad that had lasted for a very long time.

"Why are they looking for Jillian?"

"They don't want anything good, Sundeep. Listen, if you see them again anywhere, if you're driving home or at a red light, anywhere, call me immediately." She reached into her pocket to pull out her phone to give him her contact information, and he brushed her off.

"I've got your number."

Then she remembered that he'd done a couple of deliveries to the house, brought out some Nyquil and other flu medication when Mama was sick.

Rileigh walked back out to her car, got in, and sat behind the wheel without starting the engine. Her heart was pounding, then she lifted the cell phone that was still in her hand, punched favorites, and then Mitch. He answered after the first ring.

"'Lo, Rileigh, what's up?"

"They're here," she said. He didn't ask who. He knew.

"How do you know?"

"Sandeep spotted them buying gas just a few minutes ago, driving a rental, black, probably a Lexus. No more description than that."

Sandeep's convenience store was not more than fifteen or twenty minutes' drive from Rileigh's house.

"I'll get in touch with Beau, give him a heads up to be on the alert. We need to go collect Micky and get the hell out of Dodge as soon as we can."

"Copy that," Rileigh said. "Jillian was going to go by the hospital and pick her up, but I think we need to pivot. I'm closer than Jillian is. I'll give her a call and tell her I'm going to pick up Micky."

"I'll meet you at Mama's."

Before she hung up, Rileigh put in, "I heard from Jillian, by the way, just a quick text. A smiley face with David's name beside it."

She could hear Mitch let out a sigh of relief on the other end of the line.

Rileigh headed for the Yarmouth County Hospital, got lucky, and found a parking space not far from the door. She went in and immediately up to the third floor to Micky's room, and when she opened the door, the girl was sitting on the edge of the bed, fully dressed. She looked thin and pale and fragile. Rileigh searched her face without appearing to, looking for some resemblance to her sister, but she didn't find it there. Her features were strong, pretty but strong, a broad forehead, a straight nose. She likely bore a greater resemblance to her father's side of the family.

"I thought..." and then Micky stopped short. Rileigh realized she'd stopped because she was stumbling over what to call Jillian, and finally settled for, "I thought your sister was coming to pick me up."

"Change of plans. I was closer. You'll have to sit with a bag of oranges between your feet because I loaded up the car with groceries, but we need to go now."

"Something bad has happened, hasn't it?" Micky

asked. Rileigh appreciated seeing that the girl was astute, not some self-absorbed twenty-year-old who thought of nothing but herself. She was outward focused, picking up on the emotions and reactions of others.

"Yeah, I stopped by for gasoline at the convenience store on the edge of town a little while ago, and the guy who runs it, Sundeep, said that two Middle Eastern men had just purchased gas and had asked for directions to Bent Twigg Road."

"And Bent Twigg Road is?"

"That's where Mama lives."

"Is she there? There with… your sister?"

Rileigh sought to ease her discomfort.

"Yes, she and *your mother* are waiting there for us, but they're not alone. Mitch stationed a deputy at the end of the driveway where anybody driving down Bent Twigg Road would see his cruiser. I called him and told him about what Sundeep said this morning, and Mitch radioed the deputy to turn his lights on. That should be enough of a deterrent for us to get in and collect everybody and leave."

"I'm supposed to call the nurse and have her bring around a wheelchair," Micky said.

Rileigh rolled her eyes. She knew the requirement, and it was ridiculous. The hospital playing CYA in case somebody fell and broke a leg in the lobby before they left the hospital. But it would take way longer to fight than to just go along.

Rileigh, a nurse, and Micky rode down in the elevator to the lobby. Rileigh left the nurse and Micky at the curb while she went to get her car. When she pulled up under the portico a few minutes later, she was distressed to see that the nurse had left, and there sat Micky in a wheelchair all by herself. She hurriedly stopped the car, got out, and opened the car door. Micky stood up slowly from the wheelchair and walked toward the car. She didn't look so much injured as merely weak and tired, but Rileigh could see bandages on her arms beneath the short sleeves of her t-shirt and on her neck.

Rileigh closed Micky's door, came back around and got into the car, and started the engine.

"What are those?" Micky asked, looking at the pile of caramel-flavored bugles.

Rileigh smiled. "They're my favorites. I bought some when I was at the convenience store."

"Mind if I open the package? Breakfast sucked."

Rileigh smiled a genuine smile. This girl liked caramel bugles. It had to be genetic. Had to be.

Rileigh pulled away from the portico as Micky opened the package of caramel bugles and began nibbling. Rileigh kept the conversation going by describing Jeremiah Johnson's cabin, how nice it was, and how surprised she'd been that it was nice. At every intersection, she scanned the cars looking for a black Lexus but saw none.

Chapter Thirty-One

THE MAN WHO OWNED THE WHITE JETTA THAT HAD PULLED in behind Rileigh when she left the hospital and followed slowly along as she made her way to Bent Twigg Road was not driving the vehicle. He was in the car though, in the trunk — busy doing what Daniel Farley liked to think of as, "slowly assuming room temperature."

Daniel had cleaned up since he had first spotted Rileigh at the hospital coming out of the hospital room on the third floor a few days ago. He'd shaved and put on clean clothes and looked more rested.

In truth, he'd spent much of his time at the motel, where he'd crashed, tossing and turning on the bed, unable to go fully to sleep without seeing the horrible scene of blood and gore that had greeted him when he went to his sister's house to check on her after she failed to meet him for coffee at the little cafe right outside town.

He'd met his sister there every Monday morning for years, but she hadn't shown, so he'd gone to her house to find out why. And he had found her body.

Her body, and other bodies as well. All of them butchered.

Daniel Farley knew who had done it, of course. It wasn't hard to figure out. And he could have gone the normal legal route that probably most any other deputy sheriff would have gone. He could have called the law.

But Daniel Farley was not about to get the law involved, couldn't let that Hollis girl talk to authorities. He knew what she'd say. He knew what she'd accuse him and his sister and brother-in-law and others of doing. And although he didn't think she'd be believed, no way could he take the chance. So he'd gone after the killer on his own.

Fearing what she might say wasn't the only reason, though. Not even the most compelling reason. He wanted to kill the little bitch himself. Wanted to squeeze her throat and watch the life go out of her eyes. He wanted *revenge*.

And he was sure the woman a nurse had identified as Rileigh Bishop would lead him to his prey.

RILEIGH SPOTTED the flashers on Beau Mullins's cruiser — red and blue light bouncing off rocks and trees — when she made the final turn on Bent Twigg Road to head up Mama's driveway.

She smiled and let out a sigh of relief. If Beau was there, lights flashing, the Middle Eastern men might have found Mama's house, but they'd surely been deterred by the presence of the police cruiser at the bottom of the driveway with lights flashing.

She knew they were in no hurry. They had all the time in the world. No reason to go crashing into the place through an armed police officer when they could wait, bide their time, and come out of the darkness unnoticed.

Mitch's cruiser was parked beside Jillian's car, and David's Land Rover was on the other side.

"Well, the gang's all here," Rileigh said.

She considered going around and parking in the back. There was a whole lot more room back there. But Mama was sitting by herself on the porch swing, shading her eyes, watching for her car to return. And Rileigh knew that she was waiting there to meet her brand-new granddaughter.

Rileigh pulled into a tight squeeze beside David's Land Rover, then got out of the car to go around to the side and open the door from Micky. But Micky opened her own door and got out, looking around at the house and the vehicles.

"Is that her?" Mama cried out from the porch. "Is that my granddaughter?"

Rileigh looked across the hood of Mama's car to Micky's face, but it was unreadable. She'd prepared her, told her about Mama. Jillian had already given her the Dalai Lama story, so she knew that the old lady wasn't dragging a completely full string of fish. But still, Rileigh saw her brace herself for the onslaught.

"Yeah, Mama."

Thinking fast on her feet, Rileigh continued, "Why don't you go in the kitchen, bring us out some lemonade so we can drink it on the porch?"

Rileigh watched her mother's face, a study of indecision. All in the world that the old woman wanted was to run down that sidewalk and grab her granddaughter in a bear hug. But Mama was Mama, and Mama *served*. That was her role in life. She did for others. And to ask her for a glass of lemonade and her not respond was just more psychological pressure than Mama could stand.

"Okay, I'll be right out with two glasses!" Mama cried, then opened the squawky screen door and hurried inside.

Micky moved slowly but steadily around the front of Mama's car and toward the gate. She was only halfway up the sidewalk when Mama came rushing out the front door with two glasses of lemonade. She'd turned sideways, then used her butt to open the door and raced across the porch, her eyes bright. She ran the few steps down the sidewalk to Micky. And to her credit, the girl didn't flinch.

"You're her, aren't you? You're her. That hair. I can tell. I can tell you're her."

Then Mama started to throw her arms around Micky and realized that she had a glass of lemonade in each hand. Turning to Rileigh, she shoved them at her. "Here, hold these for me."

Rileigh took them, splashing lemonade out all over the sidewalk. But Mama was free. She stepped to the girl, grabbed her in a hug, but aborted the force of it at the very last minute when she saw the bandage on Micky's arm.

"I won't hug you too tight. Guess you're wondering who I am. Who's this old woman who's come running down the steps and flung her arms around me in a big hug? Why, I'm your granny."

She pulled back and looked at Micky's face.

Micky managed a weak smile. "It's very good to meet you, Grandma Lily," she said, and Mama unexpectedly burst into tears.

"Mama?" Rileigh said as Mama put her head in her hands and sobbed. Shoving the two glasses now only half full of lemonade at Micky, Rileigh took her mother in her arms.

"Mama, it's okay."

"It's just I've waited my whole life to hear somebody call me that, to hear my grandchild say it, to call me Grandma Lily."

230

Mama got hold of herself quickly and looked back at Micky.

"Let me take them glasses," Mama said. She took both of the glasses of lemonade from Micky's hands and stood holding them, grinning.

Jillian came out on the front porch then, followed by Mitch and David, and stood looking at the scene. Mama turned back to the porch.

"This here's my granddaughter. Her name's..." She turned back to the girl. "Oh my God, I never did even ask what your name is, sweetheart. They told me what it was, but I can't remember. I'm sorry. I ain't got much of a memory left. It's... it's Michaela, ain't it?"

"I'm not Michaela. I'm Micky," she said.

"Well, come on up on this porch, Micky, and meet the rest of your family," Mama said, grinning from ear to ear.

From that point on, it was Mama in a dither, and everyone else around her trying to keep her un-dithered enough so that they could accomplish what they needed to accomplish, which was to load up Michaela, Jillian, and Mama and all that they'd packed into the back of David's Land Rover for the drive to Jeremiah Johnson's cabin in the woods.

Mama flitted around like a hummingbird dancing from one flower to another. She'd hug Micky, her eyes wet, kiss her cheek, then go hug Jillian and kiss hers. Equal opportunity hugger that Mama was, she hugged Mitch, too, and David, and of course, Rileigh. Then she'd make the circuit all over again.

Rileigh spoke quietly to Mitch. "It's clear there's at least one person who's glad Micky showed up. I don't believe I've ever seen my mother happier."

Chapter Thirty-Two

It took longer than it needed to gather up all that needed gathering because Mama was so dithered, she couldn't concentrate on anything long enough to figure out what she wanted to take with her. She called a halt to all the packing for a "photo op," got David to take family pictures — Mama and Micky; Mama, Micky, Rileigh and Jillian; Micky, Jillian, and Rileigh. Rileigh took the opportunity to make sure she had good, clear headshots of everyone in the family. She would need them. And every five minutes or so, Mama would rush over to Micky, who was lying propped up on pillows on the couch in the living room, and give her a big kiss and tell her how glad she was to have a granddaughter.

Rileigh watched Micky's reaction. At first, she stiffened every time Mama started for her, but after a while, she relaxed. Mama was so effusively kind and loving and good that it would take a real asshole not to warm up to her, and Micky wasn't an asshole.

Because there was no cell service at Jeremiah Johnson's cabin, Rileigh and Mitch would have to go there to check on how they were doing, so Rileigh knew that there would be comings and goings from there. They just had to be extremely careful to be sure that nobody traced their movements. Jeremiah Johnson's cabin was unfindable unless somebody led you to it.

They'd figured out they'd need two cars to transport everyone plus the supplies that Rileigh had purchased. Rileigh would lead the way for David, and then she'd come back to town for what was to be her and Mitch's contribution to the effort.

It was going on dark before the two-vehicle caravan set out from Mama's house. As David's Land Rover passed by Deputy Mullins, who was still parked with light flashing at the foot of the driveway, Mullins cut his flashers and drove away. Rileigh was not afraid of being followed to the spot where you turned off to go up to Jeremiah Johnson's. That turn was the first of half a dozen different turns up in the woods that were not marked. Rileigh couldn't imagine that anybody, even if they knew where to turn off, could find the cabin on their own.

Rileigh was thrilled at the reaction of the castaways to their refuge in the mountains. Jillian and Mama and Micky were staggered by what Jeremiah Johnson had been able to carve out of the wilderness. She showed them the toilet and how it functioned and then took them out to the spot on the rocks on the mountainside a few feet from the porch where the frigid spring bubbled up, where Jeremiah had rigged a "refrigerator" there with a big cooler.

Mama was intrigued by the stove — and delighted by it. She had let out a big whoop as soon as she saw it. "This is what we cooked on when I was a girl," she said. It was a wood-burning stove with an oven, and it had probably cost Jeremiah Johnson a year's wages at some antique store, and even then he had to make it workable again. But everything appeared functional, a little dusty from disuse but otherwise just waiting for them to settle in.

David hauled all the supplies up the hill for them and all the bags. It felt a little like moving into summer camp to Rileigh. She and Jillian had gone every year, didn't want to leave home and almost cried, and then didn't want to come back home and almost cried.

As the shadow of the mountain lengthened and the pools and shadows under the trees formed darker and thicker puddles, Rileigh could tell that Micky and Mama were both exhausted. She had purchased a large selection of cold cuts and cheeses and different kinds of breads so it wouldn't be necessary to cook tonight, and she insisted on making them sandwiches before ushering them off to bed in their separate bedrooms. Micky and Jillian would be sleeping in one of the bedrooms, Mama would be in the other with a vacant bed for Rileigh when she came to visit, and David was ensconced on the big, comfortable couch in the den.

After dinner, Jillian got to her feet and held out her hand to Micky. "Your room's this way," she said and started toward it, and Rileigh realized that she'd orchestrated it so that she would be putting her little girl to bed — an activity that one or the other of them, and maybe both, had spent decades silently longing for.

After Rileigh got Mama to bed, she sat at the table talking to David.

"Jeremiah Johnson's paranoia has delivered to us a home away from home that's easy to guard," David pointed out. "He built the house with windows in the attic arranged so it was possible to stand in the middle of the attic and see the area behind and in front of the house at the same time."

Rileigh pointed to the room-darkening drapes. "Pull those, and this house becomes invisible."

David nodded and patted the Glock he had strapped to his waist, then indicated the AK-47 rifle he had brought with him.

"I spent nine years in the National Guard. I know how to use a weapon." He ground his teeth. "And nothing would make me happier than to put the crosshairs on one of those Arab assholes and spatter their brains all over the trees."

"Mitch and I are hoping that doesn't happen. We're hoping that you and your charges are able to stay here in safety until..."

"Yeah, until when?"

"We have a plan for the bad guys. It's dicey, it's dangerous — high risk and high reward — but we're working on it. Film at 11."

She was grateful that David didn't ask for more specifics because she didn't have any, and at this stage, the plan even sounded absurd to her own ears.

It was full on dark before Rileigh went back down the mountainside to the road. She used only her parking lights to pick out the faint trail she followed, and she actually made a wrong turn and had to backtrack, but she was glad, because it proved this place was just about unfindable, the perfect place to stash Mama and Jillian and Micky until...

David's voice echoed in her head.

"Yeah, until when?"

They had a plan, but God only knew if it would work.

And for it to work, every planet in the solar system would have to align just right.

Chapter Thirty-Three

RILEIGH FOUND MITCH WAITING AT MAMA'S HOUSE. She parked beside his cruiser and cut her eyes to the trees on both sides of the house, examining them, her hand on the Glick in the holster at her side. She went up the sidewalk quickly, crossed the porch, opened the door, and hollered out, "It's me," and went inside, closing not only the screen but the front door itself behind her. Mitch had drawn all the curtains and put down the shades. There was a warm glow of light showing from the windows on the first floor, but it was impossible to see in from outside.

As soon as she stepped into the living room, she smelled it and went to the kitchen. Mitch was stirring a pot of beans.

"Lo," he said, "I know beans aren't that good without Mama's cornbread, but I don't have a really large repertoire of items I know how to cook."

"Doesn't have to be without cornbread. Cornbread only takes ten minutes to mix and thirty minutes to cook, if you want to wait."

He smiled. "I was hoping you would say that." She

237

went to him then as he stirred the beans, got on tiptoes, and pecked his cheek.

"Thank you," she said.

"My pleasure, madame."

Rileigh set about making cornbread as she and Mitch talked. "They're all settled. And so far, they're loving it. And I got lost myself coming back down the mountain from the cabin. I count that a win."

Rileigh pulled the piping hot cornbread out of the oven with hot pads and set it on the table, then both of them took seats to enjoy the last bit of Mama's lemonade and big chunks of cornbread slathered with butter on their plates,

As they ate, they talked about their grand plan, a BTN plan — better than nothing — not a whole lot more than a wish and a prayer. It had begun to form in Rileigh's mind the night they talked about the presence of the men Big John had seen and what that meant to Jillian and Michaela.

Rileigh was haunted by the words her sister had spoken in terror.

"But if we find them, say we catch these men, this particular team. Omar will just send out another one. He's the ultimate deep pocket. He has millions and his reputation is on the line. There's nothing and nobody he can't buy. He'll just keep sending out one team after another until…"

And Jillian was right, of course. They knew about *these* two. They'd gotten lucky. But say they stopped these two, trapped them into committing a crime, got them arrested. Maybe even shot them. It didn't matter. If the first hit team didn't succeed, Omar would send out another. And another. And another. It would never stop. Jillian had avoided that fate by the new identity, Heather Priest, she'd purchased for herself when she escaped. And by the fact that she was no longer a particularly valuable piece of Omar's property. There were younger and prettier girls, taken from Sweden and Norway, in his stable. She'd been simply a house slave then who provided bed partner privileges to her master whenever his wife wasn't around and he needed an outlet.

But now she was a target. Now, he would track her down, use his vast resources to find her. And even if she and Micky could come up with alternative identities, he knew where Jillian was from. And if Jillian and Michaela intended to become other people and escape, they would never be able to return home. Ever. And that would kill Mama. Rileigh was sure of it.

She and Mitch had discussed that at length, and that's why they had come up with the BTN plan.

"So now that we don't have to worry about Mama and Micky and Jillian anymore, we can concentrate on our end of this game."

"I wish we had better cards," he said.

"You play the cards you've dealt," Rileigh said and shook her head.

There had been times when she was in the military that they'd found themselves in less than advantageous tactical position, and they just improvised. There was no other way to stay alive. You improvised. You kept moving. You got creative, thought outside the box. And that is what had formed the beginnings of her plan with Mitch.

Mitch took a bite of his cornbread and followed it with a big swig of lemonade.

"It's all about away from here," he said.

"Yeah," she said, "away from here."

People from away from here didn't realize until they interacted with the people of Yarmouth County just how insulated and clannish they were, didn't realize that they would go to any lengths to protect their own. And Rileigh intended to play her I Am a Local card for everything it was worth.

"When are you talking to your Gatlinburg friend?"

"I invited him to lunch and I'm going to spring it on him. We'll see how that goes."

"We take it one step at a time," Mitch said.

"And step one is?" Rileigh said.

"Step one is getting the assholes to show themselves. Letting them think we don't even know they're here. Luring them into our trap like a spider does a fly."

"Let's assume that part works. Step two is what?"

"Depends on how we manage to catch them, whether or not we end up having to use deadly force."

"I can't tell you how satisfying it would be to kill at least one of the bastards," Rileigh said. "But it'll be cleaner if we can pull this off without having to do that."

Mitch nodded.

"After that, we slap them in jail for long enough for us to put the rest of it together. Under ordinary circumstances, they'd be out quick, but we'll keep them locked up until—"

"We're counting our chickens before they're hatched——"

"Cleaning our fish before they're caught."

Rileigh gave Mitch a knowing look. "Or skinning our squirrels … eventually."

"You're not going to bring *that* up again."

Rileigh shrugged.

Mitch wiped the last of the crumbs off his face, then reached out and took Rileigh's hand. "Hey, the good news here is we get to spend a lot of time together."

"Yeah," she said, and winked. "*Alone* together." She

grinned, before letting the grin drain off her face. "Or at least *pretending* to be alone."

"Alone and carefree," Mitch said.

"At least *pretending* to be carefree. Which is just as confining — maybe more — than just being on the job."

"It's all we can do. But like I said, we still get to spend a lot of time together."

Mitch smiled and winked. "So, you gonna take first watch tonight or you want me to?"

"How sleepy are you?" she said.

"Not very."

"Then you take first watch. I need a reboot."

The two of them got up and washed the dishes, Mitch snatching kisses whenever he could and Rileigh aching to relax into those strong arms and let whatever will be, will be. But not now. Her mother, her sister, and her newfound niece were in danger, and Rileigh Bishop would give her life to save them.

Chapter Thirty-Four

JILLIAN AWOKE TO THE SMELL OF FRESH COFFEE AND FRYING bacon and looked over at the bed beside hers. It was empty. It was still dark outside, for crying out loud — but she couldn't help smiling. Mama had gotten up with the chickens, as she called it, and was making breakfast on the antique wood-burning stove in Jeremiah Johnson's kitchen.

Jillian got out of bed and dressed quickly and went in to see what glorious things Mama was cooking up for breakfast.

Stepping out into the dining room area, she found David sitting at the kitchen table.

He looked at his watch. "Hey, sleepyhead, it's almost six o'clock."

"What can I say? Lazy me," Jillian said.

"I tried to be quiet as I could," Mama said, "but there ain't no way to get out iron skillets and make eggs and bacon 'thout making some noise." Mama nodded toward the bedroom where Micky lay sleeping. "I figure we just need to let her sleep as long as she will."

"Yes, she lost a lot of blood. They did a transfusion, but the wounds still need to heal."

"And she's going to be getting around slow and sore for a while."

"I was thinking about that," Mama said. "And I was wishing that we'd packed them pictures and brought them here with us."

"What pictures, Mama?"

"Our pictures, family pictures," she said. "You know what I'm talking about — the ones Rileigh dragged out and was digging through when we was rushing around packing."

Jillian wrinkled her brow.

"The pictures that's all dog-eared and had so many eyes on them so many times that probably ain't no image left. Pictures of you when you was a little girl. Pictures me and Rileigh looked at and looked at and looked at." Mama's face was dark for a moment and then brightened. "You know, before you come back. I'd like to show them pictures to Micky, what her mama looked like when she was a little girl."

Jillian had lain awake last night thinking about it, replaying in her mind going into Micky's room at the hospital, telling the girl that she was her mother, watching her reaction, feeling a bond to the girl who lay there in the bed.

But if her life circumstances had taught her anything, it was not to sugarcoat reality. She was a realist above all. And it was true that she had felt a bond to the girl. But was it mother-daughter? Did genetics call out like that? Do you connect just because you share common DNA?

She didn't know how much of it she had conjured up on her own end just because she wanted to believe it. She had studied Micky's face when the girl didn't notice, studied the lines of her jaw, her cheek, her eyes, the shape of them, looking for herself in something other than the girl's hair. And if it was there, she didn't see it. But she'd also been looking for evidence of Amir Al-Saud, the Arab man who had impregnated Jillian as carelessly as dropping his DNA on the sidewalk. And she didn't see any evidence of him there either. The girl had a soft face, devoid of hard lines and the kind of structure that was common to Arab men. In truth, she didn't look like either Jillian or Amir. But maybe as she matured, she'd come to look more like one or the other of them. Jillian caught herself then, reined herself in.

That's running out ahead of your headlights, she told herself. There was no guarantee that there'd be a future for her and her daughter. And if she let herself think about the hopelessness of it, the realization that the man looking for them would stop at nothing to find them … He had no morals, recognized no laws, had no national boundaries, was an international criminal who would find anyone if he looked hard enough.

And the thought of coming up with a new identity for her and her daughter and what it would mean, leaving the mountains for good? Was she up to that now? Up to that challenge? Up to a new life that was totally cut off from Mama and Rileigh and the mountains?

In all her conjectures about the future, she refused to factor in the single most important part — David. Could she just walk out on him again? What would that even sound like? *"I know I left you standing at the altar thirty years ago and now we've rediscovered the feelings we had for each other, but I gotta go. Bye bye."*

She couldn't give David up a second time.

David reached over and patted her hand. She realized he could see her feelings on her face.

She would trust Rileigh. Rileigh would figure something out. she said she had a plan, and Jillian had no option except to believe in that plan and trust that it would work.

It was almost eleven o'clock when Micky finally peeked like a little mole out the door of the room where she'd slept. Mama spied her, and Jillian saw Mama grab herself and keep herself from rushing over and enveloping the poor girl in yet another bear hug.

"I can whip you up some bacon and eggs in five minutes. Now, tell me how you like your eggs."

"I don't need any eggs, Grandma Lily. Is there a bagel? Some butter?"

"Why, sure there is, sweetheart." Then Jillian and Mama fell all over herself to get Micky what she wanted.

It was hard not to catch the infectious joy that Mama radiated like warmth off a toaster. Her absolute delight in having her very first granddaughter made the old woman so happy, it brought tears to Jillian's eyes.

Jeremiah was not a sit-on-your-porch-so-you-can-wave-at-your-neighbors kind of guy, and there wouldn't have been any neighbors to wave at if he had been. After Micky ate, they dragged Johnson's handmade chairs out onto the porch and sat down to talk, try to get to know each other. Jillian didn't know how to proceed and decided the best place to start was by admitting that.

"I'm sorry, but I don't even know where to start, and I feel awkward and stupid trying to think of something to say."

To her delight, Micky smiled. "I feel the same way."

"How about we start at the beginning?" When she saw the pained look on Micky's face, Jillian realized that would probably be a painful thing for her. "I'm sorry, I mean—"

"That's alright. The beginning is that I grew up in a

house in northern California with two people we called Mama and Daddy, but they weren't. They were a couple who had purchased my sister Farrah, and then two years later purchased me, as babies off the black market."

"Tell me about growing up."

Micky let out a big breath, drew in another one, and said, "Let's just make this sort of a blanket statement. Our childhood was terrible. Our parents were abusive. I have no idea why they wanted children for any other reason except to abuse them, because that's all they did."

"What kind of abuse?" Jillian asked softly.

"You name it, they did it. Farrah got the worst of it because she was the older of us and Papa had already developed a ... 'special fondness,' as he called it, for her."

Jillian said, "How about you? Did he develop a special fondness for you too?" Before Micky could answer, she added, "Keep in mind who you're talking to and what I've lived. There's nothing in the world you could say that would shock or surprise me, but I also understand if you just flat out don't want to talk about it."

"I just flat out don't want to talk about it," Micky said.

As Jillian nodded, Micky continued, "But I will. To you."

She paused and gathered herself. "He had a special room in the house which was where we went to play games. It was dim there in the room. He liked candlelight, and there were candles all around. There was a big bed, and the windows in the room had been blacked out. I don't even remember the first time I went to the special room with Daddy. It's one of those things that seems like you have always been doing it, and I suppose that he started when I was very young. But like I say, Farrah got the worst of it."

"Tell me about Farrah."

"She was two years older than me and very blonde. I always thought people must surely wonder why our parents, who were olive skinned with black hair, had come up with blonde daughters that they swore were their own. Our hair was left long because Daddy," she took a breath, "Daddy liked how long hair looked on a pillow."

Jillian nodded. "I know lots of men who felt that way."

"And besides, short hair would have meant taking us to get our hair cut, and they made certain that our interactions with other people were limited to a minimum. We went to school, but we knew what would happen if we dared breathe a word of what was going on at home to our teachers. At least once a week, Daddy showed us the big hunting knife he would use to carve out our hearts. And we believed he meant every word of the threats, because he absolutely did."

As she spoke, Jillian tried to picture the sister Farrah that she spoke about. She seemed to hold her in awe. Not quite like Rileigh had felt about Jillian, but more than simple big-sister admiration. Though there seemed to be an element of some other emotion in it, and if she'd had to identify it, she would have said it was fear.

"And when I was six years old, they bought a new baby. Her name was Alyssa." Micky's face broke into a beatific smile. "Alyssa was the most beautiful baby you have ever seen. Big blue eyes and blonde hair and curls and laughter." Then the color and enthusiasm drained out of her face. "And I remember the first time Daddy took Alyssa to the room. I went to our room and stuffed my face into a pillow and screamed and cried and banged my fist on the bed. I couldn't wait to get home from school after Alyssa came. She was like my real-life doll who laughed and cried and called me Ay-la, that's what she called me, Ay-la, when she was little. She said that before she ever said Mama or

Papa. It wasn't her first word, though. Her first word was 'uh oh.'"

Jillian smiled, watched the animation on her sister's face and realized that she had one beautiful bright light in her life. And that was her little sister.

"I called her Lissy. Nobody else called her that. I used to dress her up in outfits. She didn't have a whole lot to wear, and I certainly didn't know how to sew. I was only nine or ten, but I asked my teacher if there was a book I could read in the library about sewing. She was thrilled that I wanted to read. I devoured it, begged Mama to buy materials so I could make dresses for my Lissy. I certainly didn't know what I was doing. But I started with an old pillowcase. Then I used an old sheet and finally Mama came home with a bolt of fabric she'd bought somewhere. And I made Lissy a little shirt and pants. She looked so cute in that outfit."

She stopped then. And Jillian saw what she was becoming accustomed to seeing — joy, happiness, and life draining out of Micky's face.

"That was the last one I ever made her. She died."

"What happened?"

"I don't really know what happened. I know what they told people, that she had fallen into the lake and drowned. But she didn't go to the lake. It was too far from our house. And why would she have gone there by herself? I didn't believe that. Though they produced her wet body and cried over it appropriately. I just know that it felt like the sun went completely out of my life when she was gone."

Jillian reached over and patted her daughter's hand. "I'm sorry that happened to you, Micky."

"I think Farrah knew what really happened to her. In fact, I'm sure of it. But Farrah would never tell me, so I don't know how Lissy really died."

Micky wiped the tears that had slipped from her eyes and down her cheeks and pasted the scraps of a smile on her face.

Jillian admired that she was so resilient — and hated that she found herself looking for her own smile, or for Micky's father's smile in the smile the girl held on her face by a force of will, but she saw neither.

Chapter Thirty-Five

WHIT NASH HAD BEEN SURPRISED TO HEAR RILEIGH'S voice when she called him, and even more surprised when she invited him out to lunch. She had something she needed to talk to him about. And though he professed to be very busy, she was pushy enough to get him to agree.

She picked a little Italian restaurant off of Simpson Street in Gatlinburg. That was close to his business, so he wouldn't have to take extra time to go somewhere and meet her. It was a late lunch and the crowd was gone, and she found a table near the back that was private so they could talk. She got there first and went to sit at the table and wait. She saw Whit at the front door and realized that he must be taking continuous physical therapy, because it seemed that every time she saw him, he had a little bit better control of his limbs. He had a lurching gait, of course, like everyone with cerebral palsy. But his wasn't as bad as most, and if she was remembering correctly, it wasn't even as bad as it had been the last time she saw him, when she had gone to him when Mitch and she were trying to figure out why old ladies had started to go missing from Aunt Daisy's psychiatric ward at the Carrington house. He'd been helpful then. But now? This was a bridge way farther than that.

She stood when he got to the table, and they shook hands. He definitely had better control of his muscles than he'd had when she remembered him from school when he was a senior. She was in middle school, and everybody pointed him out, but not in some derogatory way. People had always been impressed by Whit Nash because he never allowed what was wrong with him to keep him from doing whatever it was he'd decided he was going to do. And even shallow teenagers were able to appreciate that.

"It's good to see you again, Rileigh," he said and smiled as he sat. "How did you know this was my favorite restaurant?" His speech was only slightly jerky.

"I didn't. I brought you here because it's *my* favorite restaurant." He smiled broader then.

They ordered him tea, and both chose the lunch specials, which were soup and salad, and as soon as the waitress departed and they could speak privately, Rileigh got right to the point.

"Okay, this is an…" She took her hands and put them over her head, fingertips together and pointed up as if there were a roof with a steeple on the top of her head. "Umbrella of mercy."

He cocked his head to the side. "Am I supposed to know what that means?"

"Be surprised if you did. What it meant in my family was that you were about to say something that was so totally off the wall that nobody was expecting it and that they probably wouldn't like it. But once you declared an umbrella of mercy, they were bound by the solemn oath" —she held up her little finger and crooked it—"a pinky swear that they would listen to every word you had to say and not argue, and that they would give it serious consideration."

Whit wrinkled his brow, then reached his hand out with his little finger extended. "Okay, pinky swear," he said.

They locked their little fingers, and then Rileigh sat back.

"I'm sure you don't remember my sister Jillian."

"Is this about Jillian?"

"Sure, I'm surprised you remember her."

"Oh, I remember Jillian Bishop," he said. "I was twelve years old when she disappeared." When he saw her doing the math in her head, he said, "I started school two years late because I needed physical therapy before I could go to public school."

"Why would you remember Jillian?"

"Mama took me and my sisters to the Baptist church where your mother had you and Jillian warming pews every Sunday morning."

"I was only six when she disappeared, and I'm sorry to admit I really don't remember you from church."

"That's surprising, because I'm pretty memorable," he said, and he didn't say it in any caustic way, just as an observation. "But I remember Jillian Bishop. I was in love with Jillian back then."

He leaned over. "I'm a very happily married man. I'd whip out my wallet and show you pictures, but I know people really aren't interested in looking at anonymous children."

"I knew you had children. I remember the picture of your wife and two little girls, wasn't it?"

"It's three now. We have a new baby — another girl."

"Congratulations."

"I tell you that I married, and happily so, so that I can

say without embarrassment I fell in love for the first time when I was twelve. The love of my life was your sister, Jillian."

"If you had a crush on Jillian, you had to stand in line."

"And the line was long and filled with just about every adolescent and prepubescent boy in town." Whit sat back. "She was just as beautiful as an angel with that crown of pale blonde hair. I'd never seen anything like it. I gawked at her in church. Our family's pew was behind and to the right of yours, and I always prayed that Jillian would sit down on the right side of your mother, because if the Hendersons didn't show up at church, I was offered a totally unobstructed view of Jillian, and I could stare at her all through the service. I'm sure I never heard a single sermon, but other than the one about angels, and the only reason I listened to that one was because I imagined the minister was talking about Jillian."

Rileigh sat back and listened with amazement.

"But I wasn't just one of the anonymous boys who had a crush on her. It was more than that. A twelve-year-old knows what love is, and I genuinely loved her."

Whit paused.

"Let me tell you a story. There was one Wednesday night service when I was having, let's just say, stomach issues, and I had to get up in the middle of the service and make my way to the bathroom. And at that time, movement for me was always awkward and lurching. And when you're getting up to go to the bathroom in the middle of a church service, the last thing you want is to know the whole church is turning around and looking at you — and they were.

"So I went to the men's room, did what I had to do, and as I was zipping my pants, my hands slipped, and I caught my underwear in the zipper. I tried to push it back down, but I didn't have the fine motor coordination to do that and wound up zipping it tighter, catching more of my underwear. Then the zipper was completely stuck. It wouldn't go up or down. And I had no idea what to do."

"Oh, Whit," Rileigh said.

"I was horrified and mortified and frantic — desperate. But when I finally calmed down, I realized that if I pulled my shirt out of my pants — this was church, so of course it was tucked in — but if I pulled it out of my pants, it would hang down far enough that I could go back to my seat, and you wouldn't be able to see that my pants were only half zipped."

Whit sat back and gave a sad shake of his head.

"That plan was among the least effective plans I've ever made in my life. I got my shirt out, looked in the mirror to make sure you couldn't see the top of my pants, and hurried out the door. But I'd only made it a couple of steps before…"

Rileigh realized where the story was going and put her hands over her mouth.

"Oh *no.*"

"You got it. Only half zipped, my pants wouldn't stay up. I was a skinny little dude, and because I was shaky and jerky, it was like I was shaking them off. And the next thing I knew, I was standing in the church vestibule with my pants around my ankles, more mortified than any twelve-year-old boy has ever been in all of human history."

"I'm so sorry."

"So was Jillian."

"Jillian?"

"She came out of the sanctuary then to go to the ladies' room and spotted me there. I wanted to die. My entire body, from the top of my head to the bottoms of my feet, was bright red. She came over to me. She and put her hand on my shoulder, but I wouldn't, I *couldn't* look at her.

"'It's okay,'" she said. "'I can help you fix it.'"

"Then she got down on her knees and went to work on the zipper of my pants. She yanked and jerked, hurrying before somebody else came out of the sanctuary. She tried to joke about it, said things like, 'You sure stuck this thing in here tight' and 'You're stronger than you look.'

"Finally, she pulled it free. She pulled my pants back up around my waist, tucked my shirt in, zipped me up, and fastened the button."

"Thank god nobody else came out of the sanctuary."

"That's not the end of the story. She stood there for a moment with her hands on my shoulders and spoke very quietly to me. I know exactly what she said, because I repeated it to myself over and over.

"She said, 'I know you're embarrassed. You think you look like a fool. But that's not what I see when I look at you. I've never known anybody in my life as brave as you are. Every morning, you get up and face a life that's harder in every way than everybody else's. But you're so determined, you gut it out. If I were in your place, I couldn't do it — I'd whine and complain and feel sorry for myself. But you just keep going — with a smile. Please believe me — what just happened hasn't made me think less of you. I'm just proud to be your friend.'"

Whit paused again, "And then she kissed me. Not on the forehead, platonically, or on the cheek. She really *kissed* me. Then she left me standing there and went into the ladies' room."

Rileigh was so staggered by the story she didn't know what to say.

"When Jillian disappeared… we'd been invited to the wedding, of course. I was going in my very best dress suit

— in mourning. I'd screwed myself up to watch the woman I loved marry another man. But then she didn't. Then she was gone. And at first, I was glad. I thought she'd run out on him. That maybe she didn't love him and that all of my fantasies about one day being together were possible." He shook his head. "But then she didn't come back. And after a while, I settled into the reality that she was gone from my life." He looked Rileigh in the eye. "It took me *years* to get over it and move on."

"When I heard a couple of months ago that Jillian had come home, I was elated. I took my wife and kids out to dinner, told Marian that it was a celebration dinner dedicated to Jillian Bishop, who had been a real, true friend of mine when I was a little boy."

Then Whit smiled. "You asked me what time it was, and I told you how to build a watch. So, how is Jillian?"

"She's in really big trouble, and that's what lunch is about. Because I'm going to ask you to help her get out of it."

So she told him about where Jillian had been all the years she'd been gone and watched his face do what everyone's faces did when they heard that horror. And then she described what had happened in the last week, about the appearance of Jillian's daughter and what Big John and Sundeep Singh had seen and heard.

Whit looked horrified.

"The truth in long johns with the butt flap down is that we'll catch *this* hit squad and stop them — jail them, or"— she only paused for a beat—"kill them. But when we do, Omar will just send out another one… and another one after that."

"How will she ever be able to live a life?"

"She won't. The monster who *owned* her won't stop until Jillian Bishop is dead."

Whit shook his head. Then Rileigh smiled. "And that's where you come in."

He looked at her quizzically, and then she saw something like understanding begin to dawn on him as he smiled.

Chapter Thirty-Six

ON THEIR SECOND DAY IN JEREMIAH JOHNSON'S CABIN, everyone was a little more settled in, had something of a routine. Mama had worked like a beaver building a dam. She put all the supplies away, figured out what cooking utensils the mountain man had had and what he hadn't, and how she would make do with what was there.

Long about noon, Mama proposed to make rabbit stew or squirrel stew for dinner that night.

"So which one of them little rodents is you most likely to find out in the woods around here? I could make a stew with both of them, but their meats kind of clash, you know what I mean?"

"You want me to go rabbit hunting?" Jillian said, incredulous.

"Why not? 'Cause we're hiding out here? Ain't no neighbors for miles in every direction, and besides, you hear random gunshots in the woods all the time. A little bit of gunfire ain't going to tell people where we are."

"But I didn't bring my .22."

"Well, you got that pistol on your side. You can shoot one with that, can't you?"

"Mama, a Ruger .38 revolver isn't accurate for more than twenty feet. It's not exactly a weapon that you use to go hunting with."

Mama put both her hands on her hips.

"Why Jillian Bishop, ain't you got the make-do gene? You know, doing the best with what you got? Surely to God I passed that down to you. Now you take that pistol and go on out there and get me some rabbits or squirrels with it."

Jillian looked at David, who shrugged his shoulders, reluctant to take either side in this particular dispute. And then she glanced at Micky, who was smiling broadly.

"Can you actually go out into the woods and shoot a squirrel or a rabbit?" Micky asked. "I'm sure Aunt Rileigh could. But can you?"

Jillian explained that indeed she could go out in the woods with the pistol and see what she could bag. She said it fast enough to cover for the fact that she almost choked when Micky said "Aunt Rileigh."

Micky spent the afternoon outside on the porch. And then Jillian noticed that she'd gotten down off the porch and was digging around in the garden. She must like flowers, and indeed, that garden was in desperate need of somebody doing something for it. Jeremiah Johnson had obviously tried at some point to make the place a little prettier outside by planting flowers. But he hadn't been the kind of man who gave leafy creatures the time and attention they needed to thrive. Translate that: he pretty much ignored it, so it was overgrown up with weeds.

Mama came to stand beside Jillian on the porch as she watched Micky in the garden.

"I hope she doesn't end up pulling out the wrong thing, flowers instead of weeds," Jillian said.

"You know the difference between a weed and a flower, don't you?" Mama asked.

"Well, yeah, but I'm sure you're about to tell me a definition I'm not expecting."

"I don't know about the expecting part, it's just the truth. A weed ain't nothing but a plant you didn't want to be there. If you decide you want it to be there and you plant it or you let it grow on purpose, then it ain't no weed. So I suppose there's no way she could pull up weeds, because Jeremiah Johnson didn't appear to decide what was weeds and what wasn't."

Then Jillian heard Micky make an odd sound. A kind of squealing sound. Not upset, just odd. She leaned over to get a better look and Micky seemed as happy as she could be — *giggling* as a matter of fact. Mama noticed it too.

"That there's strange," Mama said.

Jillian left Mama's side and went down the steps and around to the side of the house where the garden grew. As she approached, she watched carefully what her daughter was doing. It took her a moment to figure it out and then she stopped and stood very still. Micky appeared to be making mud pies — and having a wonderful time doing it. She'd found a muddy place in the garden and had mixed up a pile of dirt with it. She now had mud all over her hands, on the front of her t-shirt and jeans, and was singing some silly song that Jillian couldn't quite catch the words to as she formed mud into flat pancake-like things and patted them on a rock.

"And we'll have this one for supper tonight," Micky said and giggled again. "It's a pancake. I like pancakes."

Jillian didn't know what to think, just stood watching in surprised confusion. Micky continued to play in the mud as happily and with as much abandon as a little kid. She'd splat her hand into it, and when the mud splashed up into her face and on her shirt, she giggled loudly.

Jillian glanced back over her shoulder to see Mama standing at the porch railing, watching the same thing she was watching with the same look of surprise and confusion on her face. More than confusion. Mama had a look that was more like alarm.

Jillian admitted to herself then that there had to be something wrong with an eighteen-year-old girl who played in the mud like a four-year-old.

Like a four-year-old. Like her sister, Alyssa, who she talked about yesterday, who was four years old when she died. Jillian felt a sensation like cold water dribbling down her back, melting ice, each drip falling slowly from one vertebra to the next.

Then David came out on the back porch and accidentally slammed the door with a bang. Micky looked up at the sound and saw Mama standing there. She didn't notice Jillian standing back behind her in the shade, but suddenly her whole demeanor changed. The abandon was gone. Even her posture changed. She sat up straighter, shook her head, looked down at her shirt with something that was close to surprise, and began to wipe her fingers on her pants leg to clean the mud off them. Jillian turned then and hurried back to the steps and up onto the porch because she didn't want Micky to know she'd been watching. And she didn't know why she didn't want Micky to know. She just didn't.

Micky came up onto the porch shortly, looking down at her jeans and her shirt, unaware that there was mud on her face too.

"Good morning." She smiled and looked embarrassed. "I got carried away digging the weeds, made a mess of my clothes, and given that I don't have that many here, that's a problem." She smiled wider. "I'm going to go in and see if I can clean this off."

And then she went slowly into the house, walking with care because of the healing wounds that still had bandages on them. Muddy bandages now. She'd seemed unaware of the bandages or the wounds when she'd been in the garden.

Jillian caught Mama's eye but Mama shook her head so Jillian closed her mouth, and they let it go.

It was a while before Micky emerged from the bedroom. She'd obviously taken a shower because they'd heard her squeal when the water touched her skin. She must have washed her clothes out in the sink and left them to hang to dry in the bathroom and put on the only change of clothes she had brought with her.

"Sorry about the squeal," she said when she came into the living room drying her hair with a towel. "It probably registered on the Richter scale like a 5.0 earthquake. I have never felt colder water in my life."

They all set the table for dinner. Mama'd wanted an early dinner so Jillian could go out in the evening when the rabbits would be plentiful in the meadow near the house and see if she could bag a few of them. But gratefully, the rabbit stew plan dropped completely out of Mama's head. Dinner was now a canned ham that Rileigh had bought and Mama had baked in the oven with all the fixings she always put on everything, along with baked sweet potatoes.

Mama sent Jillian out to the outdoor refrigerator to get the butter so they could slather it on their sweet potatoes. Jillian opened the back door and came back just in time to see Micky accidentally hit the pitcher of lemonade with her elbow and knock it off the table. She jerked back, and then to everyone's utter surprise, she totally lost her temper.

"Damn it, why'd you put that thing right on the edge of the table just begging for somebody to hit it and knock it off?" she said to Mama, who stared at her in gap-jawed surprise. "You think I'm going to clean up that mess? Hell no, I'm not. It wasn't my fault. If you'd put the damn pitcher in the middle of the table where it belonged, it wouldn't have got knocked off in the first place."

It was an angry tirade, but more disturbing than that was the look on her face. Pure rage way beyond what anybody would have expressed for the mere sin of knocking over a pitcher of lemonade.

Micky leaned over, picked up the pitcher off the floor, and slammed it down on the table, then turned and stormed into her room, slamming the door behind her.

Jillian, David, and Mama stood speechless in her wake. Jillian opened her mouth to say something when the door to Micky's room suddenly opened again and she appeared in it with a small smile on her face and a towel that she'd gotten out of the bathroom.

"We can use this to sop up the lemonade," she said as she crossed the room toward the spill. "The problem's going to be that it's got sugar in it and the floor is going to be sticky, so we'll have to wash it over and over. I'm really sorry."

Then Micky got down on her hands and knees and began to clean up the mess.

Again the others looked at each other in confusion, but Jillian was way more than confused now. She was afraid. Clearly there was something wrong with Micky, very wrong, but given what she'd said about how she'd grown up, what her childhood was like, why would that be surprising? How could she possibly have endured what she'd endured as a child and come out of it totally unscathed as an absolutely normal human being? No, it would be abnormal to have gone through what she did and *not* to have responded to it in some way. But clearly Michaela Hollis was seriously disturbed. Jillian sighed inwardly, twin emotions grappling with each other for dominance.

The first emotion was something like gratitude, that she was here to be in Micky's life, to be her mama through the difficulties she was facing, that Micky had a family now who could support her while she healed from all the emotional wounds she'd received over the years.

The contradictory emotion was despair. Not only did Jillian now have a daughter for whom she was at least morally, if not legally, responsible, she had a daughter who had emotional problems that absolutely had to be addressed. And what was Jillian supposed to do about that?

Chapter Thirty-Seven

"HOLY SHIT, THEY'RE COMING UP THE DRIVEWAY!"

Rileigh's voice on the phone at Mitch's ear was incredulous. It was shortly after sunset on Thursday, and they had been expecting the two Middle Eastern hitmen to approach from the woods, as the South Americans had done when they'd come looking for FBI Agent Lamar Devereaux. From the front corner windows on the second floor of Mama's house, you could see the front yard, the side yard, all of the woods on the side of the house, and into the backyard. The same was true from the window on the back corner of the house; you could see the whole backyard with its chicken coop, the garage, the storage building, and around toward the front of the house.

Mitch and Rileigh had been stationed there for hours, keeping their cell phones plugged in so they could chat while they watched for death to come sneaking up on them from the woods. They slept in four-hour shifts, walking a post from the front windows to the back and then to the front again, prepared for any line of attack.

The one thing they had not expected, however, was

that the two men would drive up the driveway and park in front of the gate.

"How do we play this?" Rileigh asked.

"You go down and act normal. I'll be waiting in the wings. Just don't invite them in."

Rileigh hurried downstairs where the television had been left on and sat down on the couch in the living room as if she'd been watching it. She heard two car doors slam, waited, and finally heard a knock at the door. The front door was closed, as was the screen door in front of it, with the latch fastened, which it never was. She opened the door to find two men standing there. The one on the right was short, stocky, with a broad face and a flat nose. The one on the left was tall and lean, well-muscled in a runner's kind of way beneath an impeccable Versace suit and tie, as if that wouldn't make them stick out in Black Bear Forge, Tennessee. But apparently, hiding and stealth were not their methods of choice.

She opened the front door, and the man on the left smiled.

"I'm looking for Lily Bishop." His wasn't a heavy Arab accent, but Rileigh recognized it anyway.

"What do you want my mother for?"

"I need to speak with her, please."

Rileigh allowed herself to display reasonable alarm.

"Well, I'm sorry, she's upstairs in bed. She's not feeling well. You can talk to me about whatever you need to talk to her about."

The two men shared a glance and then, with the speed of a striking rattler, the man on the left pulled a Glock out of a shoulder holster and pointed it at her. She let out a squeak of surprise and fear.

"Fine, I'll ask you what I want to ask your mother, and

if you don't give me the information I need, we'll talk to her. But let's go inside."

Rileigh backed up, shaking her head, and made no motion to open the door. The man reached out his free hand to push the screen inward and saw that it was latched, so he just banged it hard, snapping the latch off the door frame and sending it pinging across the porch.

Breaking and entering — check, Rileigh thought. Using a firearm in the commission of a felony — check.

Rileigh continued to back away from the man holding a pistol on her, moving across the entryway and into the living room. The taller man looked to be more Egyptian, perhaps Saudi Arabian or United Arab Emirates. The second man had drawn a gun by that time, both of them pointed at Rileigh.

"Let's go get your mother," he said. "We have some questions we need to ask her."

"Please don't disturb her. She has a migraine."

The short, stocky man was faster than Rileigh would have expected. In a sudden motion, he reached out and slapped Rileigh across the face — *hard.* Any other woman would have gone down, but Rileigh cried out in pain and staggered back against the wall.

"Let's try this again," said the taller man. "We want to talk to Lily Bishop. We're looking for *Jillian* Bishop. Do you understand me?"

"Jillian Bishop," Rileigh said. "That's my sister."

Rileigh shot her eyes toward the stairs as a tell and then said, "I don't know where Jillian is. We — she doesn't live here. We haven't seen Jillian in years."

"We can do this the easy way, or we can do it the hard way," said the man who had slapped her. "Now, I'm going to tell you one more time: take us to your mother so you can both tell me where to find your sister."

"Please, no," Rileigh began. The man lifted the pistol in the air, obviously intent on slamming it into Rileigh's face, but he didn't get the chance.

"Drop your weapons." Mitch's voice was commanding and came from behind them, where he had stepped out of the coat closet. The men froze.

"Drop your weapons, *now!*"

They remained still but turned their heads and saw Mitch, feet apart, hands in a two-hand grip on his pistol, the sheriff's badge on his uniform shining.

"Last chance," Mitch said.

The men dropped their guns and put their hands up behind their heads and laced their fingers. Mitch hadn't told them to do that. It was clear this wasn't their first rodeo.

Mitch called out to her. "Rileigh, come here."

She inched off the wall, cut a wide arc around the two men, and gathered up the weapons they had dropped.

"Now, both of you, down on your knees," Mitch said. The men obediently got down on their knees, keeping their fingers laced behind their heads. Rileigh set their pistols on the armoire, then went around to the back of the first man, the tall one, grabbed his left hand and yanked it behind him. He didn't cry out in pain, but she pushed it up hard enough that he felt it, and she snapped a handcuff on his wrist, pulled his right hand behind him, and snapped the other cuff on it. She went to Mitch, pulled his cuffs off his belt, and went to the second man, the one who had slapped her, and stood behind him, performing the same procedure, pushing his arm up behind his back so far he grunted but didn't cry out. Then she stepped back.

"On the floor now, on your faces," Mitch said. The men looked at him in surprise. On their knees with no use of their hands, there was no easy way to get down on the floor on their faces, which, of course, was how Mitch had planned it. Rileigh moved behind the man who had slapped her, put her foot into his back, and shoved as hard as she could, and he face-planted on the hardwood floor. Then she did the same thing with the second one, who didn't smash his face as hard because he was a little more prepared than the first man had been.

"Check them for ID."

Rileigh felt in the hip pocket of the first man, the tall, slender one, and pulled out a wallet and a passport from the United Arab Emirates.

"Mustapha Kumar," she read off the passport.

Searching the pockets of the second man, she retrieved a wallet and a Yemeni passport made out to Saleh El-Qadhafi.

"Oh, goody," Mitch said. "I was hoping Omar wouldn't hire local talent, that you'd be foreign bastards."

Then Rileigh backed away from the men and turned to Mitch.

"I'm going to see about Mom and Jillian and Michaela," she said in a frightened, freaky woman voice. "I know they heard this, they had to."

She turned and ran up the stairs, and Mitch stood staring down at the two men, who had said not a word.

"You guys are going to be the guests of the county for a while."

Mitch heard something that might have been a grunt of laughter from one of them, then Rileigh came thundering down the stairs, clearly upset.

"Oh, Mitch, they're hysterical. Michaela won't come out of the bathroom. She's locked herself in there. She's terrified. And Jillian just sat down on the bed and started rocking back and forth, shaking her head and crying, no, no, no." Rileigh paused and drew a breath. "And Mama, oh God, Mitch, I've never seen Mama like that."

She turned her gaze on the men on the floor, neither of them looking at her. "You bastards!" she cried. Without warning, she stepped to the broad-faced man who'd slapped her and kicked him as hard as she could in the leg. "Son of a bitch!"

"Call it in," Mitch said. "Let's get these bastards out of here as fast as we can."

Rileigh picked up her cell phone, called the sheriff's office, and said, "This is Rileigh Bishop. Intruders at the home of Lily Bishop, 916 Bent Twig Road."

Mitch called out so that he could be heard over her phone, "Unit one here, dispatch units two and three, code 27, lights and sirens."

Rileigh terminated the call and then told Mitch, "I need to go back upstairs and see to Mama and the others." She turned and ran back up the stairs. Mitch stood over them, as silent as a statue. The men said nothing.

As soon as Rileigh heard the sirens, she came back down the stairs.

"I had to give Mama two of her pills to calm her down, and I still can't get Michaela out of the bathroom. I've never seen them so scared."

"They should be scared," spoke the voice of the tall, thin man. Mitch kicked him hard in the side. He didn't grunt, though, made no sound at all. Deputies Mullins, Rawlings, and Crawford had responded to Mitch's call; their cruisers came flying up the driveway. They parked beside Mitch's cruiser and rushed in, weapons drawn.

"You can stand down," Mitch said. "Now get these bastards out of this house."

Mitch grabbed the man he had kicked roughly and yanked him upright; the man sneered at him but said nothing. Rawlings grabbed the other man. Mitch shoved the first one at Deputy Mullins, and the two deputies escorted the men out to their cruisers.

"Put them in county lockup," Mitch said. "Charges are assault and battery, breaking and entering, use of a firearm in the commission of a felony, and terroristic threatening and ... I'll think of more later."

Rileigh saw that Mitch didn't tell the deputies that the men would spend more than the usual amount of time in the Black Bear Forge's small jail — because the county prosecutor had agreed to "misplace their paperwork" for twenty-four hours, which would bump up against the weekend. They wouldn't get their "day in court" until Monday morning, and at that time the charges would be dropped.

What he did tell the deputies was, "Collect their cell phones and make sure you leave them turned on. I want their phones dead when they get them back, unusable until they charge them."

As soon as the men were outside, safely in the cruisers, and the deputies drove away, Rileigh slumped against Mitch.

"So, how was I?" she asked.

"I was convinced. I totally believed that Jillian and Mama and Michaela were upstairs, cowering under the beds. I don't know why they wouldn't have been."

"Let's hope so."

Chapter Thirty-Eight

First thing Friday morning, Rileigh called Whit Nash and told him the game clock had started ticking.

"They'll be stuck in jail until Monday," she said.

Whit told her that he'd just been notified that Thelma Watson had died.

"She was my second-grade teacher," he said.

Rileigh's face broke into a huge smile. She wasn't glad Thelma was dead, of course. She had liked the old woman, but still … it was very convenient. She told Whit she'd swing by his office later for a picture.

Then Rileigh dressed and drove out to Jeremiah Johnson's cabin to give the family the news about capturing the Arabs, and to explain "the plan" to her sister and niece and describe the role they would have to play if it was going to work. Thank God, Mama had gotten a pass.

"Did you bring them things I asked you to bring?" Mama asked as soon as she saw her. "Because I done got another list that's longer than that one. Do you believe I forgot my Polident? How am I s'posed to keep my dentures from flopping around in my mouth without Polident?"

Jillian came out on the porch then to stand beside Mama. Micky was nowhere to be seen.

Rileigh reached back into the car and pulled out a sack.

"Not just what you asked for, Mama. I am a Greek bearing gifts."

"What's that supposed to mean?"

"You know the Greeks … never mind."

Rileigh walked up to the house, set the sack down on the porch, and opened it so Mama could look inside.

"Steaks!" she cried. "We can grill steaks for dinner tomorrow night. That's wonderful. Everybody's so tired of bacon and eggs and bologna sandwiches, they're 'bout ready to fire the cook."

It had only been two days.

"I think they'll survive."

Mama hurried into the house with the sack. Jillian lingered on the porch, her eyes penetrating, asking the question she hadn't yet formed into words. Rileigh saved her the trouble.

"We got them," she said. Jillian's hands flew to her mouth.

"You caught them? Are you all right?"

"We're fine. The bastards drove up to the front porch and knocked on the front door." She shook her head. "They won't be that careless next time."

She watched the joy that had been on Jillian's face drain away. "Soon as we can get Mama busy with something else, you and I and Micky need to talk."

Rileigh had brought the makings of a big salad — red and yellow peppers, cucumbers, radishes, lettuce, onions and carrots. The girls left Mama to cut up all the vegetables while they went out and sat on the porch with David.

"Okay, tell me all about it," Jillian said.

Micky had emerged like a rabbit from a hole out of her bedroom when she heard Rileigh's voice and was full of questions. But Rileigh'd put her off, saying she'd explain it all to everybody at the same time.

"We caught the men who asked Big John how to find Mama's house, the ones Sundeep saw in the convenience store the other day."

"You caught them!" Micky said, wide-eyed.

"If you can believe it, they were so arrogant that they came waltzing up to the front door. And here Mitch and I had been standing watch at the windows for two days to keep them from sneaking up on us."

"So it's over?" Micky said.

Rileigh shook her head. "No, it's far from over. In fact, it's just getting started."

"But you caught them, arrested them. They're going to jail, aren't they?"

"We've got some decent charges to hold them for a little while. Breaking and entering. Use of a firearm in the commission of a felony. Assault with a deadly weapon."

"Assault?" David was alarmed.

Rileigh shook her head. "No biggie. One of them slapped me."

He ground his teeth and looked at Jillian. "I'm surprised they didn't do worse."

"If they're in jail, can we go home now?" Jillian asked.

"Nobody's going anywhere until it's all over — and it isn't, not yet. Besides, they weren't the only threat out there, remember."

"Uncle Dan," Micky said quietly.

"Tell us the story," David pressed. "What happened?"

So Rileigh described how the men came up to the front porch, broke the latch on the screen, and forced their way in at gunpoint. And that one of them had hit Rileigh before Mitch leapt out to take their guns away and arrest them.

Micky looked from Jillian to Rileigh and back to Jillian. "Why aren't you happy? What am I not getting here? It's over, isn't it? They're going to jail?"

"They're going to be guests of the county for the weekend, depriving them of their constitutional rights to a phone call and an attorney until Monday morning. After that, they'll be free, all charges dropped."

Micky was horror struck. "Free? You mean they'll get out?"

"Of course they will. You can't keep criminals locked up these days for long enough to fill out the paperwork," David sneered.

"It doesn't matter, sweetheart," Rileigh said. "It went down just as we expected it would. Easier, actually, than we were afraid it might be. This is all part of a larger plan."

"Yeah, about that plan," Jillian said and looked piercingly at Rileigh. "When are you going to tell us what that plan is?"

"Right now. But first … I know you understand this, but let's just get it out there. Locking those guys up isn't the end of it by any stretch. Even if we'd shot them dead and buried their bodies back in a hollow somewhere, eventually Omar'd send another hit squad. And another. And another."

"Micky and I are threats to him," Jillian said. "He'll never give up as long as we're alive."

Micky looked like someone had slapped her, though it wasn't the first time they'd had this discussion. Then she began to cry softly. Jillian was seated beside her and reached out to take her hand, but Micky shook her head and just continued to cry. So the rest of them sat in an awkward silence until she'd cried herself out.

"We have a plan to make sure this is the last hit squad that's ever sent to look for Jillian Bishop and Michaela Hollis," Rileigh continued. Micky's eyes grew huge. "But we won't be able to pull it off unless everybody here plays a part and plays it perfectly. Do you understand me?"

The others looked around and nodded.

"What I'm about to outline isn't something '*I hope you'll be willing to help me with.*' It's much bigger and more important than that. This plan is the only possible way to ensure that you don't have to spend the rest of your life on the run. We all have to do what we're assigned to do."

"But how?" Micky began.

"Just hush and hear me out."

When she was finished describing what she and Mitch had decided to do, all three of the people seated on the porch with her were staring at her, bug-eyed.

"You can't be serious," Jillian said.

"Totally serious. You have to do this. I know it's awful, but you have to do it."

She looked at Micky. The girl was shaking her head, a horrified look on her face. "I can't."

Rileigh'd been afraid of this.

Omar had sent the hit squad to eliminate Micky after Al-Saud's son sent his father a picture of the DNA results. They'd come to Black Bear Forge looking for Lily Bishop, knowing Micky would hook up with her family and they'd all be in one spot.

"You didn't have to upload a photograph to send in your DNA, did you?"

Micky didn't answer, just shook her head and stared at Rileigh with huge eyes.

Perhaps the Arabs had gone looking for a driver's license photo of Micky, but there wasn't one. She had no passport.

"The Arabs know where you're from, though," Rileigh said. *Which is more than we know*, but she didn't say that. "Maybe they went to your house, got a picture of you from your parents."

Micky's face went totally white at that suggestion. "No. My parents wouldn't have talked to them."

"These people don't take no for an answer. If they went to your parents, they got whatever they wanted from them."

"They couldn't because … they couldn't have found my parents." The protest had all the earmarks of an excuse made up on the fly.

"And why is that?"

"Because they … they have a motor home, and they tour around the country in it. And nobody ever knows exactly where they are. They don't have a schedule, and they just go wherever they feel like going. They would be hard to find if somebody went looking for them."

Rileigh let it go at that. But Micky threw up roadblocks at every encounter and was not as helpful as someone ought to be to the people trying to keep her alive. Rileigh didn't believe that her parents were out roaming around somewhere in a motor home. That's what Micky wanted her to believe, but why?

There'd been a newspaper story about the murder in the bus station, and a photographer had snapped a picture of Micky being loaded into the ambulance. But it wasn't a very clear picture, and the Arabs likely hadn't even connected the person they were looking for to the stabbing. But who knew?

"What about you, Jillian? Does Omar have pictures of you?"

"Lots of them." That's all she said.

So it seemed that the hit squad *probably* only had a description of Micky — no photos.

Micky was shaking her head back and forth.

"I can't do what you ask," she said. "I *can't.*"

"If this plan doesn't work, you're going to be hunted for the rest of your life. Always waiting for someone to jump out of the darkness at you — tomorrow, next week, next year, on your wedding day. Eventually, they'll catch you and slit your throat."

Rileigh hadn't meant to sound so harsh and was surprised that her words sparked what looked like anger in Micky's eyes. Just a flash and it was gone. But Micky said nothing, just ground her teeth, and then she seemed to fold in on herself.

"I can't. I'm sorry … *no.* I want to go lie down." Her voice was timid and weak as she got to her feet and moved slowly back into the house, leaving Rileigh and David and Jillian on the porch.

As soon as she was out of earshot, Jillian turned to Rileigh.

"How will you do it without her?"

"We'll figure out something. It's better not to use her at all than for her to blow the whole thing. If she's not stable enough to do this, maybe that's for the best."

"We've had some odd encounters with Micky in the last couple of days," Jillian said.

"Really? Tell me."

Jillian told Rileigh about the serene morning when she actually thought they were making progress at getting to know each other. Micky had told her about Alyssa and described how much the little girl had meant to her.

"She called the child Lissy. She adored her."

Jillian paused, and David said, "But then there's everything else. Tell her about the flower garden."

So Jillian described watching Micky play in the mud in the flower garden, as childlike as a four-year-old. "That's how old Alyssa was when she … died."

Then Jillian told Rileigh about Micky flying into a fit of rage over spilling the lemonade.

"It's obvious to me that Micky has serious problems," Jillian said. "That kind of mood swing doesn't happen to normal people. But then, think about it. Why would she be normal? How could she be if she grew up in a home where every day was filled with abuse?"

Rileigh nodded sadly.

"I'm wondering," Jillian continued, "what do you think about seeing if Dr. Al-Masri would talk to her? Maybe she could help her."

"Dr. Al-Masri agreed to see you, to take you on as a patient when she wasn't taking any new patients, as a favor to me. Her schedule was packed. I can't ask her to see someone else. But maybe I could talk to her, see if she'd be willing to see Micky to evaluate her, to figure out what kind of counseling she needs. And then we'll go find somebody to provide it."

Jillian nodded.

"That sounds like a plan." She stopped, then simply repeated the word out loud. "Plan."

RILEIGH PICKED up the photograph at Whit's office as she'd promised and went directly to Stop The Presses, located between Adrien's Authentic Hand-Made Jewelry and Rogers Brothers Barbecue, which boasted, "If it's bad barbecue, it ain't R's."

Stop The Presses offered tourists a bogus front page of the Gatlinburg News-Journal with pictures, headlines, and stories about whatever they'd like. Samples were displayed on all the walls. One showed a frowning tourist beneath a banner front page headline: "Police Arrest Serial Killer Joe Jones." Next to it was a newspaper with a photo of the same tourist, grinning this time, beneath the headline: "Joe Jones Named Sexiest Man Alive." Newspapers displayed winners of the Master's Golf Tournament, Best Actress Oscars, Olympic gold medals and million-dollar lottery tickets.

Rileigh went from Stop The Presses to Henderson's Floral to order flowers. Lots of flowers.

Chapter Thirty-Nine

RILEIGH SLEPT IN ON SATURDAY MORNING, TRYING TO catch up on the sleep she'd missed alternating guard duty with Mitch. When she got up, she fixed herself a cup of coffee and then called Dr. Al-Masri on her private cell phone number.

"Hello, Rileigh, how are you?"

"I'm good, Dr. Al-Masri."

"Aaliyah."

"I would say I can't complain, *Aaliyah*, but I can complain and I would complain if you had the time to hear it, but you don't. Listen, I have an issue."

"Is something wrong with Jillian? She's been doing so well."

"Nope, it's not Jillian. The issue is Jillian's daughter."

"Daughter?"

"I wondered if she told you about it."

"Okay, I'm sitting down, fill me in."

Rileigh described what had happened in the past week, how it came to be revealed that Jillian had had a baby when she was in the United Arab Emirates, a little girl, the daughter of a very rich Arab merchant, and that the baby had been taken away from her and sold on the black market.

"All right," Dr. Al-Masri said, "I didn't say this and you didn't hear it, but I've never had a patient whose life had been shattered like Jillian's for three decades."

Then Rileigh talked about how Mama had wanted to find her past lives by posting her DNA and how a girl in California named Michaela Hollis had also posted her DNA and was a match.

"So she came here to find Lily, her grandmother, and her mother, Jillian," Dr. Al-Masri said. "How did Jillian take that?"

"If that had been all she'd had to deal with, she'd have been fine … but it wasn't." Rileigh shook her head. "You ain't heard nuthin' yet. The girl also found a match to her father's DNA."

"The Arab?"

"Right. The students in an anthropology class at Stanford University posted their DNA on the website, and apparently the father's son was in that class."

"What happened?"

"Michaela went there, totally innocently, thought he'd posted his DNA because he was also looking for his family. Not! He had a total meltdown, called her a gold digger trying to rip off his family. She saw him call somebody and tell them the whole story — up to and including the part about how she had matched to Lily Bishop in Black Bear Forge, Tennessee."

"Is this going where I'm afraid it's going?"

"It is indeed. Michaela was on her way here to Black Bear Forge when she was the victim of a stabbing."

"They found her that fast?"

"No, it didn't have anything to do with Jillian. Remember, Michaela's parents bought her on the back market, and she grew up in a horribly abusive household — she ran away, and Mitch and I believe that's what the stabbing was about."

"I'm sensing there's even more awful to this story."

"Yup. We found out that two armed Arab men were in town asking about Lily Bishop. Omar — that's Jillian's, uh…"

"You don't have to explain. I know who he is."

"Omar wants to get rid of Michaela and Jillian, and he will stop at nothing to do that."

"What did you do?"

"Right now, Jillian, Michaela, Mama, and David Hicks are in hiding in a mountain cabin, while Mitch and I take care of the threat from the Arabs — which we did last night. We captured them breaking into Mama's house."

"So they're in jail?"

Rileigh nodded.

"Oh, thank God."

"It's not that simple. They'll get out on bail, and even if we manage to stop these two, Omar will just send more."

"So you're saying that Jillian and her daughter are going to be on the run for the rest of their lives?"

"Not if I can help it. Mitch and I have a plan — but that's a whole other story, and it's way too long to explain. But Jillian isn't the reason I called you."

"Why did you call me?"

" Jillian told me yesterday that Michaela has displayed some really bizarre behavior."

"Such as?"

Rileigh described how she had played in the mud like a little girl, then exploded in a rage over knocking over a pitcher of lemonade.

"Her mood swings are — strange. Unhealthy. That's what I wanted to talk to you about."

Before Dr. Al-Masri could say anything, Rileigh rushed on. "I'm not about to ask if you'd take Michaela on as a patient, but I was wondering if perhaps you could evaluate her and tell us what kind of psychotherapy we should get for her."

"The symptoms you've described could be half a dozen different disorders, all of them common to abuse victims and prisoners of war. I'd need to spend some time with her to get an idea of where her abuse has most damaged her."

"Would you be willing to do that?"

"Of course I would, Rileigh. I'd be glad to."

"'Thank' and 'you' are really pitiful words to describe how grateful I am for all you've done for me and my family. But they're all I've got, so thank you."

"If they're all you've got, save them for somebody else. I'm happy to do it."

"You're the best. I'll talk to Jillian and Micky, then give you a call and we'll set something up."

"Just so you know, I'm going to be in the Gatlinburg office on Monday. I don't know how that might work with your schedule, but if you wanted to bring her by late afternoon after I finish with my last patient, I'd be glad to talk to her then. If that doesn't work, I'll work her in some other time."

"Oh, thank you so much."

"I thought you were going to save that for somebody else."

"I changed my mind."

Rileigh hung up and smiled, thinking to herself that Dr. Aaliyah Al-Masri was one of the most genuinely caring people she had ever met, and maybe she'd be able to help them find help for Micky. She had certainly done something close to a miraculous job with Jillian.

Speaking of Jillian, Rileigh needed to tell Jillian about her conversation with Aaliyah.

It would need to be a quick trip to Jeremiah Johnson's house. Rileigh still had half a dozen items on her to do list to pull off the plan she and Mitch had hatched. She came around a corner on the main road and saw a white Jetta pulled over on the side of the road about fifty yards before the turnoff to Jeremiah Johnson's house. She looked around to see who the car might belong to and saw no one. The car made her uneasy, but she pushed her concern out of her mind. Just getting off the main road here wouldn't lead you to Jeremiah Johnson's house. It wasn't exactly at the end of a yellow brick road.

Rileigh found Jillian on the front porch, shelling the black-eyed peas Rileigh'd gotten at Buy Low.

"Wish I could stay for supper," she said, looking at the peas, but the grand plan still had all manner of pieces parts to assemble, and she needed to get back to town .

"I talked to Aaliyah a little while ago and told her about Micky."

Jillian looked up expectantly.

"I wasn't expecting a diagnosis — she said there are several different disorders that might result in that kind of behavior."

The hopeful look went out of Jillian's eyes.

"But she did say she'd be glad to talk to Micky, do an assessment, and help us figure out what treatment she needs."

Jillian nodded. "I'm not surprised she was willing to help." She smiled. "I told her once that she had a heart of gold and she said, 'so does a poached egg.'"

"She said she'd be in the Gatlinburg office on Monday

and could see Micky late that afternoon if we could swing it."

Jillian stopped shelling the peas and looked into Rileigh's eyes.

"It'll all be over by then, won't it?" she said softly.

Rileigh nodded. "Everything we have control of, yes. By then, it'll be a done deal."

Rileigh almost added, *Or not.* But she didn't. It *would* be a done deal. The plan *would* work. It had to.

Chapter Forty

JILLIAN GOT UP EARLY SATURDAY MORNING. MAMA WAS already up, of course, as was David. He looked exhausted, and she suspected that his proclamation that "this couch is as comfortable as my bed" was a pile of the warm sticky substance you find on the south side of a horse going north. Or maybe he was worn out from keeping watch, from not sleeping on purpose. Whichever it was, she was grateful. She took in his unshaven face, the dark circles under his eyes, and his bedhead, and she loved him so much at that moment that she could barely catch her breath. She couldn't lose David. Not now, not after finding him again after all these years. No matter how bizarre she thought Rileigh's plan was, Jillian would do whatever was asked of her. She owed David that, owed the two of them a chance for a life together.

About mid-morning, she went out onto the front porch to shell black-eyed peas and Rileigh paid a brief visit to tell her that Dr. Al-Masri had agreed to evaluate Micky and recommend a plan of treatment for her. She told David what Rileigh said, and they decided to wait until after dinner to talk to Micky about it. She was still upset over Rileigh's plan, and there was no sense piling on if they didn't have to.

Mama set about grilling the steaks that Rileigh had brought. It wasn't like Jeremiah Johnson had a barbecue grill, no apron hanging from a hook in the kitchen that said May The Forks Be With or An Apron is Just a Cape on Backwards. No grill or apron didn't stop Mama, of course. She took one of the grates out of the oven in the kitchen, got David to build a circular pile of stones near the back porch, and placed the grate over the stones. They had no charcoal, but Mama lit a fire, let it burn down, and then put cedar and pine and other slow-burning woods in it to make a bed of embers.

David had taken over at that point, said he was a man who knew how to grill, proclaiming solemnly, "I grill, therefore I am." When the steaks were done, he took them inside, filling the kitchen with an aroma that brought a smile to everyone's faces. Jillian liked her steak well done, and she sent it back for David to cook it a little more. Mama had baked some potatoes, plus they had the leftovers from the huge salad.

After dinner, they cleaned up the kitchen, and Jillian determined that now was a good time to broach the subject with Micky of going to see Dr. Al-Masri.

"You remember I told you that a friend of Rileigh's is a psychiatrist and I've been going to see her for counseling?" Micky smiled and nodded. "Well, I was wondering if you'd be interested in talking to a counselor too."

She held up her hand when she saw Micky's eyebrows go up. "Hold on, hold on, I didn't want to go either. The last thing in the world I wanted to do was to go sit in a room with a stranger and pull all the scabs off all the wounds, go to all the places I had managed to stay away from for years, so I get it."

Mama interrupted then. "Tell her about them pillows and them stuffed animals." Without waiting for Jillian, Mama hurried on. "That was the first thing she told me when she come back from her first session — 'bout how the chairs and couch in Dr. Al-Masri's office is full of fluffy pillows and big old stuffed animals. Not cause she talks to children, but 'cause sometimes grownups need something to hold onto, somewhere to bury your face when you cry."

Jillian tried to grab the conversation then, but Mama was on a roll.

"And tell her how the first thing she told you was when you was in her office was you didn't have to put a good face on it, that it was just fine not to be just fine."

Micky said nothing, just looked at Mama, the look on her face utterly unreadable.

"I'm not suggesting that you sign up to go to Dr. Al-Masri for therapy. You can just talk, and she'll get an idea where would be the best place to go for treatment."

Micky repeated the single word. "Treatment."

"You told us how you grew up — the constant abuse. There's no way to walk away from that kind of thing unscarred. And I know what most people do with emotional pain — they bury it, won't acknowledge it even exists ... because it *hurts* to talk about it. But I also know that when I finally opened up and talked about it, I could let it go, not carry it around with me everywhere. There's a freedom in that, I promise you."

When Micky's face was still unreadable, Jillian put down the dish towel she was using to dry a dinner plate, reached out, and touched her arm.

"Given what you've lived through, there's a whole lot

of pain in your past to unpack, and that would be the place to unpack it."

Micky stared at her mother for a few seconds with her face blank. And then she went off like a bottle rocket.

"You think I'm *crazy*, don't you!" She shrieked the words so loud and angry, Jillian took an involuntary step back. "You think there's something wrong with me and I'm nuts. Well, I'm not crazy, there's not a damn thing wrong with me. I didn't let them break me, okay, I didn't let them damage me, I stood up to them and spit in their faces." She spun on her heel then and marched toward her bedroom, throwing words over her shoulder. "I don't need a damned shrink. There's nothing wrong with me!"

Then she went into her room and slammed the door behind her, leaving Mama, David, and Jillian in shock.

There was a stunned silence, then David said, "That went well, don't you think?"

With humor, timing was everything, and Jillian couldn't resist the smile that flitted across her face.

"I certainly wasn't expecting *that*," Jillian said.

"She just don't understand," Mama said. "She just don't realize how much help Dr. Al-Masri has been to you, how you don't have them PTSD things so often anymore, how you're getting on with your life because of talking to her. She's just a kid. she don't realize how much good it'll do her."

David stepped forward and put his arm around Jillian's shoulders.

"Remember that *no* is not *no* forever."

Micky didn't come out of her room before bedtime, and when Jillian went to bed, her daughter appeared to be sound asleep. The next morning was Sunday, and on Sunday mornings, your bum was supposed to be on the pew at church. On this particular Sunday, the bums of the

Bishops were hiding out in a cabin in the mountains. But even so, it was Sunday, and Mama proclaimed that it was the Lord's Day. After which she got out her Bible, opened it to the 23rd Psalm, and read it aloud. Then, to Jillian's absolute amazement, she proceeded to preach a mini sermon about what it meant. David and Jillian sat respectfully on the couch while Mama talked, and when she was done, Jillian was afraid for a moment that they were going to have to sing a hymn. Gratefully, Micky saved them from that fate.

The door to her bedroom opened, and she came out. She smiled and looked a little confused that everyone was staring at her.

"What's the matter? Do I have toilet paper stuck on my shoe?"

"No, it's just a... we were listening to Mama's..." She didn't want to call it a sermon or a mini sermon, so she settled for, "devotional. Are you hungry?"

Mama had never been one to tiptoe around the elephant in the room. She went to Micky, took her hand and said, "We're all surprised at your reaction to the suggestion last night that you might like to go to counseling with Dr. Al-Masri."

Jillian rolled her eyes, afraid that Mama had totally stepped in it, and was surprised when Micky looked at Mama in confusion.

"Counseling with Dr. Al-Masri?" She turned toward Jillian. "She's the shrink who helped you, isn't she?"

Jillian took a moment to get her bearings and answered the question.

"Yes, she's a friend of Rileigh's. And she's agreed to talk to you to see if maybe you might, you know, maybe she could find somebody who could help you deal with all that's happened to you."

Jillian was stumbling and bumbling because the girl standing beside Mama didn't appear to know that Jillian had already said all this once.

Micky smiled a little and ducked her head.

"I know I didn't respond very positively to that suggestion before," she said. "Okay, so I sort of lost my temper. I'm sorry." She stopped then and when she continued, her voice sounded hollow. "I guess that sort of proves it, doesn't it? That it would be a good idea for me to talk to somebody."

Jillian crossed the room and put her arms around her daughter, proud of her.

"I think it'd be a good idea."

Micky looked up then, her eyes going from Jillian to Mama to David and back to Jillian.

"Well, if we all think this is a good idea, it couldn't possibly be a bad one, could it?"

They all stood for a moment, awkward, and then Micky asked, "Is that coffee I smell?" That broke the tension in the room.

"Would you like some?" Jillian asked, then went to pour her a cup.

Mama put her arms around Micky and enveloped her in a wordless hug. And Jillian could see Mama's face over Micky's shoulder, could see the smile that bloomed there like a rose in spring and the tears that fell instantly and spilled down her cheeks. Mama had a granddaughter, and she couldn't be happier about it.

Later that afternoon, Micky suggested that they play a game.

"I saw that Aunt Rileigh brought us a Monopoly game. I just want you to know that I rule at Monopoly."

David raised an eyebrow. "Well, that's convenient, because I also rule at Monopoly." He rubbed his hands together and made a wolfish sound. "I'm game for a challenge."

They played Monopoly — Micky bankrupted every-body — and then Scrabble. One of the letter tiles fell on the floor and Micky reached out her foot and picked it up with her toes.

"Couldn't have done that if I still had only nine of them," she said, wiggling her toes in the air.

After the games, they had dinner, then went out to sit together on the back porch, listening to the birds in the trees and the crickets under the porch, the little tree frogs and critters that came out at twilight.

"I never realized there was so much chatter in a forest," Micky said and gestured toward the trees.

"Yeah, there's a whole world out there of critters and every one of them likes to come out and sing at sunset," Mama said. Then she stood. "I've got a surprise for all of you."

As she went into the kitchen, the others looked at each other, grinning, because Mama's surprise was no surprise. She'd been preparing it all afternoon, and they'd smelled it, of course. How could you not? But when she brought the fresh lemon meringue pie out of the house and onto the porch and set it on the table, it looked so scrumptious that Jillian felt a twinge in that little spot in her jaw just under her ear that twinged when she ate something super sweet or super sour.

Mama cut slices for everybody and handed them out.

"Micky's birthday is soon," Mama said, "and if I'm gonna make a big ole cake, I'm gonna need somebody to make a grocery run."

Jillian took a bite of her pie. "Ahhh. I have just been transported directly to heaven, do not pass go and do not collect two hundred dollars."

It was a little while before Jillian noticed that Mama was just standing there, looking around.

"What? Mama? Did you forget something?"

"Listen up, child. The woods will talk to you. They don't never lie, and they'll tell you the absolute truth — if you've got ears to hear it."

Mama stood silently. "Jeremiah told me about that," she continued. Jillian remembered that Rileigh'd told her she thought Jeremiah Johnson had a crush on Mama, because he was always bringing her fresh game or a string of fish that he had caught.

"My daddy said the same thing about coal mines," Mama continued, her eyes searching the trees. "He said, a mine will talk to you if you've got the ears to hear. And mostly what it'll tell you is get out now while you still can."

Then she fell silent. Jillian was quiet too, listening to the woods. And it took her a moment to realize that what Mama had noticed was that the woods were silent now. When Micky noticed, she looked questioningly at Jillian and then at Mama.

"Those critters out there making noise, why are they quiet?"

Mama reached down and picked up the pie and said softly to the others, "You need to get your plates and go on in the house right now."

"But why?" Jillian asked.

Mama shook her head.

"Critters know. When there's a predator around, they get quiet."

Chapter Forty-One

Mama decided right before she went to bed that she would love to have a bread-and-butter sandwich. She did that sometimes, had weird cravings at odd hours. Jillian didn't know if it was a result of the dementia or just from getting old.

Picking up the flashlight, Jillian went out the back door and across the porch and walked the fifty yards or so to the clearing into the trees where Jeremiah had built his ingenious refrigerator.

She reached for the handle of the cooler.

Then a voice out of the darkness froze her in place.

"Don't move."

She squeaked out an involuntary cry, not a scream, and felt hands grab her from behind and the cold barrel of a pistol jammed into her back.

"Make one more noise like that and it'll be the last sound you ever make."

The voice was gravelly, almost sounded like a growl, and Jillian knew who it must be.

"Now, where's Farrah?"

For a moment, Jillian was confused. "Farrah?"

"Don't play dumb with me, bitch." He shoved the pistol deeper into her back. "She's in there, isn't she?"

That's when Jillian realized he was talking about Micky's sister, Farrah. "Farrah's not here. The last time Micky saw her was on a bus on their way here to Black Bear Forge. She hasn't seen her since."

"*Micky?*" The man barked out a derisive laugh. "Right, so Michaela's in there, is she? That'd be a neat trick." He poked her with the barrel of the gun again. "Fine, Michaela will do nicely. Now come on."

He grabbed her arm and twisted it painfully up behind her back and shoved her through the trees and out into the clearing, across it, up the steps, across the porch to the door. When he growled into her ear, she could smell the foul stench of cigar smoke, beer, and rotted teeth on his breath.

"You make the least little squeak and I'll blow your backbone out through your belly button. Now, open the door."

Jillian reached out and opened the door, pushed it inward, and stepped inside, hoping that someone, Mama or Micky or David, would glance her way and could tell by the look on her face that something was wrong. But David was busy working a crossword puzzle at the table, and Mama and Micky were in an animated conversation about cross-stitching, sitting together on the couch. The man shoved Jillian in front of him into the room, and the sound of the scuffle caught everyone's attention.

David jumped to his feet. "What the—?"

The man growled, "One more inch, pal, and she's one dead bitch."

David froze in place where he was. Jillian looked at Micky then, and the look on her face was abject terror.

The man let go of Jillian's arm, and she stumbled a step, pulling her arm around her and rubbing where he had twisted it painfully. She turned then and saw the man who'd come at her out of the darkness. He was scraggly, and the whiff of body odor she had caught was more pronounced in a smaller space. God only knows when he'd last had a bath. His clothes were tattered and wrinkled, his salt and pepper hair a tangle. A week's growth of beard on his face was not the attractive kind that made a fashion statement. His pale blue eyes were fixed on Micky, and hers on him, looking at him like a mouse looks at a cobra.

"Damn," the man spit the word out. "I thought I never was gonna find this place. Whoever built it must have been one reclusive son of a bitch."

He looked around at the interior of the cabin and shook his head. "Gonna be a shame to burn it down." Then he turned his gaze to Micky. "Get over here, bitch." He shoved Jillian toward Mama, who was still seated on the couch, then swung the barrel of the pistol toward Micky. "You gone deaf? I said, get your ass over here. We're leaving."

Still, Micky didn't move. She appeared to be frozen in place by fear.

"We're gonna have a good time, you and me. Better time than we've ever had, and we've had some good ones." He snarled out a nasty laugh. "I'm gonna make you pay. I'm gonna do to you what you done to them. I'm gonna cut off little pieces. Only I ain't gonna wait till you're dead. I'm gonna do it while you're still alive so as you can feel it."

Jillian had seen evil in men's eyes countless times. She'd known men whose desires were sick and revolting. But she'd never seen a look like that in the eyes of the ugly stranger who obviously was Micky's Uncle Dan. There was such pure evil there, it was chilling.

"You've got one more chance to come over here, bitch." Then he swung the barrel toward Mama, sitting beside her. "Before I put a bullet in the old lady."

Micky squeaked out a cry. "No, please don't."

To Jillian's utter surprise, she heard her mother speak, and her voice was level, no tremor of fear in it.

"You planning on planting us, ain't you," Mama said. "You're going to have to kill us all." Mama crossed her arms on her chest. "Just so's you know, I ain't gonna go quiet."

The man grinned a crooked grin.

"Get your ass over here, bitch, and I'll kill these people *before* I burn the house down. Otherwise, I'm just gonna tie them up and let them fry."

The man stepped toward Micky then, his eyes focused on her in hatred.

Jillian didn't even see David move. He was that fast. She felt the sense of motion next to her, but before she could turn and see what was going on, he had already kicked the gun out of the man's hand, followed up the kick with a step and some kind of karate punch that she'd never seen the like of. Then she saw his elbow streak out and crush the man's nose all over his face. The blow sent the man to the floor in a heap.

David collapsed on top of him, his knee on his chest.

"Get his gun," David said.

Jillian rushed to where the gun had slid on the floor and picked it up. Micky collapsed back onto the couch and curled up in something like a fetal position.

"You sure kicked his ass," Mama said, smiling approvingly at David.

"I'm assuming this is Uncle Dan, right?" David said to Micky, who nodded mutely. Then David turned to Jillian. "Didn't I see a roll of duct tape in one of those drawers?"

Mama sprang to life then. Give her a purpose — somebody needed something — and she was all business. She hurried to one of the kitchen drawers, pulled out the duct tape, new, still in the plastic. She handed the duct tape to David. He pulled off a piece, bit into it, ripped it free. With his other hand, he yanked up the man's head by the hair, not gently. He swiped the blood off the man's face so the tape would stick, then slapped the piece of tape over his mouth. Then he quickly bound the man's hands and feet together with the tape. When he was done, he stood with Jillian gaping at him.

"I had no idea you could do something like that," she said.

"I've been teaching karate classes for over twenty years, and this is the first time I ever got to use any of it." David went to Jillian and put his arm around her. "You need to get in the truck and go down the mountain as far as you have to go to get cell service and call Mitch." Reaching into his pocket, he pulled out his keys and handed them to her. She fumbled, and only then realized that not only were her knees shaking, but so were her hands. She turned, took one step toward the front door, then turned back abruptly, threw her arms around David, and kissed him — hard, on the mouth.

By the time Mitch arrived, the man had come to, had fought his bonds for a moment until David pointed the gun at him and told him to be still. He tried to talk too, mumbled, making word sounds, but the tape on his mouth kept him silent as blood from his shattered nose gushed over the tape and dripped off his chin. Mitch came into the house with his weapon drawn, then saw the man lying on the floor, relaxed, and put his pistol back in its holster.

"I ought to make you haul his ass out to the car," Mitch

said. David looked at him questioningly. "There's a tradition in law enforcement. It's called you bag it, you rack it."

As Jillian held the gun on the man whose nose was still bleeding, Mitch and David hauled him to his feet and cut the duct tape off so he could walk, shoved him out to Mitch's cruiser, and threw him into the back seat. Jillian stood at the door watching. Micky had never left the couch, where she was still cowering with Mama sitting beside her, ineffectually patting her hand in reassurance. Mitch smiled at David and extended his hand. David shook it, then Mitch got into his cruiser and drove away.

MITCH HEADED CAREFULLY down the mountainside trying to follow the barely visible trail. He flipped on his lights when he got to the main road as he drove into town, then hauled the man out of the back seat of his cruiser into the sheriff's office and handed him over to Deputy Rawlings. He pulled the man's wallet out of his back pocket and looked at his driver's license. Roger Daniel Farley, 188 Mill Pond Road, Singer, California.

As soon as he got back to the office, Mitch would call the sheriff's department in Burkett County, California and leave a message asking the sheriff to call him back tomorrow. It was too late now to talk to anybody, even though it was three hours earlier there. He'd get the scoop on Farley tomorrow, find out if there were any outstanding warrants on the guy. Micky had said it was a small county and this guy was a deputy sheriff, so Mitch was anxious to talk to the sheriff and get the story.

But none of that was the most important thing now. The two Arab men who'd been sent by Omar to kill Jillian and Micky would be in court when it convened at nine a.m. — briefly, and then they'd be released. And as soon as they were, Mitch and Rileigh would put their plan in motion. This guy could cool his heels in a holding cell until Mitch and Rileigh were done.

Mitch looked at his watch and shook his head. Wouldn't be long now. A couple of hours and it'd be showtime.

Chapter Forty-Two

THE TWO ARAB HITMEN, SALEH EL-QADHAFI FROM YEMEN and Mustapha Kumar from the United Arab Emirates, had been released from custody less than half an hour ago and were in their rented Lexus driving toward the Knoxville interstate when Mitch took a deep breath, flipped on his lights and his siren, and roared up behind them.

The car obediently pulled over to the curb. All four deputies' cars converged on the scene then, appeared out of nowhere, screeching to a halt to block the road in front and behind the car. The deputies leapt out and trained their weapons on the vehicle. Mitch approached it from behind, with his weapon drawn,

"Get out of the vehicle," he called.

"You can't do this," said the driver, El-Qadhafi. "All the charges were dropped!"

"Get out of the car or I will shoot you where you sit," Mitch snarled.

The two men looked at each other and then slowly opened their doors.

"Keep your hands where I can see them!" Mitch snapped, and the men held their hands out above their heads and moved with exaggerated slowness. He nodded first to Deputy Mullins and then to Deputy Rawlings.

"Get their weapons." The deputies holstered their own weapons before approaching the men with their hands in the air. Mitch and the other deputies kept the men in their sights.

"You so much as twitch and I will blow your brains all over the side of that car."

As the deputies relieved them of the pistols in their shoulder holsters, El-Qadhafi spoke in a low, threatening voice. "You're going to regret this, Sheriff Webster. You weren't in court this morning, so maybe you didn't get the memo — the prosecution dropped all the charges. You have no legal right to—"

Mitch stepped forward and buried his fist in the man's belly, knocking him up against the back door of the car, where he slid down to the ground, gasping for breath.

"That's so you understand that the rules of engagement have changed since I busted you," Mitch spat. "You have no rights, and I don't give a fuck about the law. We clear?"

Mitch used his foot to shove the man over onto his side, then he roughly yanked his hands behind his back and slapped handcuffs on him. As Deputy Mullins cuffed Kumar, the man glared at Mitch defiantly but said nothing. Pulling El-Qadhafi to his feet, Mitch dragged him back to his cruiser, opened the back door, and shoved him roughly into the back seat. Mullins shoved Kumar in the back passenger side door and slammed it shut.

Mitch didn't so much as glance down at the newspaper dropped haphazardly in the floorboard of the back seat.

Since El-Qadhafi was still bent over in pain, his face would be inches from it, but perhaps he wouldn't see it, or would ignore it if he did see it. Who knew? This whole thing was a crapshoot.

Climbing into the front seat, Mitch started the engine and pulled away. He could see in his rearview mirror that Deputy Rawlings had gotten into the vehicle the two men had exited and was following along behind.

"What's this all about, Sheriff? You know you have no cause," Kumar said.

"Shut up!" Mitch growled. "One more word out of either one of you and I will pull over to the side of the road, drag you out of this car, and so help me God I will beat both of you to death with my bare hands."

The men were silent after that. Mitch couldn't see the man seated directly behind him, but he did see Kumar look down toward the floorboard. Maybe he was reading the newspaper. It was folded, with the top half, the bold headlines, and the pictures there clearly visible.

Deputy Crawford pulled his cruiser in front of Mitch, and Deputy Mullins pulled in behind the Arabs' rented Lexus. All of the sheriff's vehicles had their lights flashing, but no sirens. Mitch drove on the bypass to Gatlinburg, took Exit 24, and wound through a neighborhood with expensive homes perched on the mountainside before pulling through a parking lot jammed with cars and around to the side entrance of a building. He got out of the car, opened the driver's side back door, and yanked El-Qadhafi out. Deputy Mullins pulled his cruiser in beside Mitch's, got out, and dragged Kumar out the other door.

"Where are we?" El-Qadhafi asked, his voice still a little breathless from Mitch's gut punch. "What are we doing here?

"You're not gonna be nearly as chatty after I pistol whip you and break out all your teeth."

The man looked startled by Mitch's ferocity but remained silent. As Mitch and Deputy Mullins dragged him and his partner into the building, both men looked around, taking it all in. Of course, it was obvious where they were. You only had to look around to see that. The bigger question that was surely looming in their minds was, "Why?" And Mitch was about to provide an answer

They were at a large, ornate building in Gatlinburg that a sign identified as Dargenio's Funeral Home and Mortuary. There were mourners lined up on the sidewalk leading into the main entrance, and the line went all the way down the street as far as you could see. Mitch dragged his captive, followed by Deputy Mullins dragging his, into the building through a side entrance. The four emerged into a waiting room that opened onto a hallway and paused there while Mitch stepped out into the hallway and spoke briefly to a young woman in a dark gray suit with a black name tag. A newspaper stand just inside the door held the same issue of The Gatlinburg Daily News that had been in the floorboard of Mitch's car, and someone had left a newspaper from the rack lying face up on one of the waiting room chairs.

Mitch stepped back into the waiting room and grabbed El-Qadhafi's elbow, then dragged him out into the hallway, where they followed the young woman past a sign that gave directions to four viewing rooms. They passed VR1, where a nameplate on the door identified the deceased as Thomas Thurgood, and they could hear the soft sound of crying from inside where the Thurgood family was grieving the loss of their father/brother/husband/son/friend Tom. A sign on the door of VR2 noted that visitation for Juanita Hernandez would begin at 5 p.m. The hallways were crowded with people, who glanced questioningly as they parted and made way for the law officers and their two handcuffed prisoners.

The young woman was leading them toward VR4 at the far end of the hallway, where the long line outside the building terminated in the crowd standing outside its closed doors. Then she veered left into a short hall where a side door opened into VR4. She stopped and gestured toward the door.

"Please, don't take long," the young woman said. "You saw the crowd that's waiting."

Mitch felt the Arab man stiffen slightly, but that was all, when he saw the names written on the nameplates on door.

Lily Bishop.
Jillian Bishop.
Michaela Hollis.

Mitch hoped the reason the man's reaction was muted was because he wasn't taken completely by surprise — that he'd read the story on the front page of the newspaper in the floorboard of Mitch's car.

The headline stretched six columns across the top of the front page: *Bishop Family Rocked By Triple Tragedy.*

Beneath the headline was the picture of an elderly woman who was identified as Lily Bishop — but the woman wasn't Lily. Beside it was a photo of Michaela and Jillian, one of the pictures David had taken the day they'd moved into Jeremiah Johnson's cabin.

There was a small picture of Rileigh in her deputy sheriff's uniform in a quote box on the far right above the words: "I still can't believe it — my whole family's gone."

The lead of the story was simple and stark.

"One of the founding families of Black Bear Forge in Yarmouth County lost three of its own over the weekend. Lily Frances Gillespie Bishop, 72, died on Friday from an apparent heart attack. Jillian Reneé Bishop, 46, Lily Bishop's daughter, and Michaela Marie Hollis, 20, her granddaughter, both died on Saturday. The coroner has ruled their deaths a double suicide. (*Full obituaries, page A10.*)

"They are survived by a remaining daughter, Rileigh Joseph Bishop, 33, of Black Bear Forge.

"The Gillespie family settled on the bank of Stinkin' Creek shortly after the end of the Civil War, and succeeding generations of the family have lived in Yarmouth County ever since. Lily Bishop retired in 2007 from a thirty-year career at the National Park Service. Jillian Bishop was a member of the 1978 class of Yarmouth County High School and (see *Tragedy, Page A4*).

Mitch pushed open the door of the viewing room, shoved the Arabs inside, and closed the door behind them. Soft music played in the background of a dimly lit room so jammed with flowers that it looked and smelled like a florist shop. There were dozens, maybe hundreds of different flower arrangements jockeying for space along the back and side walls of the room, two and three deep in places. Roses and carnations and bouquets of lilies were everywhere, and huge pots of greenery towered in the air. Each of the arrangements had an attached card to identify who had sent it.

At the far end of the room, centered in front of two groups of chairs that would seat fifty people each, were three caskets, two open and one closed. They rested beneath soft spotlights, and a table at the head of each displayed a nameplate and a photograph. Encircling each of the caskets were tables with more pictures of the deceased.

The center casket, with a big picture of the woman who'd been identified in the newspaper story as "Lily Bishop," was surrounded by pictures spanning a whole lifetime: her wedding photo, standing in a starched white dress beside a skinny young man in a black suit. There were pictures of her at someone's graduation, pictures of her at a wedding, in her garden, fishing in a johnboat, sitting in the stands at a Little League game, building a snowman. There was a monitor on one of the tables displaying pictures on a continuous loop — Lily sitting in the swing on her porch, then a picture of her with a small child on her lap opening a package in front of a Christmas tree, and so on.

There was a similar display on tables around the open casket on the left. But there were not nearly as many pictures, and all of them were dated. A little tow-headed girl on a tricycle. A little girl with blonde braids on a bicycle. A teenager in a prom dress. Another picture of a slightly older blonde teenager in a different prom dress with a different boy on her arm. A picture of her standing proudly at graduation in her cap and gown with a gap-toothed little girl clinging to her leg, looking up at her adoringly, and the engagement picture of her and David that had been in the newspaper. There were only a handful of pictures besides those — recent pictures taken with a much older David and Rileigh. There was no wedding picture. No pictures of her holding a newborn in her arms or the hand of a toddler learning to walk. All of the pictures of the woman identified as Jillian Bishop were before age 18 and after she was 45.

The casket on the right was closed, covered with a huge blanket of white roses. The only photo was the one that'd been in the newspaper story about her death — the whole photo that showed Michaela Hollis smiling into the camera, with Rileigh on one side and Jillian on the other.

Mitch dragged the man from the door up the aisle between the empty chairs to the center casket, where a blanket of yellow roses lay across the closed end and an old woman lay inside with her hands crossed primly on her chest.

"That's Lily Bishop."

The man said nothing. Mitch grabbed him by the neck and shoved his face down close, inches from the face of the corpse in the casket. With his hands cuffed behind him, he couldn't resist and didn't try.

"Look at her, dammit. Look at her."

Mullins had brought the other man into the room, and Mitch grabbed him and forced him to do the same thing. Then he hauled both of the men to the casket on the left where the young woman was laid out. She had pale blonde hair and pale skin, looked to be in her mid-forties. There weren't as many flowers around her casket as there were around the old woman's. The blanket of flowers on the end of the casket was made of red roses.

"That's Jillian Bishop," Mitch said, grabbing the man's face and shoving it down to within inches of the face of the body in the casket. "Your boss *owned* her" — he slathered the word with loathing — "for almost three decades, and then you *killed* her. Look at her."

Then he yanked the man up, pushed him toward Deputy Mullins and shoved the man named Kumar's face down into the casket. Pointing toward the casket on the other side of Lily's, Mitch said, "You can't look at Michaela's face … because there wasn't much of a face left after she put a shotgun in her mouth and pulled the trigger. Tell your boss that his client can rest easy. Hussain Amir Al-Saud's *daughter* blew her brains out."

Mitch gestured toward the closed doors at the far end of the viewing room. "All those people out there are lined up to come in here and say goodbye to people you murdered."

El-Qadhafi spoke then for the first time, sneering, "I didn't lay a hand on any of them."

Mitch punched the man in the face and he staggered back, tripping over one of the flower arrangements and sprawling to the floor.

Deputy Mullins stepped up and grabbed Mitch's arm to keep him from going after the man.

"You *killed* all three of them. Lily's heart gave out, afraid of what you'd do to Jillian. Jillian wouldn't let you drag her back to Omar, would rather die than have that happen ... so she took sleeping pills." He paused. "And Michaela found her."

He ground his teeth, stepped back and grabbed Kumar's arm, and told Deputy Mullins, "Pick up that piece of shit and get him out of here."

Mitch and his deputy dragged the two men out of the funeral home where their rented Lexus was parked beside the two cruisers. Then Mitch shoved them up against the wall of the building and snarled into Kumar's face.

"That woman you slapped Friday night was Rileigh Bishop — Lily Bishop's daughter, Jillian Bishop's sister, and Michaela Hollis's aunt. And my *fiancée*. She's the last surviving member of her family, thanks to you. I dragged your sorry ass here so you'd know I mean what I say when I tell you that the only reason you're still breathing is so you can take a message back to your boss. If I ever see you again, you're a dead man. You may be all-powerful where you come from, but you're swimming in my pond now." Mitch gestured at the crowd of people at the front of the building, watching curiously. "Ask those people — not one of them will say they saw me throw you up against this wall. You have no rights here — not to a phone call or a lawyer. The law's whatever I say it is, and if I ever see you or anybody else your boss sends in my county after today, I will shoot on sight, bury the body so damn far up in a hollow nobody will ever find it, and a whole county full of upright citizens will put their hands on a Bible and swear in court that they didn't see a damn thing." He paused, snarled into El-Qadhafi's face. "Are we clear?"

The man said nothing.

As fast as a striking rattler, Mitch drew his pistol and jammed the barrel up under El-Qadhafi's chin, shoving his head painfully back against the brick wall.

"Cat got your tongue now? *Are. We. Clear?*"

"You made your point, Sheriff."

Mitch grabbed the man and threw him onto the hood of the car on his belly and removed the handcuffs. Mullins removed Kumar's cuffs. Then Mitch handed El-Qadhafi the car keys and looked at his watch.

"You've got fifteen minutes to get out of Gatlinburg." He gestured to his deputies. "We'll give you an escort. After that, you're prey."

Mitch turned on his heel and stomped back to his cruiser and stood beside the door. The two men got into the rental car and fell in behind Deputy Crawford as he drove his cruiser out of the parking lot and away.

Mitch waited until they were out of sight before he went back into the building. When he stepped into the hallway, he could see Whit Nash at the other end near the front entrance of VR4, where a crowd was waiting to file into the room to pay their respects to Mrs. Thelma Watson, who'd been an elementary school teacher and principal in Gatlinburg for thirty years. Whit was explaining that there'd been a problem with the AV system.

"It'll be fixed in another minute or two and you can go in," he said. "I'm very sorry."

There was a little mumbling and grumbling in the crowd as Nash went back into the room, where three of his employees were scrambling to move all of the flower arrangements back around the only casket that remained in the room. And rearranging pictures on both the tables so that all of them were photographs of Mrs. Watson, whose name was now the sole one in the slot beside the front doors of the viewing room.

A few minutes later, Mitch watched as Whit Nash opened up the double doors and welcomed the crowd into the room. As the people streamed through the front door, Mitch went out the door on the back of the room to the dressing room, where Jillian was standing beside a coffin in the white dress she'd been wearing when she lay in it.

Rileigh was beside her, with her arm around her shoulders.

Jillian's eyes locked on Mitch's face.

"Did they buy it? Did they believe it? "

Mitch smiled and only then realized that relief had flooded through his body as he watched the men drive away. The looks on their faces … yeah, they'd believed it.

"You were perfect," Mitch said. "And as for buying it — there's no way to know for sure, of course, but …"

He glanced over his shoulder at Deputy Mullins, who'd followed him into the room.

Beau's smile was huge and genuine.

"They fell for it all right, hook, line and sinker," he said.

David put his arm around Jillian and squeezed her tight, then she turned away.

"I have to get this"—she shuddered involuntarily—"gross makeup off me." She hurried into the bathroom.

The casket that Jillian had been lying in was rolled over to the side of the room and Rileigh looked at it, then at Mitch. He knew how hard it must have been for her to see Jillian laid out as if she were dead, and he pulled her close.

"It's over now," he said.

"You sure?"

"Yeah, I'm sure. It's over."

Chapter Forty-Three

JILLIAN INSISTED ON GOING TO WHIT NASH'S OFFICE before she left the funeral home to let him know how much she appreciated what he had done for her. Rileigh'd told her what he'd said about his stuck-zipper episode when he was a teenager, and Jillian had teared up at the story.

"I told him he was brave," she said, "and I meant it."

Then Rileigh, David, and Jillian went back out to Jeremiah Johnson's cabin where they had left Micky and Mama. Micky had been so horrified by the plan and by the part she'd adamantly refused to play in it that she couldn't even face going to the funeral home, so they'd left her snug in the cabin in the mountains.

Mitch went back to his office to finish up a pile of paperwork on his desk and then to question Micky's Uncle Dan. David had made short work of the man on Sunday night, and Mitch had kept him in the county lockup waiting for questioning until he had time and attention to focus on him.

"Well, how did it go?" Micky asked the moment they stepped into the cabin.

Jillian smiled, and it was an easier and more relaxed smile than Rileigh had seen on her face in a long time.

"I think they bought it," she said.

"Are you sure?"

"There's no way to be sure, but Mitch thinks so, and so did Beau Mullins."

Micky still looked dubious.

Jillian put her arms around Micky and told her that everything was going to work out.

"There's no reason not to be optimistic," she said. "We've done every possible thing we can do, and now we need to let it go and trust that what we did worked."

David gathered up most of his things and packed them up in his Land Rover to take home. He was planning to go back into town and get some work done, but they'd all agreed that they would have a final dinner tonight at Jeremiah Johnson's cabin after Jillian and Rileigh took Micky for her first appointment with Dr. Al-Masri.

"All you people got something important to do," Mama had announced as Rileigh, Jillian, and Micky prepared to leave for Gatlinburg. "Well, I got something important to do, too. I'm making homemade bread for dinner tonight."

Homemade bread in the oven of a wood-burning stove. Rileigh didn't even know she'd brought yeast to the cabin. Her mother never ceased to amaze her. There didn't seem to be anything she didn't know how to do, and if there was, she simply learned how and then did it. Mitch had commented on several occasions that Rileigh was a carbon copy of her mother, and she'd never seen much resemblance, certainly not what he saw, considering that her mama was sweet and compliant and kind and nonviolent, and Rileigh was all those things, too … now and then. Just not very often. However, she did agree that their can-do attitudes toward life meshed like the inner workings of a fine gold pocket watch.

As they drove down the mountainside late that afternoon, Rileigh had to admit that she could see now how it was possible that Dan Farley had found them. Obviously, he'd been watching the hospital and had followed her when she left. He'd been the driver of the white Jetta that she'd seen parked at the foot of the trail when she'd come up it the last time. And all those repeated trips up and down the mountain had scuffed the almost indiscernible trail to the point that if you looked hard enough, you could see it.

Rileigh and Jillian had talked about going shopping for a birthday present for Micky while she was in Dr. Al-Masri's office. The girl would turn twenty on Wednesday. They decided instead to just do basic clothes shopping for the girl. She only had a couple of pair of jeans and some tees. She needed everything. They'd go to Walmart and pick up some basics and surprise her. But both of them went in with Michaela to meet Dr. Al-Masri.

"Good morning, Rileigh. Jillian, how are you?"

Dr. Al-Masri got up from her desk and came around to greet them, giving Rileigh and Jillian both hugs.

"And this must be your daughter," she said to Jillian. Jillian smiled. "I'm really glad to meet you, Michaela."

"It's Micky," Michaela said.

"I'm glad to meet you, Micky. Your mother and your aunt are lovely people, and I look forward to talking to you."

Dr. Al-Masri showed Micky back to her therapy room as Rileigh and Jillian walked out. When they got in the car, Jillian turned to her sister.

"I know exactly what she's saying to Micky right now, if she's saying the same thing she said to me. She's telling her, 'It's okay not to be okay. You can cry or scream or yell or stomp your feet or do whatever you feel like doing. No behavior is out of bounds. No emotion is over the top. Be real.'"

"I think hearing something like that would be freeing."

"Oh, it wasn't freeing. It scared me to death."

"Why?"

"Because I'd kept everything so locked up inside, I felt like a bottle of Coke that somebody'd shaken up, and if I even touched the cap, it would explode off the end and all the Coke would spew out, leaving the bottle empty."

"Is that what happened?"

"More or less," Jillian said. "You remember, I wasn't in very good shape after my first few appointments. But it got better."

"I'm really glad Dr. Al-Masri is talking to Micky. We need her help to tell us at least enough about what's wrong with your daughter that we can get her the help she needs."

"My daughter." Jillian said the words in an odd way, but they'd arrived at Walmart by then, so Rileigh didn't have a chance to ask what she meant. It was clear, though, that something was bothering her.

Rileigh and Jillian cruised the aisles of Walmart, picking out generic garments for Micky because they didn't know her taste. Several tee shirts in different colors with no markings at all. A couple pair of jeans, white underwear, and bra. Jillian did, however, opt for a night shirt that had a pink and blue unicorn on it, and when Rileigh raised an eyebrow, she said, "I never got to buy"—she paused for a heartbeat—"my little girl anything when she was a child."

When they returned to Dr. Al-Masri's office, they found Micky standing outside on the curb waiting. As soon as they pulled up, she jumped into the back seat.

"What's up?" Rileigh asked.

"Dr. Al-Masri had an emergency just a few minutes ago and she had to rush out. She told me what it was, but she used some kind of technical term I didn't know. Let me have your phone, Aunt Rileigh, and I'll Google it and see what it means."

Rileigh handed Micky her phone, and Micky did the magic with it that all kids her age knew how to do and read off a description of "paranoid schizophrenia" and a "psychotic event."

On their way out of town, they stopped by Red-Eye Gravy to get a milkshake to surprise Mama. Micky dug through the sacks of purchases from Walmart and squealed over the unicorn nightshirt. When they walked into the house, Rileigh held out the surprise vanilla milkshake to Mama. But Mama blew right by her without even noticing and enveloped Micky in a bear hug. Rileigh shook her head. She was so, so glad to have a granddaughter.

Chapter Forty-Four

MITCH SAT AT HIS DESK, RIFLING THROUGH THE PAPERWORK that he ought to be working on, but his mind kept straying to the events of the morning. At the time, he had been concentrating so hard on being convincing, on being believable, that he hadn't taken his eye off the ball long enough to examine the faces of the two Arab hitmen. In flashes, he could see their faces, their reactions to what he was saying and what they were seeing. But in truth, he really wasn't sure whether they had believed the ruse or not.

But he couldn't tell Rileigh that. He would never tell Rileigh or Jillian that. The Bishop family needed to be out from under the shadow of a hawk flying over them all the time, ready at any minute to swoop down and snatch Jillian up in its claws. That was no way to live. He wanted very badly to believe that the two hitmen would go back and tell their boss that the job was done and that Jillian Bishop and Michaela Hollis were no longer a threat. But only time would tell if that were true.

He picked up a part-time deputy job application form

that had been filled out by a young man who'd come by last week when Mitch was far too busy to interview him, read the first part of the form twice, and realized he had not concentrated enough on it even to remember the guy's name. This was useless. He got to his feet and looked at his watch. He'd hoped to be able to talk to the sheriff in Burkett County, California, before he went in to interrogate Roger Daniel Farley. But he hadn't received a call back, and he might as well go see what Mr. Farley had to say for himself.

The prisoner had been brought from a holding cell into what passed for an interrogation room at the Yarmouth County Sheriff's Department. When not in use interrogating prisoners, it was the break room for the deputies and staff. But it did have the requisite chains attached to the table that could be affixed to handcuffs to keep a prisoner in place.

As soon as Mitch walked in the door, the man lurched at the manacles and chains binding him, as if he could somehow break them and attack Mitch.

"I ain't done a damn thing," he snarled. "She's the one done it. I just came looking for to take her back."

"She who?" Mitch asked.

"You know damn well who I'm talking about. You people are the ones who've been hiding her away up there in that cabin." The man sat back in the chair and sighed. "Took me four damn days to find it."

"Why don't you relax and tell me your story," Mitch said.

"My story is that I came here looking for Farrah Hollis because she killed my sister and my brother-in-law and a couple of other people, murdered them and then ran, and I came after her."

Mitch kept his face impassive, didn't allow the man to see his response.

"So you're saying that Michaela Hollis killed some people in California? Because I just spoke to the sheriff's office there and their outstanding murder warrants have charged *you* with those crimes." That was a total bluff, but he launched it out there hoping to get a reaction, and he did.

"Hell no, I didn't kill them. I didn't have any reason to kill them. That's crazy talk. She's the one who did it. She's the one who's crazy."

"If Michaela Hollis is crazy, you certainly gave her reason enough, you and your brother."

That rocked the man back on his heels, but only for a second.

"Damn it. I'm not talking about Michaela. I'm talking about Farrah."

Mitch continued to question the man, creatively twisting reality to convince him that he was wanted in California for murder, but the guy stuck to his guns. No matter what Mitch said, he still contended that Farrah Hollis had killed his sister and brother-in-law and two other people.

Finally, Mitch had had enough, looked up at Deputy Rawlings, who was standing in the doorway. "Get this piece of shit out of here and lock him up," he said.

Now Mitch sat again at his desk, drumming his fingers, trying to make all the pieces of the puzzle he just gathered up fit together, but they didn't. He had interrogated Roger Daniel Farley but was never able to budge his story. And much of what the man said was very, very troubling if it were true. There was absolutely no reason to believe that it was, of course, except for Mitch's gut. Right now, it was telling him that the guy cooling his heels in a holding tank on the other side of the building had not lied to him.

Mitch was just about to call the sheriff in California when the dispatcher poked her head into his office.

"Deputy Crawford just found a white Jetta parked up in the trees on McCandless Lane," she said. McCandless Lane was directly on the other side of the mountain from where Jeremiah Johnson's cabin was located. A white Jetta was what Rileigh had seen parked on the state road beside the turnoff to the cabin.

"Thank you, Sheila," Mitch said. But Sheila remained standing where she was. "Is there something else I need to know?"

"You must be psychic," the dispatcher said. "Crawford said that there was something odd about the vehicle, a distinct odor coming from the trunk, but he didn't have the keys to open it. So he called Miller's Automotive, and they're towing it into the compound so you can break into it."

"Strange odor."

"Yeah. Like dead-body strange odor."

Mitch had Farley returned to the interrogation room.

"What are they going to find in the trunk of the white Jetta we just found abandoned on McCandless Lane?" Mitch asked. The man clinched his jaw.

"I ain't saying nothing else. I want a lawyer. Get me one."

He hadn't asked to see a lawyer until now, and Mitch didn't like that. It seemed to imply that the man was telling the truth before, that he had not committed the murders in California Mitch had accused him of. But the strange smell coming from the trunk of the white Jetta scared him enough that he'd lawyered up. Mitch ordered Farley returned to the holding cell and told Sheila to call the prosecutor's office, that the guy was going to need a court-appointed attorney.

About ten minutes later, he finally got a return call from the Burkett County Sheriff's Department in Singer, California.

Mitch's conversation with Sheriff Edmund Blair was brief and chilling. The sheriff told him that Roger Daniel Farley had been telling the truth, at least part of it, and that Mitch's bluff had hit close to the mark. Farley did, indeed, have four active murder warrants out for him. His sister, Charlotte Hollis, and her husband, Joe, had been murdered in their beds. But it was the identities of the other two murder victims that had stolen Mitch's breath. Apparently, Farley had been telling more of the truth than Mitch believed. His story was that that Farrah Hollis had killed his sister and her husband and some kid and then likely stole the kid's vehicle and ran. He had gone to the bus station and found the abandoned vehicle there and discovered that she'd bought a ticket. So he'd followed the bus, looking for his chance.

More than that, though — he had kept insisting that the girl Mitch and everyone else had been calling Micky Hollis was not Michaela Hollis at all. She was Farrah, Micky's sister.

"You don't know jack shit," Farley had said. "That's Farrah Hollis, not Michaela. Michaela's dead. Farrah killed her."

Sheriff Blair confirmed the identities of the two other murder victims beside the Hollises. One of them was Carson Granger, who'd been an aid who worked in a homeless shelter. The other was Michaela Marie Hollis.

Mitch ended the call with the sheriff and was about to have a deputy drag Farley back to the interrogation room when the phone on his desk rang again. Sheila informed him that the caller was Dr. Aaliyah Al-Masri.

"Hello, Dr. Al-Masri. What can I do for you?"

"I'm making a judgment call here," she said, sounding uncertain. "But I have to. I can't do anything else."

"Excuse me?"

"I'm sorry. I didn't mean to be vague. The law requires that I report to authorities whenever I believe one of my patients is a danger to themselves or others. I am allowed to break patient confidentiality if I believe there is a clear and present threat of harm." She took a breath. "I just spoke with Michaela Hollis, and I believe she's dangerous."

Mitch sucked in a gasp.

"Did you tell Rileigh that?"

"I couldn't. Michaela got up to go to the bathroom at the end of our session, and she slipped out the front door, and Rileigh must have picked her up at the curb. I've been calling Rileigh's number repeatedly, but she doesn't answer."

Mitch was on his feet and running as he spoke. "I'm on my way there right now," he said. "You need to keep trying to reach Rileigh. But first, tell me what's going on."

As Mitch's cruiser screeched out of the parking lot and he flipped on his lights and his siren, Dr. Al-Masri told him the story.

"I'm sure Rileigh told you that I agreed to talk to Michaela Hollis this afternoon to assess her condition and recommend to Rileigh and Jillian what kind of therapy I think would benefit her best." She paused for a breath. "But I didn't talk to Michaela Hollis. I talked to Farrah Hollis."

"What do you mean?"

"In my professional opinion, the person I spoke to in my office a little while ago suffers from dissociative identity disorder."

"I think I know what that means, but you better tell me anyway."

"DID occurs when a person suffers trauma that fractures their sense of self. Unable to deal with the horror, they become someone else so they don't have to face it. The dominant personality in the young woman I spoke to is Farrah Hollis. And Farrah Hollis displays the total lack of empathy of a psychopath."

Mitch gasped and hoped she didn't hear him.

"She came quietly into my office, then changed on a dime, became sarcastic and nasty and angry and arrogant. And though she didn't confirm it, I believe she has killed people." Dr. Al-Masri paused before continuing kindly, "I'm afraid that ... I believe she ... *killed* Michaela Hollis, and then 'became' Michaela Hollis, the version of Michaela she called Micky."

Mitch felt a punch to his gut, but he kept driving.

"The suppressed rage in Farrah Hollis is staggering. I suspect she killed the people who purchased her on the black market as an infant and then abused her. But in her mind, a greater offense than abuse is selling your own baby to strangers. Jillian gave Michaela up, and the baby was sold on the black market."

Mitch heard Dr. Al-Masri take a big breath.

"The Michaela personality is not aware of the existence of the other personalities, but Farrah knows about all of them. She thinks Michaela is a fool, and she uses Michaela to get what she wants. She only comes out personally whenever she needs to."

Dr. Al-Masri's voice went low and intense.

"Mitch, I believe Farrah Hollis is a danger to Jillian. I believe she wants to kill Jillian because Jillian gave Michaela up, and I believe she'll kill Rileigh and Lily, too, if they get in her way."

Mitch said nothing, just pushed his foot down harder

on the accelerator — because Rileigh would most definitely get in her way.

Chapter Forty-Five

MAMA'D FINISHED MAKING THE LOAVES OF BREAD FOR supper and was letting them rise before she put them in the oven, and when she finally did acknowledge the existence of the milkshake Rileigh had brought her, she sat down with it contentedly on the couch and started slurping away.

Rileigh set to unpacking the Walmart sack when Micky reached into it and pulled out the nightshirt with the pink and blue unicorn on it, held it up for Mama to see.

"Isn't this absolutely adorable?" she said and smiled.

Mama allowed that she had "never seen nothin' cuter."

Micky dropped the nightshirt on the couch beside Mama and went into the kitchen where Jillian was washing her hands at the sink. She'd scrubbed and scrubbed to get off all the mortuary makeup that Whit had put on her face and hands to make her look like a corpse, but she'd been so repulsed by having to wear it that she imagined she still had some of it under her fingernails.

"You want some of this milkshake?" Mama asked Rileigh as she removed Micky's tee-shirts and underwear from the Walmart sack. She shook her head, then Mama called over her shoulder to Jillian, "You can have the last sip."

A voice Rileigh almost didn't recognize replied from the kitchen.

"Oh, it'll be her 'last sip' all right, that's for damn sure."

Rileigh looked up, startled, and saw a scene that didn't make any sense at all. Micky was standing behind Jillian. She had a hunk of Jillian's hair in her hand and was using it to yank Jillian's head backward. And she was holding a butcher knife to Jillian's throat.

"Looking around for Micky, are you?" said the young woman with a knife to Jillian's neck. "She's not here. Michaela Hollis, aka Micky, has left the building. She's only around when I need her for camouflage."

She shook her head.

"But my bastard uncle is gonna start running his mouth soon, so the jig is up here. I need to do what I came here for."

"Micky," Mama said in an anguished voice, "what are you doing, sugar?"

"Shut up, old woman or I'll slit your throat next."

"But Micky…"

"But Micky…" the young woman mocked sarcastically. "I'm not your precious Micky."

"Then who are you?" Rileigh asked.

"I'm Farrah."

"The sister Michaela told us about the night she was stabbed?"

The young woman holding a knife to Jillian's throat barked out a laugh.

"She got all huffy about that stinky old man I offed, and I paid her back for being nosey."

Paid her back? Farrah stabbed … *herself?*

"Don't act like I did some terrible thing to poor Michaela. Poor *Micky* abandoned me, was gone for a whole year. Wanna know what happened to *me* during that year?"

"What happened to you?" Rileigh asked, trying to appear casual as she inched her hand up to the pistol in the holster at her side.

"Micky was gone, so I was all they had. And Papa had a party, invited his friends. They all got roaring drunk, handed me off from one to the next. And one of those bastards knocked me up."

Jillian gasped at that, and the girl yanked her hair back harder, held the knife so tightly against her throat that a thin line of red formed there and began to drip down and stain the top of her tee.

"Knocked up. And so what are they gonna do about it? That's what Micky wanted to know when she came back. What did they do about it? Stupid bitch. She knew damn well what they did. They got rid of it."

"So they took you to an abortionist?"

"That's the same thing Micky said — took me to an abortionist, like they were going to go to that much trouble, spend that kind of money just for me."

"So you … had the baby?" Rileigh asked.

"Hell, no I didn't have the baby."

"But you said—"

"I said they wouldn't *pay* for an abortion. Papa did it."

Rileigh sucked in a gasp.

"Your father—?"

"Yeah Papa. He aborted the baby. It was all Micky's fault. But I made her pay for it." She threw back her head and laughed an ugly laugh. "She didn't see me drown that snot-nosed Alyssa — got fingernail polish on my best sweater."

Alyssa. That was the little girl Micky talked about, the

small child Micky had adored, made clothes for and dressed her up like a little doll. Farrah had killed her.

"But I made her watch me kill Mama and Papa. Then I used the knife on Micky. Stabbed her in the heart."

Mama sat with her eyes open too wide, staring in horror at Micky, shaking her head, confused, didn't understand how *Micky* could describe how she had *killed* Micky. It made no sense to Mama, Rileigh knew. But it made perfect sense to Rileigh. Everything made sense to Rileigh now.

The behavior Jillian had described hadn't been mood swings. When Micky had played in the mud like a child, she *was* a child. The meek and gentle Micky who'd gone into a raging tirade — she hadn't been Micky at all. It all fit now. The girl was obviously suffering from Dissociative Identity Disorder. Rileigh had only come upon it once in all her years of police work, but she had mentioned it to Dr. Al-Masri in Memphis, and the psychiatrist's face had grown very serious.

"It's not some carnival trick or plot device in a movie," she'd said. "It's a real disorder. People with DID have lived through horrific circumstances, and the only way they can cope is to disassociate, to make the bad things that have happened to them happen to somebody else."

Aaliyah had warned ominously, "People with DID are who they believe themselves to be."

Rileigh was sure Aaliyah had picked up on it when she talked to Micky earlier. But Rileigh didn't see Dr. Al-Masri after Micky's appointment ... because Micky had met her outside.

Farrah was growling venom into Jillian's ear—"Payback's a bitch, but it's payback time"—as she held the knife tighter against Jillian's throat. The line of red grew wider; blood was dripping freely down.

"And it all started with you. You lied — you told Micky

you were forced to give her up. Bullshit. You sold Micky on the black market to the highest bidder, sold her to the Devil himself."

Jillian's eyes were wild. She looked pleadingly at Rileigh, seemed to be working her throat as if she wanted to say something, but Rileigh shook her head and she kept silent.

Rileigh heart hammered like a lunatic woodpecker as terror grabbed her guts in a fist and squeezed. Jillian was literally an inch away from certain death. A second, maybe two left to live. There wasn't time for Rileigh to draw her pistol and fire. And even if there had been, she would chance hitting Jillian. The distance between them was too wide. She couldn't jump Farrah, couldn't get to her before she used the knife.

She had only seconds.

What could she do?

Her mind scrambled.

Micky wasn't Farrah's only other personality.

"Lissy!" Rileigh cried. "I made you a new dress. Come see."

Farrah's eyes snapped toward Rileigh, then her eyes unfocused.

"A new dress?" she said in a child's voice and relaxed her hold on Jillian's hair.

Rileigh leapt across the space between them, then grabbed Farrah's wrist and twisted it, and the knife clattered to the kitchen floor. Then she flung her onto the counter, pulling her arm up painfully behind her back.

"Ouch!" the little girl's voice cried. "That hurts!"

"Get me the duct tape," Rileigh ordered Jillian, who simply stared at her, uncomprehending. And then suddenly Farrah began to buck, struggled violently to get free. Rileigh shoved her arm farther up toward her shoulder.

"Stop it!" Farrah snarled. "You're going to break my damned arm."

"Be still or you bet your ass I'm gonna break your arm. And that won't be the only thing I break."

That freed Jillian from her trance. She turned toward the drawer where they'd put the roll of duct tape they'd used only last night to bind up the man who had come to kill Micky — the man who had called her Farrah.

MITCH WENT roaring up the trail that led to Jeremiah Johnson's cabin, slid his cruiser to a stop, leapt out, took the steps on the porch two at a time, and burst into the living room with his weapon drawn. The women inside looked at him in surprise, and as he took in the scene, he slowly holstered his pistol.

Rileigh was carefully dabbing at a wound on Jillian's neck that surely had been caused when somebody held a knife to it. Micky/Farrah was duct-taped to a kitchen chair. Mama sat on the couch, her head down, crying softly.

Mitch should have known Rileigh could handle this, and he was enormously proud of her. Though he didn't say that, not now anyway. But he would say it later.

He walked to Rileigh and put his hand on her shoulder as she worked on Jillian's neck.

"You alright?" he asked.

She nodded, then gestured toward her mother sitting on the couch crying. "She's not. She took it hard."

Mitch looked up into Jillian's eyes and saw such sorrow there.

"How about you?"

"I'm fine," she said stoically, though he could tell she was anything but. "Actually, I wasn't really surprised," she continued. "I knew she wasn't … really my daughter." She nodded toward the girl duct-taped to the chair, who was no longer struggling to be free but who glared at them. If looks could kill, there wouldn't be a single person alive in the room except her.

Rileigh was surprised by that. "You figured it out? How?"

"It just didn't feel … right. I realized that what I had mistaken for some *connection* when she was in the hospital was really just sympathy on my part for a young girl who had been through hell — just like I had. But I didn't know for certain until last night when we were playing games. She picked up a Scrabble tile off the floor with her toes, lifted her foot, and wiggled her toes and said they worked just fine now that they'd been separated."

Jillian sighed.

"It was the wrong foot. The baby I cared for all those years ago… my *daughter* … her toes were grown together on her right foot, and Micky was wiggling the toes on her left."

Jillian glanced at the girl taped to the chair but didn't make eye contact.

"I knew then she wasn't the baby I'd given up, but it was clear she'd known the person who was — knew her toes had been separated, just confused which foot. And it was also clear that she wanted us to believe she was my daughter, had used the detail about the toes to *trick* us." Jillian sighed. "Which meant she was up to something, wanted something … and, of course, she had to have known my daughter — who'd sent her DNA off to that site … so where was *she?*"

Jillian's voice broke then.

"I never considered that maybe she had … *killed…*"

She couldn't go on. Rileigh leaned over and touched her forehead to Jillian's.

They were silent for a moment, the only sound Mama's soft crying.

"So why did you come roaring out here?" Rileigh asked Mitch.

"I got a call from Dr. Al-Masri. She said the girl she'd spoken to earlier was 'a danger to herself or others.' She tried to call and warn you, but you didn't pick up."

"My phone never rang," Rileigh began, then she stopped. "The ringer. Micky asked to use my phone as we were driving away from Aaliyah's office. What do you bet the ringer's turned off?"

"When I questioned Dan Farley," Mitch said, "he claimed he had come looking for Farrah Hollis — that she had killed his sister and brother-in-law. I talked to Burkett County, California Sheriff Edmund Blair, and he said the man I had in custody had outstanding warrants for four murders. The couple who lived in the house where Michaela and Farrah grew up had been murdered in their beds. He found a body outside on the driveway — a young man named Carson Granger, who'd worked in a homeless shelter for migrants — so he's the young man who convinced Michaela to send her DNA off to that ancestry site." Mitch paused and looked sympathetically at Jillian. "And Sheriff Blair said there was another body in the house, too — Michaela Marie Hollis had been stabbed in the heart."

All eyes went to Farrah, who glared hatred back at them. Mitch glanced at Mama, sitting on the couch crying. She had been so delighted to finally have a grandchild.

Chapter Forty-Six

MITCH HAD MADE IT ABUNDANTLY CLEAR TO EVERY MEMBER of the Yarmouth County Sheriff's Department that even if there was a nuclear explosion on Main Street in Black Bear Forge, he was not to be called.

"Say Mrs. O'Leary's cow kicks over a lantern and all of downtown is burning to the ground … what should you do?" he asked Sylvia, the dispatcher, as other deputies looked on in amusement.

"Grab a fire extinguisher, but don't call the sheriff."

"Check. But what if somebody releases a hungry Bengal tiger in the senior citizens center. What should you do then?"

"Call Bernie, let him handle it." Bernie Sandlin was the 82-year-old almost-blind animal control officer. "Just tell him Gertie Potter's tabby got loose again. He'll never know the difference."

One of the looky-loo deputies — maybe it was Jeb Rawlings — burped out a lone bleat of laughter at that, then choked down the rest.

"Just *don't* call Sheriff Webster," Sheila continued.

"Ah, but what will you do if somebody releases all the creatures from the *Gremlins* movie in the Forge elementary school?"

Sheila made a *humph* sound in her throat. "Those kids'll beat the shit out of them and I won't need to call anybody."

That brought the house down.

It had become an inside joke now, and everyone was in on it. All the deputies teased Mitch about having to come in from his day off to cover a shift for them.

"You know that bad knee I got in the Airborne jumping out of perfectly good airplanes? It's been acting up, and—" Deputy Beau Mullins began.

"I don't care if you jump out of an airplane and your chute doesn't open. Your smashed ass had better show up on time for your shift tonight."

Rileigh watched in amused admiration as Mitch lectured the dispatcher and the various deputies about the sanctity of his off-duty time. He and Rileigh were going out tonight come hell or high water.

"Just checkin', just checkin'," Beau said, backing off with a grin.

Rileigh and Mitch had stopped by his office to pick up his huge "golf umbrella." Forecasters were predicting a big storm, and that umbrella was roughly the size and shape of a circus tent. Mitch wanted to cover the "high water" base should the need arise. The stop-off also provided an opportunity for everyone to see for themselves that he and Rileigh really were going out on the town, with him decked out in a civilian suit, looking, Rileigh thought, good enough to eat. And her in a gorgeous, slinky satin dress, blue not green, but Mitch had told her a couple of weeks ago that it really didn't matter anymore what color she wore. Every time he looked into her eyes, they were jade green. That's what he saw. And she was just fine with that.

They were going to the just-opened Italian restaurant Mama Mia's in Gatlinburg, on the street where work continued on the rising-from-the-ashes version of the Bahama Mamas restaurant that had burned down the night of their first aborted big date.

Mitch finished his spiel and — to the accompaniment of catcalls and whistles — ushered Rileigh back out the door in front of him. They were in date mode, which meant that doors were opened for her, chairs were pulled out. It didn't matter to her, but it definitely did to Mitch, so she tried to relax and enjoy being treated like a princess — because that's exactly how Mitch treated her.

Rileigh was enjoying every minute of all of her life right now, as a matter of fact. Somehow, seeing her sister in a coffin had driven home more profoundly to Rileigh her sense of gratitude that Jillian had survived and was safe, that she had been granted a second chance at life with her sister. Jillian, for her part, had recovered well from the ordeal of Farrah Hollis showing up and pretending to be the baby Jillian had given away all those years ago. Rileigh accepted and respected the fact that Jillian never mentioned pretending to be dead in order to throw off pursuit from the Arabs, and nobody ever talked about it. There was no way to be sure, of course. But every day that passed made it more obvious that the Arabs had bought the ruse, that they believed Jillian Bishop and her daughter were both dead — so no one would ever come looking for them.

Everyone had been concerned about Mama, though. She'd been so delighted to have a grandchild, *finally*. And to witness her beloved grandchild turn into a deadly, heartless killer right before her eyes had shaken Mama to the core.

She'd been emotionally fragile for several days after that, and then one morning she got up and the old Mama was back, just like she'd always been — happy and cheerful. And when Jillian accidentally made a reference to Michaela, Mama had looked up and asked, "Who's Michaela?" So clearly, her dementia had wiped those unpleasant memories out of her mind.

Rileigh had managed not to get out in front of her headlights on this date with Mitch. She refused to daydream about the "what comes after dinner" part of the evening, managed to stay in the moment, soaking up the wonder of feelings she'd heard other people talk about but had never imagined she could experience — until Mitch.

The first spoonful of zuppa Toscana reminded Rileigh why Mama Mia's was one of her favorite restaurants. Mitch had calamari fritti and raved about it. That was followed by risotto and lobster for Rileigh and veal scaloppine for Mitch, topped off with double portions of tiramisu. They heard the promised storm hit as they sat in the restaurant, the rain pounding against the roof drowning out the soft music, the crack and rumble of thunder seeming to shake the building.

After they finished dinner, they discovered they couldn't leave the restaurant. Other patrons were backed up from the entrance, looking through the glass doors at the howling wind that hurled raindrops at the glass like buckshot, pelting the sidewalk and the awning. They stood with the others for fifteen minutes waiting for the rain to abate. When it didn't, Mitch hauled out the golf umbrella and held it overhead as he ran to the car, then drove up front so that Rileigh could get in without getting soaked.

"Can you see well enough to drive?" Rileigh asked.

"You told me once that it was always best to drive at

night in the mountains because you could see the head-lights around corners."

"I said at night, not at night in a torrential downpour."

Traffic inched along, all the drivers held hostage by the timid driver out front, too scared to move faster than five miles an hour.

"Let's ditch the bypass," Rileigh said. "Taking the long way around will probably take half the time."

"On it," Mitch said and pulled out of the line of cars and down a side street. Back streets and then back roads, narrow and pot-holed and steep. Mitch was totally lost after the third turn, but Rileigh's internal mountain GPS never faltered. At the four-way stop on Shamrock Lane, a car approaching from the left blew through the sign and roared past to become a set of taillights in the darkness. Mitch turned into the road behind the car, following the twin red taillights for half a mile when the lights suddenly brightened — brake lights! — and then vanished.

"What the....?" Rileigh began. Who turns off their lights in the middle of a storm?

"Stop!" Rileigh cried. And if Mitch had hesitated to ask her why, it would have been too late. He didn't ask though, just hit the brakes to stop the car, which hydroplaned fifty yards or so before coming to rest about ten feet before the asphalt in front of them ended in a jagged edge.

The narrow road had washed away in that spot. The car that'd been in front of them had been washed down the mountainside.

"Flares!" Mitch cried. He flipped on his emergency flashers and was out his door one step ahead of Rileigh, who met him at the trunk. As he yanked it open, she kicked off her shoes so she could run. Mitch reached into the trunk and grabbed four flares, handed her two, and then they ran back up the road the way they'd come.

They stopped and Rileigh twisted off the cap of a flare, held it away from her body and rubbed the rough end of the cap against the exposed top of the flare, like striking a match. Even in the downpour, the flare burst into bright light. They placed two lit flares in the center of the road, then lit two more to wave over their heads to get the attention of approaching motorists.

The first car they flagged down contained a family from Arkansas. The driver was an ex-Marine, and he and his teenage son wanted to help.

"We have to stop the traffic coming from the other direction!" Mitch shouted above the drumming of the rain on the car roof. "You wouldn't happen to have any rope?"

"Affirmative," the Marine said. "We're rock climbers."

Rileigh suddenly understood the strange look the man was giving the two of them.

Pointing to Mitch, she said. "He's the county sheriff and I'm…"—she paused for a beat—"I served two tours in Afghanistan." She nodded at her drenched dress and Mitch's soaked sport coat. "We may look like civilians, but we're not."

"Coulda fooled me."

The man and his son opened the back of their van and dug through gear. He shoved rain jackets at Mitch and Rileigh, then hauled out coils of light nylon rope as strong as steel cables.

"I've got a trunk full of flares," Mitch said. "If you two can hold down the fort on this end…"

"We got this," the man said, and Rileigh was sure they did. That freed her and Mitch to find a way across the gaping hole in the road to the other side. A slab of asphalt about eight feet across had been washed away by the flood of water rushing down the mountainside.

Mitch worked quickly to tie the rope securely around his waist in the light from his car's headlights pointed across the broken road surface, secured the line to a nearby tree trunk, and handed Rileigh the coil of rope.

"Don't let the rope get tangled," he said unnecessarily.

And Rileigh realized to her horror that she didn't want Mitch to do it. She knew he was planning to take a running start and leap across the gap, and she didn't want him to. It was *dangerous!* But allowing her feelings to get in the way of doing the job was even more dangerous. If she ever let herself to go down that path... nope, not happenin'.

"Try not to trip, okay?" she told him.

He nodded, backed up, then tore out through the downpour toward the broken edge of asphalt, leapt as far as he could, and landed inelegantly on his belly on the other side, with his feet and legs in the rushing water. Clawing his way out of the water, he got to his feet, gave her a thumbs up, untied the rope, and ran down the road into the growing darkness. A moment later she saw his form backlit by a flare. He lit another to set opposite it, then held up a third in his hand, waving it above his head.

He'd been standing there for only a few minutes when headlights appeared out of the darkness and he flagged down the vehicle, made it stop. It was a family in a minivan with five children. And if Mitch hadn't been there...

When other volunteers took over the task of warning oncoming traffic, Mitch crossed back over the break in the asphalt, moving along the rope tied between two rocks slowly and not in a grand leap. He found Rileigh trembling from the cold.

"There's blankets in the car, and we can turn on the

heater full blast," he said, taking Rileigh's elbow and shoving her toward the car.

Rileigh opened her door and then paused, turned, and slipped out of the borrowed rain jacket, handing it to Mitch.

"We need to return this," she said, then started to get into the car.

"Wait ..." he said and she turned back toward him. The rain was pounding on her head. She could feel the individual drops trying to crack open her skull. She could barely see through the torrent of it running down her face, could only imagine what her dress must look like. And her shoes were ... somewhere.

"I've been wanting to ask you something all night," he said.

"What is it?"

He let out a breath. "Will you marry me?"

Chapter Forty-Seven

SUNDAY DINNER AT RILEIGH'S MOTHER'S HOUSE HAD become a weekly strategy session where Rileigh and Jillian and David and Mitch worked out the logistics of the double wedding they were planning.

Jillian and David had been planning to get married long before Mitch popped the question in the pouring rain on Ramblin' Creek and Rileigh threw her arms around him and kissed him passionately and said, "Of course, I'll marry you." (Although she later teased him, said she'd have agreed to anything just to get out of the rain.) When they finally got back to Rileigh's house through the storm, it was almost three a.m. and Mama and Jillian had been sitting up waiting for them. The storm had knocked out all cell coverage, and they were terrified Rileigh and Mitch had been in an accident.

When they'd stumbled into the living room, drenched, Mama had rushed to go get towels while Jillian tried to console her sister.

"I'm so sorry that your date was ruined."

"Ruined?" Rileigh said. "This was the best date I've ever been on in my life!" Jillian gawked at her. "Don't you think so, Mitch?"

"Absolutely." He beamed with his arm around Rileigh.

"Absolutely what?" Mama asked as she came rushing into the room with towels. "You need to get out of them wet clothes. You want me to make you some hot tea? Hot chocolate? Rileigh, why don't you run upstairs and jump in a hot shower."

And then she realized that nobody else was talking and that Jillian was staring at her sister with an odd look on her face.

"What? What am I missing?" Mama said, looking from one to the other. "Come on, out with it."

"Rileigh just said she had been on the very best date of her whole life," Jillian told her.

"Getting caught out in a storm like that's the best date of your whole life?"

"Totally … on steroids, industrial strength absolutely," Rileigh said and smiled and snuggled up to Mitch.

There was a beat of silence. And into that silence, Rileigh dropped the words, "The best date of my life, because Mitch proposed and I accepted."

After that, there was nothing but squealing and howling and celebration that was way louder than the rain pounding on the roof and the boom of thunder. The only sound that rose above the celebratory din was when Jillian cried, "We could have a *double wedding*!" and then the noise level cranked up another hundred decibels.

Now, as the date approached — they called it "Wedding Squared," because two had become four — Sunday dinners were spent planning out the double wedding that both the brides-to-be said they wanted to keep simple …

and Mama kept upping the ante from "let's do this" to "how about we do *this?*" And within a week, the ceremony had taken on all the trappings of a royal wedding — minus the coaches and footmen — swelling bigger and bigger with every "we have to invite so-and-so" and "oh, we can't *not* invite so-and-so" until it was nothing short of a full-blown mountain "whoop-ti-doo."

Jillian was engaged in a discussion with Mama in a vain attempt to dial back her enthusiasm when Mama cried out, "Why, we can use Grandma's silver candelabra!"

"I didn't know your grandmother had a silver anything," Jillian said.

"If she did, why didn't she hock it and use the money for something more practical?" Rileigh wondered aloud.

"Like running water," Jillian offered.

"Or indoor plumbing," Rileigh chimed in.

"Or electricity."

"Oh, you girls go on with your bad selves," Mama chided them. "You know the silver candelabra I'm talking about. The one that's in the back of the chifforobe."

If there was, indeed, a silver candelabra in the back of the chifforobe in the corner of the dining room, Rileigh'd never seen it. And it could not possibly have been handed down through the family from dirt-poor Grandma Cummins, who'd once told Rileigh that when she was growing up, "We didn't have a pot to piss in or a window to throw it out of."

As if Jillian were reading her mind, she whispered, "Maybe Rhett Butler gave it to Mama."

"It was probably the Dali Llama."

Jillian set down the mashed potatoes she was passing to David, then got to her feet and went around the table to the old chifforobe, said to be the home of a mythical candelabra that neither Jillian nor Rileigh had ever seen. She opened the side doors, digging around in the miscellaneous flotsam and jetsam that'd been jammed into it over the years. Unloading it, she pulled out an old Monopoly game and a Scrabble game, missing half the letters, Clue — "Colonel Mustard in the library with the rope" — a harmonica, a bicycle pump, bookends shaped like unicorns, plastic figurines of three of the four California raisins — "heard it through the grapevine" — several sets of matched salt and pepper shakers from national parks, a pile of recipe books, two rose vases ... but she saw no candelabra. What she did see, though, was a small box wrapped in brown paper like it had come in the mail but had never been opened. She reached back into the dark interior, grasped the box, pulled it out, then stood up and asked, "What's this?"

Looking down, she saw that there was no marking of any kind on the box except who it was addressed to: Rileigh Bishop, 639 Bent Twig Road, Black Bear Forge, Tennessee. No zip code, but it didn't need one since there was no postage on the box. Jillian's eyes shot to Rileigh's, who didn't know what had surprised her. And then she looked at Mama.

"Oh, no!" Mama said. "Oh, no, oh, no, oh, no!" And she put her face in her hands like something terrible had happened.

"What's the matter, Mama?" Rileigh jumped up from the table, hurried to her mother, and put her arms around her. "Mama, what's wrong?"

"I think this is what's wrong," Jillian said and held up the box wrapped in brown paper, then handed it to Rileigh.

"Where did you get that?" Rileigh began and then

realized what she was holding. It took her a few moments to connect the dots. And then she said, "Mama, when did this box come?"

"I hid it there and I forgot that's where I hid it. I'm so sorry. I should have just burned it. I wish I had. But it was so early in the morning that I was afraid I'd make noise and one of you would come down and find me. And then I forgot all about it being there."

"Mama, when did this come?"

"It's been a right smart while," Mama said vaguely.

"There's no postmark on it," Rileigh said, turning it over in her hand.

"It was leaned up against the screen door."

Rileigh felt like Mama had slapped her.

"On the front porch?"

Mama looked up at her and nodded. And understanding flowed like a chill wind around the whole room as they silently stared at the box.

Someone had *come up on the porch* and put that box up against the screen door. Mitch was on his feet in an instant. He came around the table and took the box out of Rileigh's hands.

"We don't need this right now," he said.

"It's addressed to *me*," she said and snatched it back. "And I'm going to open it."

Mitch let out a sigh and everyone stared at the box as Rileigh picked up the butter knife and cut the paper off to find a cardboard box inside. And when she opened the cardboard box, she found a card with a crudely drawn frowny face on one side. On the other side was a tombstone with her name on it. Beneath her name was the number two. The frowny face card lay on top of a small wooden box with a keyhole. Rileigh tried to open the box, but it was locked. She looked down at the box and up at Mitch and then it hit her.

"Mitch, do you still have that key on your keychain?"

The key she was referring to was the key that had been sent to her shortly after FBI Agent Lamar Devereaux had been killed. It had been in a box with a piece of dried and tanned human skin and a card with the number 3 on it. They'd traced the DNA of the piece of skin to a murdered gang member in Chicago but had never figured out what it was the key unlocked.

As Rileigh watched Mitch move keys out of the way on his keyring, she was certain that the small key he finally located would fit perfectly into the lock on the box in her hand.

He took the key off the ring and handed it to her. She set the box down on the table, inserted the key, and turned the lock. When she did, the box sprang open, startling everyone into a communal gasp. It was a jack-in-the-box. Inside was a clown head on a spring, bouncing around. The clown was not smiling, though. Its face was contorted in a hideous, grotesque frown.

A card attached to the front of the clown said: "BANG! You're DEAD this time."

"Dead … *this time?* What does that mean?" Rileigh asked.

"I suppose it means you weren't dead *the last time.*" Mitch said.

"The last…?"

Then she knew.

"This is about the day somebody shot at me and blew out my car window, and I swerved off the road and ended up in the Pigeon River. I was supposed to be dead … but the killer *missed.*"

The head on the spring bounced around and around. Rileigh watched it, as mesmerized as a mouse by a cobra.

When she spoke, Rileigh's voice was barely above a whisper. "This is a promise that he won't miss next time."

THE END

THE END

About The Author

Lauren Street has always loved a mystery. As a kid growing up in bible belt country she devoured every whodunit book she could get her sticky little hands on and secretly investigated all of her (seemingly) normal boring neighbors. Sometimes their pets and farm animals too. All grown up now and living in the UK with her thoroughly unsuspicious (and often unsuspecting) husband, she writes domestic psychological thrillers about families torn apart by secrets and lies. And she sometimes still peers over garden walls to check up on the neighbors.

Also By Lauren Street

The Bishop Smoky Mountain Thrillers

Hide Me Away

Fuel To The Flame

Closer By The Hour

A Gamble Either Way

Calling My Children Home

Too Far Gone

Here You Come Again

A Friend Like You

The Company You Keep

One By One

Come Back To Me

Replaced with Nolon King

Replaced

In Her Place

Irreplaceable

The Salazar Redwood Forest Thrillers

The Girl Who Couldn't Stop Dying

The Girl Who Couldn't Get Out

The Girl Who Couldn't Be Found